ROBERT J. SHOOP
Compulsion

former
KSU prof

ISBN: 1461047560
ISBN-13: 9781461047568
Library of Congress Control Number: 2011905276

Acknowledgments

I am indebted to the following friends and colleagues who read and commented on various drafts of this book. Mary Shoop, Katha Hurt, Doug Kurtz, Dan Barber, Tonnie Martinez, Hope Goodman, Doug Robertson, Denny Dunklee, Mary Devin, Teresa Miller, Susan Scott, Ronnie Whalen, and Connie Butler.

TABERNASH, COLORADO

Adam never owned a dog and really wasn't interested in having one. He didn't form attachments easily. To him every attachment was a loss waiting to happen. He'd already lost his mother to cancer, his wife to divorce, and of course Julie, his childhood friend and first love was abducted and murdered. When, Adrian, his best friend, died Adam promised to take care of her five-year-old Blue Heeler, Bronco.

Against Adam's better judgment they quickly became inseparable. Bronco's excitement for life and soaring energy countered Adam's tendency to fall into depression. He cantered out in front as Adam rode his mountain bike to town, ran ahead as Adam jogged along the forest trails, and lay at his feet as Adam snoozed on the deck.

For four years Bronco slept at the foot of Adam's bed until the night Adam heard a deep-throated growl and woke to catch a glimpse of a mountain lion's tail leaving his bedroom. Bronco weighed over forty-pounds, the lion just clamped his teeth down around the poor dog's neck and carried him away. Adam knew there were mountain lions in the valley, but never expected one would invade his home.

Adam grabbed his Glock from the nightstand and chased after the lion. By the time he reached the deck, they were gone. He knew Bronco was probably dead by now, but he didn't want him rotting under a pile of leaves. The scores of recovered bodies and dozens of autopsies he'd observed during his twenty years as a police officer taught him more than anyone should know about how the intestines store bacteria that wait until death strikes to aid the decomposition process. Just as importantly the thought of the cat getting away with abduction and murder infuriated Adam.

Adam paced the deck waiting for sunrise. He hadn't handled his service pistol since he left the Columbus, Ohio, Special Victims Unit but thought it made sense to take it with him when he headed into the dense forest that surrounded his cabin. He liked the familiar feel of having his duty holster pressing against his lower back. He also admitted reluctantly that he liked the adrenalin rush of the hunt.

Mountain lion season didn't open until December, but Adam knew if he found the big cat he wouldn't hesitate to kill it. The anticipation of stalking through the forest looking for a 160-pound predator that could leap twenty-five feet and was fearless enough to enter his house and take Bronco revived Adam's hunter instincts.

With the first rays of daylight Adam set out stalking the predator. He held on to the hope that Bronco might have broken free. He told himself Bronco could still be alive. Although he saw mountain lion tracks and fresh scat, after a day slogging through the mud and undergrowth he hadn't seen Bronco or the lion. He was familiar with the feeling he got when he failed to find a killer, and he hated it. After seven hours he reluctantly abandoned the hunt, went home, and rinsed off in a hot shower. Fortified with a tumbler of Glenfiddich he slipped into the hot tub and allowed his many regrets to run roughshod through his mind. He'd failed in his promise to Adrian to look after Bronco. Just as he failed as a husband and failed to protect Julie.

I should've known better than to get attached to the damn dog, he thought. Not caring about anyone or anything is the smarter way to go. The freaking lion came right into my bedroom and snatched my friend. The cat was just like the other predators Adam spent his life tracking. Like the rapists and child abusers, the puma just took what he wanted. Adam knew a tall scotch and a hot tub filled with 105-degree water was a treacherous combination.

Chapter 1

TABERNASH, COLORADO

A strident buzzing startled Adam out of his stupor. Cursing for leaving his cell phone on the deck he hoisted out of the hot tub and scrambled up the steps.

Snatching up the phone he mumbled, "This is Adam."

A woman's voice asked, "Mr. Faulkner?"

Annoyed that a sales person got his restricted cell number he was about to flip the phone shut when the caller said in a rushing voice, "My name is Sarah Abbott. I desperately need your help. Monica told me you could help me. Will you help me?"

"Please, Ms. Abbott, slow down. I can hardly understand you. How do you know my sister?"

"We live in the same apartment building in East Cambridge. I've known her for about a year."

Adam seldom talked with Monica since he took a disability retirement from the Special Victims Unit four years ago and they both left Ohio. They were never close. What in the hell was she thinking, giving out his cell number, he wondered? More gruffly than he intended, he said, "There are hundreds of private investigators in Boston. I'm in Colorado. Why are you calling me?"

The answer came in a voice filled with pain. "I was sexually molested. He's still out there. He killed a little girl. You've got to help me find him."

She was still speaking so rapidly Adam wasn't sure he understood her. I really don't need this, he thought. He tried to keep annoyance out of his voice when he said, "Please slow down. Take a deep breath and start at the beginning."

"I was raped by my teacher when I was in middle school. I thought I'd put it behind me, but a lawyer on the Today Show said a teacher could not have raped his client if people who had suspicions would have told someone. Mr. Faulkner, I never told anyone what happened to me. I just tried to forget. Now I'm having migraines and night terrors. I've got to find out if he's still out there. No one at my old school knows where he is. I need to be sure he's not molesting other children. Otherwise, I'm afraid I'll never get over my guilt."

Adam chose his words carefully. "Ms. Abbott, I'm truly sorry about what happened to you. I hope you find the man you are looking for. But this sounds like a pretty straightforward missing person case. As I said, there are hundreds of competent PIs in the Boston area that will be able to help you. I wish you good luck." Again he started to snap his phone shut.

"Wait, Mr. Faulkner! Please don't hang up. There's more. When I was back at my old school I browsed through a stack of old yearbooks looking for a photo of my music teacher. An annual from a couple of years after I was there was dedicated to the memory of a seventh grader named Molly Lincoln. The dedication said Molly died while she was attending a summer music camp. Mr. Faulkner, Molly looks just like I did when I was her age. A couple of years after Mr. Shepherd molested me, I think he murdered Molly."

Adam's vision blurred and he heard a rushing sound as he slumped back against the deck railing, almost dropping the phone. Images of Julie's music teacher flashed through his head. Did Shepherd kill Julie? He heard Sarah repeating, "Are you there, Mr. Faulkner? Are you there?"

This can't be happening, he thought. "What's Shepherd's first name?" he whispered.

"Tony. His name is Tony. Tony Shepherd. He was my music teacher. Monica told me he might be someone you know." After a short pause Sarah again asked, "Mr. Faulkner? Mr. Faulkner? Are you still there?"

Adam struggled to regain his senses. This news combined with sixteen ounces of scotch clouded his thinking. "Yeah, I'm still here," he mumbled. "I can't talk right now. Please call back first thing tomorrow morning," he said and snapped his phone shut. He gripped the deck railing in both hands and stared into the forest. His mind was racing. Could this be the same Tony Shepherd? Could Shepherd have murdered Julie? For fifteen years Adam tracked down child molesters of every description. Each conviction was a payment on the debt he felt he owed Julie for failing to keep her safe. He couldn't get his head around the idea that Tony Shepherd may have killed Julie and could still be teaching.

Adam poured another scotch and sat on the deck until long after the sun disappeared behind Long's Peak. The beauty of the evening was lost on him. He didn't notice the cloudless sky studded with brilliant stars or the silhouettes of the pines, black against the indigo night, or the haunting call of the Great Horned Owl that perched near his cabin. He saw only Julie's face. He knew the name might be just a coincidence, but the thought of finding Julie's killer after all these years boggled his mind.

Adam tried to remember what Tony Shepherd looked like. He'd never been in Shepherd's class, but often passed him in the hall. Julie was always talking about him. It seemed that everyone loved Mr. Shepherd.

Finally, the scotch did its nightly duty and allowed Adam to shuffle into his bedroom and pass out across his bed.

Chapter 2

Julie left the recreation center and headed for the bike rack. She pulled up the hood of her grey sweatshirt and tied the drawstring, dropped her gym bag into her bike basket, and got on her yellow Schwinn Breeze. She paused for a moment and then, instead of taking her usual route downtown, she turned north and peddled into the park.

It was the first Saturday Adam could remember when they didn't ride their bikes to Poppy's Diner to share chocolate malts, Poppy Burgers, and a large orders of fries. As Julie passed the duck pond she edged to the far right side of the lane as a vehicle pulled up behind her. She motioned for it to go around, but it didn't pass. It stayed back a few yards neither speeding up nor slowing down. Adam watched Julie stand on the pedals and pump her legs harder trying to get away. The next moment the small truck was right beside her. Adam couldn't understand why Julie didn't cut off the road and ride where the van couldn't follow. Julie glanced over her shoulder at the driver and coasted to a stop.

The driver called out as the van rolled up beside her, "Hey Jules. How ya doin?"

"Great, Mr. S." Julie smiled. "You've got a new van. Cool."

"Yeah. I just picked it up from the dealership. Wanna be my first passenger."

"What about my bike?"

The van blocked Adam's view of the driver. "There's plenty of room in the back," the driver said as he slid open the side door.

Adam tried to run toward Julie, but couldn't move. "Julie! Stop! Don't get in the van," he shouted.

Their eyes met and Julie smiled and waved as she looked out the passenger window as the van pulled away.

Adam was still shouting as he kicked off the soggy sheet and lunged from the bed. His naked body was drenched in sweat. Gasping, he took several deep breaths trying to slow his racing heart. The damn dream again, he thought as he sat on the side of his bed, opened his clinched fists and pressed his hands to his face. Over the past twenty-five years Adam had dreamt about Julie Romano hundreds of times. Sometimes he saw her walking ahead of him, but he couldn't catch up. In other dreams he heard her call his name, but he couldn't find her. Usually the dreams came when he was working on a sexual abuse case. He knew what caused tonight's dream.

Fully aware that sleep would evade him for the rest of the night Adam rummaged through his dresser and retrieved a tattered arcade photo booth strip. The four black and white photos of Julie and him when they were both fourteen, mugging for the camera, had faded to sepia. But when he looked at the snapshots he saw Julie's reddish blond ponytail, the flecks of brown in her green eyes, and the sixteen freckles sprinkled across her nose and cheeks. He smiled as he remembered her quick laugh and how much he loved the way she said his name. He saw her playing baseball, football, and basketball with the boys. She was the first one to dive head first after a loose ball. As a result, she always sported a collection of scrapes and bruises on her knees and elbows. He recalled her favorite expression, "tape me up and get me back in the game, coach." She swam like a fish, was fearless off the diving tower, took a hard charge in basketball, and skied with wild abandon. She won the NFL's

Punt, Pass & Kick contest when she was thirteen, beating boys who later starred in college. Julie and Adam were inseparable and they were in love. Each knew they would go to the same college, get married, have three children, and spend the rest of their lives together.

Deer Falls was a close-knit borough of about 3500 people situated at the foot of Black Mountain in Pennsylvania. At first the police treated Julie's disappearance as a runaway. They speculated that she had fought with her parents and left town with her boyfriend. Everyone in town knew she was missing within hours of when she was expected home. No one wanted to believe that one of their children could be abducted, but those who knew Julie, knew she didn't run away. The only plausible explanation was that someone took her.

Betty Hughes, the gymnastics coach at the Deer Lake Recreation Center, said Julie left practice on her bike; no one reported seeing her again. Julie's house was only two miles from the recreation center. Her bike was found in the weeds beside a dirt road in the park. Every residence, barn, business, factory, and pond was searched and then searched again. The police conducted hundreds of interviews.

For a time Adam was considered a person of interest. When Julie disappeared Adam's parents were touring the Southwest in a rented motor home and couldn't be contacted. Adam thought he was too old to travel with his parents. After weeks of arguing they agreed to allow him stay home alone. He'd joined a few friends on a spur of the moment camping trip to Harvey's Lake, just a few hours drive from town. The police deduced Adam disappeared about the same time as Julie.

Two days after Julie went missing Adam showed up with scratches and bruises on his face and arms. His physical condition, combined with his angst upon learning of Julie's disappearance, heightened the level of suspicion. The police reacted with skepticism when he told them he injured himself in a rappelling accident. The investigators asked if Julie and he were having sex, if they fought, if she dumped him, if he were jealous of another boy, or if he accidentally hurt her. He answered their questions honestly in a monotone voice interrupted at times with bouts of sobbing.

Adam was inconsolable. He blamed himself for Julie's abduction. He knew if he hadn't gone camping, Julie would be safe. For weeks he devoted every waking hour to looking for her. He showed her photo to everyone he met.

The police interviewed Julie's friends, neighbors, teachers, and anyone else they could think of. It took months for the police to run down every lead. Finally, the search wound down and the reporters stopped writing about Julie. Eventually, the police stopped returning Adam's calls.

Adam was never the same after Julie disappeared. His intense longing for her intruded on everything he did. At first he searched for her at all their favorite places. Later he avoided everything that reminded him of her. The realization that Julie's wasn't coming home caused an overwhelming anger and profound sadness and despair that wouldn't go away. He lost his appetite, was unable to sleep, couldn't concentrate on his schoolwork, and had his first thoughts of suicide. He knew no one would ever love him like Julie. It seemed that his sadness would never let up. Both his father and his football coach told him he had to be strong, that his pain would go away faster if he didn't dwell on it. Eventually Adam acquired a taste for the scotch he stole from his father's liquor cabinet.

Two years after she went missing, Julie was back on television and in all the newspapers. "The sheriffs' office confirmed the discovery of the skeletal remains of a young woman in a wooded area outside of Deer Lake. They are investigating the identity and cause of death of what appears to be a 10 to 16-year-old female."

A follow-up story several days later reported that Jack O'Donnell, a retired history professor, found a black plastic trash bag contained skeletal remains, hair, some bits of clothing, and a small silver half heart charm with 'Adam' engraved on its face while gathering firewood on his property. The age of the remains, combined with dental records and the charm, left no doubt that Julie Romano had been found.

Fourteen is too young to lose your innocence, your sense of safety. When someone kills the one you love, you never get over it. Adam wished people could be trusted to do the right thing, but deep down he believed evil people populated the world. However, in a strange ironic twist, instead of becoming fearful Adam became fearless. Since he couldn't guarantee his safety, he stopped worrying about it.

Chapter 3

Adam rolled out of bed and called for Bronco before remembering his friend was gone. He was still thinking about his dog as he slid open the door to his deck. Each morning the air was a little crisper than the day before. The sweep of wind rocked the fifty-foot lodge pole pines that kept the cabin in continuous shadows, except for the shafts of light that filtered through during the early afternoon. He loved his trees and worried that the recent infestation of pine beetles was going to take away his seclusion.

After taking a few deep breaths of mountain air, Adam donned his typical fall running gear, a faded long sleeved Willie Nelson t-shirt, a pair of faded cargo shorts that were getting a little too snug, and a pair of two hundred dollar cross-trainers. The shoes were supposed to give him some relief from the pain caused by his battered back. They didn't.

As he headed into the forest for his usual morning run he paused and listened to the sound of the trout stream as it skipped and jumped around the red and gray boulders as it flowed twenty yards from the cabin. He was still learning about Pole Creek's life cycle as it changed from a wide dark torrent fed by the snow pack thaw in the spring to a much narrower and slower moving brook in the fall. Across the creek a swath of Quaking Aspen had colonized a burned area of the forest. The slightest whisper of a breeze caused the golden leaves to tremble incessantly. Adam smiled as he remembered his first autumn at the cabin when he thought the Aspen leaves were hundreds of Western Swallowtail butterflies.

Forty-five minutes later he returned to the cabin. The shifting breeze brought the clean scent of pine. The temperature was falling, but he couldn't force himself to go inside. He moved to the mountains to be alone. He knew he made the right decision. Yet, on mornings like this he wondered what it would be like to have someone in his life.

Directly below the deck a family of ground squirrels had burrowed under the pad of his hot tub. He smiled at the memory of Bronco trying to herd the rodents away from the cabin. Adam was about to turn away when the squirrels dove into their burrow. A sharp-shinned hawk swooped down, barely missing the last kit to disappear into the ground. Adam's first instinct was to try to figure out how he could protect the young squirrels from the silent killer. By now he had become hardwired to try to protect the innocent from predators. As the hawk flew away Adam shrugged and grudgingly acknowledged he couldn't save everything or everyone.

As he stood to go back inside his lower back spasmed and he lurched against the deck railing. Bad back, no family, few friends; not where I expected to be when I reached forty-five, he thought. The damaged back and full pension were all he had to remind him of his fifteen years on the Columbus Special Victims Unit. After five years mostly working the street beat and drug cases he joined the SVU where he worked sexual assault and child abduction cases.

His time with the SVU ended five years ago on a Friday evening, shortly after 3:30 a.m. when he stopped a car that reportedly belonged to Frank Stork, a deadbeat wanted for producing child pornography. As Adam approached the driver's door, Stork rolled out shooting. The first slug hit Adam high in the right shoulder, spinning him around. The second shot hit him in the middle of his back, fracturing a vertebra and proving fatal to his career. Adam tumbled down the embankment beside highway 33 and stared up at the passing headlights until help arrived.

After six months of physical rehabilitation Adam accepted the offer of medical disability and moved to Colorado where he accepted an occasional investigation job. Adam's back never completely healed. Some days were better than others. On the worst days he took a handful of painkillers, muscle relaxers, and anti-inflammatory pills, and did a lot of stretching. By lunchtime he was usually doing pretty well. Most evenings a twenty-minute soak in the hot tub and a couple of swigs of scotch took the edge off the pain and allowed him to sleep. Living alone, he didn't have anyone to complain to, and mostly he liked it that way. He had voice mail to take his calls and an accountant to do his taxes. Otherwise, he worked alone. Adam refused to take cases involving pre-employment verification, identity theft, harassing e-mails, computer crimes, divorce, or pre-marital screening. Although child assault and abduction cases caused him a great deal of emotional pain, he knew what it felt like to have a loved-one taken and he owed it to Julie to help when he could. He didn't have a web page. He wasn't even listed in the yellow pages. The cases he took were the result of referrals from police officers or attorneys with whom he had worked. Clients usually came to him when their local police ran out of leads or simply dropped the ball.

Adam told people he left the police force because of his injury. He actually left when he no longer believed he was making a difference. He used to look up to the veteran investigators, real masters, guys that he worked with who were his mentors. Later he realized that to a man every one was a cynical son-of-a-bitch. Adam felt himself becoming just like them. Over the course of his career he felt himself changing in subtle and not so subtle ways. He knew if he stayed on the job much longer he was going to become a lousy cop and a worse person.

He needed to get away from daily contact with the worst of the worst and get some perspective. Adam admitted to himself that getting shot gave him the excuse he was looking for. Several weeks before he was shot, he had remarked to Jack Haw, his partner, "If it's true that the average adult laughs seventeen times a day, someone is using my share of laughs." Shortly after that he left the force, sold his house, and moved into his fifty-year-old cabin.

Adam entered his kitchen, poured himself a mug of coffee, went back outside, and sat on the top step of the deck. It didn't take long for his thoughts to turn once again to Julie Romano and Tony Shepherd. If Shepherd is still alive, I'll hunt him down and kill him, he thought grimly. The buzz of his cell phone roused him from his brooding.

Chapter 4

TUPICO FLATS, NEVADA

As Jim Schafer watched the gym fill with incoming students and their parents he remembered how much he loved the beginning of the school year. It's such an exciting time, filled with possibilities. He could tell at a glance which girls to steer clear of and which ones will fall in love with him. He casually walked toward the nearest group of mothers and their amazing daughters.

Jim had learned he must seduce the parents and other teachers before he could start grooming the students. He knew he had succeed when a mom told him she wished she were back in school so she could be in his music class. After twenty years of practice, he had become an excellent child molester.

Over the years he learned to attend every school function, schmooze with all the parents, and take on the school responsibilities that no one else wanted. He smiled at the thought of how grateful his principal and the other teachers were when he volunteered to be the student government advisor. They didn't think he knew what he was getting into - weekly meetings, weekend car washes, helping decorate the gym, chaperoning dances, and in general having his time monopolized by fourteen-year-olds.

Jim smiled and half listened as the president of the parents group told him he was her daughter's favorite teacher. This woman was practically gift-wrapping Cindy for him. Lucky for her Cindy wasn't his type. Some of these parents are in denial about their teenage daughter's sexuality. Most parents know boys become sex crazed when they hit puberty, but some just don't want to admit their daughters are interested in sex, too. They certainly never suspect the admired and respected teacher they are talking and laughing with tonight may be grooming their daughter tomorrow. It made Jim shudder when he thought about the risks he took when he was known as Tony Shepherd. Tony Shepherd was a fool.

Jim barely got out of town after Molly's accident. Within a few months after her death he had filled out the paperwork to have his name legally changed to James Schafer. He cancelled all his credit cards, rented an apartment in another state, and had his name changed on his new teaching certificate. Next he applied for an Individual Taxpayer Identification Number from the IRS. Knowing that many employers don't check the number, accepting the card as proof, he then put the valid ITIN number onto a fake Social Security card giving him the proof needed to get a job and file taxes. When Jim Schafer left Summer Haven, Tony Shepherd no longer existed.

Chapter 5

Tupico Flats was a rural mining town in northern Nevada. It was the perfect hunting ground for Jim. Most teachers didn't want to go to Tupico Flats and face low salaries and no social life in the evenings or on weekends. As a result, the school district took just about anyone they could get.

By the second week of school Jim had spotted four potential little darlings. Emily Grover was the first to catch his eye. Unfortunately, she went out for soccer and didn't enroll in his beginning band class. Petite and freckled Amanda Arnold had real possibilities until he brushed up against her as they passed in the hall. She had spun around and almost took a swing at him, stopping when she saw he was a teacher. He looked at her with a lopsided smile and said, "Excuse me." She gave him a dirty look and continued down the hall. If a target showed any fight, Jim left her alone and moved on to more passive prey. Brianna Wilson seemed to be a promising candidate. She was flat chested, tiny, shy, and she signed up for band. Jim crossed her off his list as soon as he met her mom at the open house. He watched Brianna and her mom talk and laugh as they walked into the gym. It was clear that they were very close. Mrs. Wilson was also a volunteer in the mentoring program. She would be in and out of the school on a weekly basis. Brianna was quite tempting, but self-preservation made Jim move on.

The fourth possibility was thirteen-year-old Lizzie Sutton. Jim noticed how insecure she was about her body and her general appearance. At the parent-teacher open house she stood a few feet from her mom. They didn't speak with each other. Lizzie stood with her arms across her chest and mostly looked at her shoes. Mrs. Sutton seemed distracted and was clearly anxious to leave. Jim had done his homework. He knew she was working two jobs and didn't have much time to spend with Lizzie or attend school functions. Mrs. Sutton looked at her watch several times as she waited for the principal to finish welcoming parents, students and teachers to the new school year. None of the other girls talked with Lizzie or even acknowledged that she was in the room. He smiled to himself as he thought, Lizzie doesn't know it, but she's about to fall in love.

As Jim stood to the side of the cafeteria and watched Lizzie he knew he must have her. His desire was intense and immediate. He didn't allow himself to fall in love any more, but Lizzie looked so much like his first love that old feelings surfaced. Jim's face contorted in anger as he remembered Julie Romano.

It was really her fault. Every time I looked at her she was smiling at me. She was always the first student in the classroom each morning. When I asked her if she wanted to stay after school and help me grade papers she jumped at the chance to be with me. I just wanted to be near her, to smell her, to touch her, to taste her. I could tell she wanted me by the way she walked, and dressed, and laughed at all my jokes. It was clear that she wanted to make me happy, he recalled bitterly.

Jim really hadn't planned on hurting Julie. He hadn't even expected to see her that Saturday morning. He'd just picked up his new van from the dealer and was taking a shortcut through the park. Then, there she was. She was wearing green shorts and a gray sweatshirt. As he drove up behind her he watched her muscular bottom and legs pump up and down. He remembered thinking, look at the way she's dressed. What man could resist that little flirt? When she saw me she lit up. Clearly, she wanted me.

He became even angrier as he remembered how she had jumped in the front seat as he loaded her bike in back. She was the happiest girl he'd ever met, always smiling and laughing. She tossed her head back and laughed when he tried to speak in German, "Willkommen zu meinem neuen Auto."

She looked over at him, still smiling, and said, "You're really funny, Mr. S., this is so much fun. I'm so glad you stopped."

Jim couldn't resist her. I'm only human, he thought. He drove deeper into the park and pulled the car off the road and up under some trees. Julie looked at him in surprise. Before she could say anything he leaned over and tried to kiss her. Jim suddenly felt terrible pain in his mouth and saw blood running down the front of his shirt.

Thinking back on that day, even after all these years, Jim was certain that if Julie hadn't split his lip when he tried to kiss her everything would have been fine. But she started kicking, and fighting, and screaming. He couldn't let anyone hear her. She was so strong. She just wouldn't shut up.

Jim remembered the heat of her body as he pressed down on top of her. She squirmed and bucked as he clamped his hand over her mouth and nose. He was relieved when she stopped struggling. He took his hand away when he thought she finished playing hard to get. Julie was dead.

He knew he had to hide her. He had to get out of the park before he was discovered. But he just sat there. This wasn't supposed to happen, he thought. He couldn't make his mind form a coherent thought. He knew he must get rid of her body, but couldn't think of what to do. He pushed her into the back of the van near her bike and just started driving. Eventually, he stopped at a grocery store and bought a box of large trash bags and some paper towels. When he noticed a few drops of his blood on her shirt he pulled it over her head and put it in a bag. Then he stuffed her in a trash bag, drove a few more miles from town, and carried her into the woods. He stuffed her in a hollow beech tree, and hoped she would stay hidden. He wiped a towel over her bike and threw it into a field on the way back to town. When he got home he wiped down the van and burned the towels and shirts. For weeks Jim was afraid the police were going to arrest him, but after only one interview they left him alone.

Jim forced himself to stop thinking about Julie as a new group of students entered his band room. He smiled as he thought: I admit it. I love young girls. Fortunately, this school provides an endless supply. Some people might say I'm sick. He smiled as he thought, society isn't very sympathetic to people with my disability.

He used to wish he were like other men. For years he prayed to be healed. Now he knew it was useless to try and fight his demons. He went into education because that's where the young girls were. He frequently thought, I'm good looking, married, clean-cut, don't smoke, drink, or do drugs. What parent wouldn't want their daughter to spend time with me?

As he glanced at his new students he reflected that most of my girls would agree that I am the best thing that ever happened to them. It's really not all about sex. Young girls are funny and smart. I feel so comfortable when I'm with them. I love teaching them about life and love.

Young girls had always liked Jim. His mother told him it was because he had the most beautiful eyes she'd ever seen. She said they were periwinkle blue. He often got asked if he was wearing tinted contact lenses. Jim still thought about his mom every day. After his dad ran out on them, Jim remembered his mom being very lonely. From then on it was just Jim and his mom. Jane Shepherd was quite petite, only five feet tall and very thin. She supported them both by working as a bank teller and giving piano lessons on weekends. Jim loved sitting at her feet watching her teach and listening to the metronome. He was a natural musician and was composing and improvising by the time he was nine.

Jim and his mom were constantly together. His earliest memories were of taking baths with her. She called him her "little man." They slept naked in the same bed. He liked to remember how much his mother liked to play the licking game she taught him. They bathed together until Jim started middle school. He remembered how they laughed together when she washed his penis and testicles and called them "her spaghetti and meatballs." If Jim's relationship with his mother set him on a destructive course, what happened in David O'Connor's attic sealed his fate.

Chapter 6

As Jim waited for his students to settle into their seats his thoughts turned from Lizzie to memories of David O'Connor's sister Debbie. Jim was cursed with an almost photographic memory. He had detailed memories of events from twenty years ago. He found himself thinking about his childhood more and more lately. He could remember the details of the afternoon he spent in David's attic as if it were yesterday. He remembers thinking that in order to get home and masturbate he had to walk through David's kitchen to get out of the house. He was afraid David's mother would notice his pants tenting out in front of him. She was ironing with her back to him but turned as the door opened. "Hi Tony, what do you think of those airplanes?"

He quickly hid his erection behind a kitchen chair. "Very cool, Mrs. O'Connor."

He was there to see David's model airplane collection. The planes were amazing, but they weren't what caused his painful erection.

An hour earlier he had followed David up the flight of stairs that led to the attic. The only flooring was a series of four-by-eight sheets of plywood laid end-to-end the length of the attic. The attic smelled of musty old clothing and airplane glue. Tiny particles of dust and insulation floated over-head. Old furniture, broken luggage, faded and broken Christmas decorations, and boxes of clothing and books were stacked on the floor joists. Strips of pink fiberglass insulation filled the space between the joists. Two small gable vents allowed outside air and light to filter into the large room. Hanging from the rafters were about two-dozen amazingly detailed model airplanes.

Tony had followed David down the planks to the far end of the room where they sat on an old trunk that was covered with ratty quilts. David picked up one of his father's books, *Airplanes of World War One*, and they looked up some of the planes. David and his dad spent a lot of time together, and David knew the history of every plane. There were German biplanes, an America Curtis Jenny JN 4, about a dozen British planes including the Sopwith Camel, and a half-dozen French planes. Tony's favorite was the Russian Saveljev Quadriplane. He was amazed that a plane with four wings could actually fly.

David and Tony turned their attention from the book when they heard footsteps on the stairs and saw David's little sister, Debbie, and a girlfriend coming toward them. The girls stopped a few feet in front of them, turned their backs to them and pulled their panties down around their ankles. They bent over and wiggled their bottoms back and forth just inches in front of Tony's face. David just laughed and shook his head. Tony was dumbstruck. He was pretty shy and had never had a girlfriend. The only other naked girl he had ever seen was his mom. Having two naked bottoms right in front of his face was overwhelming. Thoughts of his mom and these girls jumbled around in his head. As he reached out and tried to put his hand between Debbie's legs she quickly bent over to pull her pants up. His fingers brushed against her as she danced away. Both girls laughed hysterically as they charged down the stairs.

After the mooning incident Tony started to spend more time at David's house. He hoped David was his passport to seeing Debbie naked again. Debbie and her friend obviously want me, he thought. Maybe they'll let me touch them next time. Several weeks later, Tony rode his bike to David's to pick him up for school.

"Hi Mrs. O. Is David ready?"

"Not yet. He'll be down in a minute." Mrs. O'Connor invited Tony in to wait. "Do you want any toast or juice?"

"No thanks."

"Sit over there while I finish ironing Debbie's dress. She has a speech contest after school today and wants to wear her 'lucky' dress."

The room was warm. The kitchen chairs and table were stacked high with folded laundry. Tony sat on the floor with his back against the wall. A few minutes later Debbie came into the room wearing only a pair of pale green panties. She asked her mom if her dress was ready. When she saw Tony she clutched her hands across her chest, screamed, and dashed from the room. Once again it was Mrs. O'Connor, her ironing board, and Tony's erection sharing a very small space.

Tony quickly moved to the door. "I'll wait for David outside," he said.

His erection was throbbing, but there was nowhere for him to find relief.

This was the beginning of Tony's intense sexual fixation on young girls. From that day forward he became sexually aroused each time he saw girls of similar age and appearance as Debbie. He had no interest in girls his own age.

For the rest of his life muddled memories of being in bed with his mother and the vision of the two naked girls in the attic filled his dreams and daydreams. He knew there was something wrong with him. Although Tony wanted to stop thinking about naked young girls, he just couldn't. He was possessed by a fierce obsession that tyrannized him.

Tony's sexual fixation on young girls intensified after his family's financial collapse. When his mom lost her job at the bank and was forced to sell their house and move to a cheaper apartment, he was forced to leave his familiar school and comfortable house and go on public assistance. After that he never had fashionable clothes or money to go on dates. He was afraid that girls his own age would reject him. It was then that he began to masturbate compulsively. Instead of developing dating relationships with real girls, his sexual outlet was shallow and fantasy based. He felt totally powerless over the situation. He tried not to think about his mother, so he used images of Debbie and her friend as a masturbation fantasy, sometimes masturbating up to five times a day. Eventually, fantasying about girls in their early teens was the only way he could become sexually excited. Soon these fantasies were not enough, he needed real girls.

Not many families in his neighborhood could afford air conditioning. On hot summer nights most people left their windows open. It didn't take Tony long to locate the bedrooms of the half dozen or so junior high school girls who lived within walking distance of his apartment. Because his mom got a job working nights, and usually stayed out drinking after work, it was no problem for Tony to leave his apartment after dark and cruise the neighborhood. A few blocks from his apartment Mrs. Moore often left her bathroom window slightly open when she took a shower. Tony wasn't interested.

Intuitively he knew that if a father or older brother of one of his targets ever caught him peeping in windows, he would get hurt so he learned to creep silently in the shadows avoiding houses that had dogs. Over time he developed a route that led him past five bedroom windows that often provided him with the stimulation he was looking for. Wendy's house sat back from the road and had shrubbery planted on the side. Her room was on the ground floor on the side with the bushes. If Wendy's light was on, he would sneak across the back of the property and sit in the shadows to be sure no one was in the back yard. He would then move silently up to the house and slip behind the bushes. From his vantage point he could see almost every inch of Wendy's bedroom. The room was small, painted yellow, and furnished with a bed, dresser, small desk, and reading lamp. Sometimes Wendy was in her room when Tony arrived or she entered while he was lurking outside her window. Usually she would be fully dressed and would read or do her homework at her desk. She typically changed for bed in the bathroom, but every so often she would undress in the bedroom. These were successful hunts.

Wendy was a little older than he liked. She was almost fifteen. However, she was small for her age, undeveloped, and looked vaguely like Debbie. Although she usually got undressed and put on her robe pretty quickly, occasionally she would walk around the room naked. One night while she was naked, she turned her back to him and bent over to rummage in her closet for something. Tony opened his pants and began masturbating. His breath came in ragged gasps as he ejaculated on the side of Wendy's house. His relief at returning home without getting caught combined with his genuine humiliation at what he had just done caused him to sob with regret and embarrassment. Tony promised himself he wouldn't ever do it again.

He was afraid and confused as he thought, why do I do this? I know it's wrong. What will I do when I see Wendy in school tomorrow? She is one of the few girls whose nice to me. She'd be so humiliated if she knew I was spying on her. I wonder if other boys do this.

Sometimes Tony's resolutions to stop stalking young girls changed his behavior for weeks or even months, but he always started again. Tony had to exert all of his will power to keep from touching the young girls he followed in shopping centers, school hallways, and everywhere else he went.

Tony played trumpet in the school band. His school loaned musical instruments to students who couldn't afford them. Being in the band began to change Tony's personality. The band was like a family. Although he was still too shy to try and date girls his own age, he started to come out of his shell and became more confident. Hanging out with other band members, he discovered that people thought he was funny. He could make almost anyone laugh. He learned how to charm people into being nice to him.

When he graduated from high school, he won a music scholarship to the state university. That, combined with giving piano lessons at Doug's Music Store, allowed him to leave home and go to college. He wished his mom could come to college with him. He missed her desperately. Her weekly letters weren't enough. He liked his classes but was intimidated by the other students who seemed so much more sophisticated then he. No one befriended him. He started volunteering at the local youth center, teaching music to low-income children.

One day as he walked across campus after his freshman year of college he discovered over one hundred middle school boys and girls who were attending a summer music camp. He was earning extra income working in the library. He planned his lunch break so he could walk across campus at the same time the campers were going to the student union for their lunch.

It was a cool June morning, but he was sweating. He had to exert all of his limited supply of self-control to keep from putting his hand on the bottom of the 13 year-old-girl he was closely following. She had blond hair, was amazingly tanned, and was wearing white terrycloth short-shorts. He could clearly see the shape of her ass cheeks as she walked up the steps in front of the student union. Suddenly, his preoccupation was interrupted when a camp counselor stepped in front of him, poked him in his chest, and said, "Hey pal, what're ya doin?"

Tony froze, then stammered, "What do you mean? I'm not doing anything."

"I've been watching you," the counselor said. "Every day this week you've been hanging around the band girls. Why are you following them? Are you some kind of pervert?"

Two other counselors began walked toward Tony, and several of the campers stopped, their eyes on him.

"You're crazy," Tony said. "It's a free country. I'm just taking a walk." He turned and rushed away. He was overwhelmed with relief when he realized no one was chasing him. Shaking uncontrollably when he got back to his dorm room, he locked the door and knew he wouldn't go near the band girls again.

What's wrong with me? He wondered. People are noticing me looking at young girls. I'm going to get beat up or arrested if I keep this up. He knew he was fixated on middle school girls. He also knew he could go to jail if he continued to stalk them. As he lay on his bed agonizing he had an epiphany. It all suddenly became crystal clear. If he became a middle school music teacher he wouldn't have to hunt for girls. They would come to him.

Chapter 7

TABERNASH, COLORADO

Adam had been up since five a.m. waiting for Sarah's call. He was tempted to hit *69 and call her. He regretted not finding out more details during yesterday's call, but he had been too addled to cope with what she was telling him. Adam did the math in his head. Shepherd was in his first or second year of teaching when Julie disappeared. If he were twenty-two then, he would be fifty-three today. If Tony Shepherd killed Julie and was still teaching, there was a school out there with a monster in its midst. Adam slammed his hand on the kitchen counter and said out loud, "Shepherd, you have no idea what's in store for you."

His cell phone buzzed at exactly eight o'clock. Adam's hand shook as a wave of anticipation arose within him. Was it possible, after all these years that he would face Julie's killer?

Adam snapped open the phone and asked, "Sarah?"

"Hello, Mr. Faulkner. Thank you for letting me call you back."

"Sarah, I apologize for hanging up on you yesterday. My best friend was abducted and murdered when she was only fourteen. Her music teacher was also named Tony Shepherd."

"I know. When I told Monica the name of the music teacher that raped me, she told me about Julie and the name of her music teacher. We wondered if it could be the same guy. Monica thought you would help me when you heard the name. That's why I called you."

"Well it's not going to be as easy as I had hoped."

"What do you mean?"

"Last night I went on line and began to look for him. I subscribe to the same databases that the police use. I can access tax records, vehicle registration, credit card records, teacher licensure, and employment records."

"Did you find him?"

"Well, yes and no. I found him, and then I lost him. Shepherd taught at my school in Deer Lake, Ohio for two years. He left the year after Julie was murdered. Then he went to Summer Haven, Pennsylvania and taught at your school for four years."

Sarah interrupted, "Are you sure he's is the same guy?"

"Yes, Sarah. The man who molested you is the same guy who murdered Julie."

"What do you mean, you lost him?"

"After he left Summer Haven he disappeared. I can't find him on any database. I've even checked death certificates."

"You aren't giving up are you?"

"Not bloody likely. Some of these creeps do whatever they can to disguise themselves. They move around a lot, often just before they are suspected or investigated. Some change their appearance by gaining or losing weight, growing or shaving beards, shaving their head, changing the color of their hair, getting or discarding contact lenses or they start to wear glasses. Some stop using credit cards and don't register to vote. If they're married, some put all their assets in their wife's name. Some even change their names. But I promise you I'll find him."

"How?"

"Like I said, these guys change what they can, but there are some things they can't change or don't think about changing.

They will sometimes drive the same type of car, or go to the same church, or smoke the same type of cigar. They often retain the same habits and hobbies. It just means that a lot legwork will be required."

"I don't have a lot of money. How much do you think this is going to cost?"

"Finding Shepherd won't cost you a thing. I'm going to get this bastard for Julie."

"When do we start?"

Adam was prepared for this. "'We' don't start. I work alone. I promise I'll keep you in the loop. I'll call you the minute I find him."

Sarah's heart sank. She wanted to be there when Adam found Shepherd. "Mr. Faulkner, please let me help you. I really need to be part of this. He took something from me. I didn't do anything about it then. Now I want to be part of bringing him to justice. Let me come out to Colorado so we can talk. Please!"

Adam was sympathetic. He understood what she was feeling. "Okay, he agreed reluctantly, but I'm not promising how much you can be involved," Adam said, but he knew he already had.

Chapter 8

TUPICO FLATS, NEVADA

Lizzie kept her eyes focused on the floor and held her books across her chest as she walked down the hall toward Mr. Schafer's classroom. Without lifting her head she watched the other girls pass by. In May, when she left on summer vacation, none of her classmates had started to mature physically. Over the summer many of them had developed breasts. She couldn't help being envious. She was painfully aware of her own flat chest as she watched boys flock around Hannah whose breasts were ginormous. She wondered why boys were so dense. When she entered the band room, Mr. Schafer was passing out music folders.

Schafer liked to imagine that every girl in the class was staring at him. When he was younger, he was sure the girls liked to look at his butt when he wrote on the black board. Keeping fit is part of the package, he thought, but my looks aren't enough now that I'm in my fifties. Still, I have to do what I can to stay young looking. As motivation, Schafer likes to pretend he was walking behind one of his music students when he was on his elliptical trainer, thinking about what he would do when he caught one.

He smiled to himself as Lizzie entered the classroom. She looked like a frightened fawn that might startle and take flight at the first sound. Her breasts are still tiny, just starting to bud. She's perfect. I've ignored her so far. Today it begins, Tony thought hungrily.

Over the years Schafer has learned that he didn't need to use force to get what he wanted. It was more satisfying and much safer when the girls were willing. It still frightened him to think of how stupid he was with Julie, Sarah, and Molly.

His narcissism allowed him to deny any responsibility for Julie's death. He thought of her death as an unavoidable accident. Shortly after Julie's death, Schafer moved to Pennsylvania where he took the job as the middle school band teacher at Summer Haven Middle School. He was so frightened by what had happened with Julie that he swore he would never touch another student. He knew what he had been doing was wrong. He tried to be a good professional.

In an effort to satisfy his sexual fantasies he began hiring prostitutes. He drove to larger cities, went to adult bookstores, and picked up adult newspapers with lists of local call girls. He went to hotel rooms and called modeling agencies. "Look, what I need is a girl that looks very young, the younger the better. It doesn't matter how old she really is, she has to look like she is in middle school." When the prostitutes arrived, he gave them clothing to wear that made them look like school girls and coached them on how he wanted them to act. None of the prostitutes were good enough actresses or looked young enough to satisfy his fetish. Within a month of taking the Pennsylvania job he saw Sarah for the first time.

Schafer had been patiently grooming Sarah since the first week of school. She had been taking private music lessons two or three times a week when he decided it was safe to get more intimate. He nearly got sick to his stomach when he recalled his last tutoring session with Sarah. He was Tony Shepherd then. He remembered saying, "Sarah, because you're my most favorite band member, I'm going to let you help me select the new band uniforms. You'll be the first person to see them. They're still in the shipping carton."

Sarah couldn't believe her good luck. A delighted smile broke out across her face. "Really? Thank you, Mr. S.," she bubbled.

Shepherd lifted a bright red jacket and silver slacks from the large box and handed them to Sarah. "The uniform manufacturer sent us several samples to select from. Take this uniform into the storage closet and try it on," he said. As soon as she closed the door, Shepherd moved around behind the storage closet and silently slid a Newport Jazz Festival poster to the side to expose a pinhole he had drilled that morning. Knowing that he would be having sex with Sarah in a few weeks heightened his excitement as he watched her undress.

Sarah was beaming when she came out of the closet. The red and silver uniform had a cape with an outline of an eagle embroidered across the back. She twirled around and around looking at herself in the mirror.

"Sarah, you look awesome. What do you think?"

"I really like this one, Mr. Shepherd."

"Try on the one without the cape and see if you like it better. Then there's a red and white one to try, too."

After Sarah tried on the three uniforms, she got dressed and came out of the band closet. Shepherd mistakenly thought she was ready for the next step. "I'm afraid I've kept you too long, he apologized. The activities bus just left, Sarah, but don't worry, I'll drive you home."

She smiled and tried to act like she rode in Shepherd's car every day, but she failed. She got in the car and beamed happily as she noticed a few teachers watching her drive away with Mr. Shepherd. They drove in silence for a few minutes then

Mr. Shepherd asked, "What radio station do you usually listen to, Sarah?"

"I don't care," she said, too embarrassed to say she was never allowed to select the radio station in her aunt's car. Sarah felt so grown up riding with Mr. Shepherd. She regretted that it was getting dark. It would really be something if her friends saw her with the most popular teacher in school. After Shepherd tuned the radio to the local rock station he let his hand drop and rest on Sarah's knee. Sarah tensed but didn't pull away. She didn't know what to do. No one had ever done this before.

Shepherd was more excited than he expected to be. Seeing Sarah getting undressed earlier took him back to that afternoon in David's attic. Feelings of excitement and loss of control came flooding back. He knew it was too early to even think about doing anything. He knew he had to get Sarah home without touching her. When he stopped at the cross street he intended to turn left and travel the ten blocks to Sarah's house. Instead, he turned right.

"You turned the wrong way, Mr. Shepherd!" Sarah said in a surprised voice. She turned in the seat and looked out the back window, "Mr. Shepherd, turn around. My house is back there." She said pointing out the window.

Shepherd smiled his most reassuring smile and said, "Whoops. I'm sorry. I forgot where you live. Hey, since we missed the turn, let me stop up here and get some gas. He was now about five miles away from the school. "It is just up here a few more miles, Sarah." As they drove along the deserted road Shepherd slowly slid his hand up under Sarah's skirt and lightly caressed her thigh. Sarah tried to scrunch away from him, but the seat belt held her in place.

"Sarah, you are soooooo beautiful. Do you have any idea how sexy you are? He crooned. "I can't control my self around you. You're driving me nuts." Sarah didn't say anything. Her mind was racing. She couldn't believe Mr. Shepherd was doing this. As he talked, he slid his hand farther up her leg.

"Please don't do that, Mr. Shepherd," she whimpered.

He moved his hand to her crotch and caressed her through the front of her underwear. She couldn't get any farther away from him. He then slid the tips of two fingers under the elastic of her panties.

Sarah was sobbing and hyperventilating. She didn't know if she was going to throw up or pass out. "Stop it! What are you doing? Please stop!"

"Be quiet, Sarah. It is all right. I want to be your boy-friend. This is our first real date."

Shepherd forced his finger inside of Sarah. The pain was unbearable. She was having difficulty breathing. She knew she had to get away. Her hand fumbled with the seat belt.

Shepherd drove down the county road that led away from the highway trying to figure out where to take her. He knew the county cemetery would be deserted. There was a road that led to the old section of the cemetery where he would be able to see any approaching cars. It was getting dark and he thought he'd be safe if he drove back behind the equipment shed.

He drove into the deserted cemetery and pulled off the road and coasted to a stop behind some tall Azaleas. He unzipped his pants and pulled his erect penis out of his pants. He grabbed Sarah's hand and forced her to hold him. Sarah squeezed her eyes tightly shut. He pushed her face down between his legs and forced her mouth open. Sarah was hysterical with fear.

"Its okay Sarah, don't be afraid," Shepherd said.

Sarah pulled free and sobbed, "Please stop! Please take me home."

Shepherd was angry and didn't want to stop, but he remembered what happened with Julie. "Okay. I'll take you home. But, you better promise not to tell. If you tell anyone what happened I'd say you are a liar. I'll tell your aunt and all the teachers that you asked me to have sex with you. Who do you think they will believe? Your aunt and uncle will hate you. Everyone will think you are a little whore. You might even be kicked out of school."

Tony pushed himself back into his pants and zipped up. He backed his car onto the dirt road and he headed toward Sarah's house. At the first stop light when they got back into town Sarah unfastened her seat belt, swung open the door, and leaped from the still rolling car. Startled, Shepherd slammed on the breaks and shouted after her, "Where are you going? Sarah! Come back! I'm trying to take you home." He could only watch as she ran into a Big Boy restaurant.

Shepherd was sweating. He didn't try to chase her. He realized he couldn't confront her in the middle of the restaurant. He was also afraid if he caught her, he might hurt her.

That night Shepherd tried calling Sarah, but there was no answer. The next morning there was a note in his school mailbox telling him that Sarah had dropped band. For weeks Shepherd lived in constant fear that he'd be called to the principal's office or that a police officer would enter his classroom and put him in handcuffs. But nothing happened.

Sarah avoided Shepherd as much as she could. She convinced her aunt that she needed to drop out of band because she needed the time to study for her other classes. She never told anyone about what happened. Although the memories of what happened with Julie and Sarah frightened Shepherd, what happened with Molly had almost caused him to commit suicide.

Chapter 9

TABERNASH, COLORADO

From the time she settled into her seat on the 747 her mind reeled with concerns about spending time with a man she didn't know. She was worried about Adam's scruples. In general, she was uncomfortable around men and knew she couldn't work with any man she didn't trust. She needed to meet him face-to-face and see what it was like to be near him. Sarah's plane arrived in Denver at 10:30 a.m. In two and a half hours I'll be in Winter Park sitting across from him. I can always call it quits if I get bad vibes, she thought.

Today was the fourth day Adam spent the morning walking through the forest looking for Bronco. Although he knew there was little chance he would see Bronco again, he still held out hope. For the first two days Adam thought it was possible that Bronco broke free. Bronco is pretty strong. He might be out there somewhere hurt, he thought. By the third day Adam knew his rescue mission had become one of recovery. When he returned to his cabin he had stood on the deck watching the trees sway in the wind and thinking about Bronco. Even now, he stared into the forest hoping his friend would appear. It wasn't a fair fight, he thought. The cat outweighed Bronco by a hundred pounds. Bronco didn't have a chance. Adam felt familiar feelings of guilt. It's my fault. I left the door open. Bronco would still be alive if I had done what I was supposed to do, he thought. Although it was only early November, this morning's freezing temperature and blowing snow forced him to accept that Bronco was never coming home.

Berthoud Pass received seventeen inches of snow last night. Living in the mountains made Adam very aware of the weather. He knew it was unlikely Sarah would make it over the pass in time for lunch. He wasn't surprised when Sarah called and told him she was in Idaho Springs. She'd been delayed by a snowslide on the pass and was told the road would be cleared in a few more hours. They agreed to meet at five o'clock.

Adam started most days by splitting firewood. Some days his back wouldn't let him do much, but today he felt great. After an hour, he'd worked up quite a sweat. As he walked toward the garage to put away the axe, he admired his Jeep-Wrangler Rubicon. I never thought I'd own a Jeep, but I love it. He smiled as he recalled the hours he spent off road rock crawling and trail riding.

He'd always been a Porsche guy, but moving to the mountains made it impractical to drive his Roadster on a daily basis. He stored her from early-November until May. During good weather there is nothing more fun than dropping Gisela's top and running the continental divide between Clear Creek Canyon and the upper valley of the Fraser River. When Edward Berthoud surveyed the pass in 1870, he said it might be suitable as a wagon road but not as a railroad. Although recent road improvements made the pass less treacherous, it is still arguably the most notoriously challenging pass in Colorado.

As he got in the jeep and headed for Antonio's, a snowplow drove past and left a two-foot high wall of snow at the end of his drive. Adam barely felt a bump as he blasted onto the dirt road that ran past his house. He regretted allowing Sarah to come to Colorado. His quest to find Julie's murder was a private thing. He didn't want or need any help. It also crossed his mind that she might be a witness to something he didn't want anyone to see. Yet, he understood that without Sarah's call he would never have had a chance of finding Julie's killer. A grim smile crossed his face as he thought about what he would do when he found Shepherd.

Antonio's, Adam's favorite restaurant in Winter Park, was definitely a blast from the past. Open only on Wednesday, Friday, and Saturday, the menu consisted of two items: cheese pizza and pepperoni pizza both sinfully greasy. Adam is a regular customer.

Before the tourists hit in late November, Antonio's served as the local hang out for retirees, local business folks, and a handful of year round ski bums. He enjoyed being recognized and welcomed at his favorite haunt. Some bars and restaurants gave him a local discount. He nodded to the Banana as he entered. The Banana's real name was Kenny Williams. Someone once told Kenny bananas were a good source of potassium, manganese, Vitamin C, and Vitamin B6. Since then he was seldom seen without a banana in his hand. He was a white water rafting guide in the summer and a backcountry ski guide in the winter. He was also about twenty years older than Adam. His white ponytail, puka shell necklace, and "make love, not war" jacket patch clearly identified him as an aging hippie. "Yo, Adam. You're not gonna try to ski again this year, are you? Man, last year you looked like the stiff old Tin Man in serious need of some oil."

Although there was more than a little truth to what the Banana said, Adam smiled and replied, "I found the oil, Banana. I'm ready to help you look for your brain."

Adam had skied a few times with Tom, the bartender. He stopped to talk with him about the coming season. They quickly reengaged their long-standing debate about the merits of snowboarding versus skiing.

"Ol'Pops, don't be so lame.," Tom urged. "Boarding is epic. Plus all the wicked women ride."

"Look, Tom, you know I hate snowboards. They're like the motorboats that pollute the air when I'm on the lake sailing. Boarders scrape off the moguls and are out of control half the time."

"Time has passed you by, my friend." Tom patted Adam on the back condescendingly and continued, "You just can't keep up, old timer."

Enjoying the banter Adam replied, "If you're just looking for speed, more speed, and nothing but speed, skiing beats snowboarding virtually every time."

"Sounds like bar talk. Don't let your mouth write a check your body can't cash. Let's settle this on the hill."

"I may have a few years on you, but I'm still the Big Dog. As soon as they have enough snow to open Retta's Run..."

Tom interrupted, "No. No. No. That's a sucker bet and you know it. No snowboarder can negotiate those mogul trenches. Let's make it fair. First one down the tree run between Sleeper and Riflesight Notch buys the other a fifth of his favorite scotch."

"You're on," Adam said as he shook Tom's hand.

Adam was still smiling as he turned and headed to his favorite corner table. He knew a skier would win the race if he were of equal ability to the boarder. He'd race Tom, but he knew his bad back, extra weight, and twenty-year age difference gave him no chance of winning.

A large wood-burning fireplace dominated the center of the room, but it was not the center of attention. Rather than being decorated with fake pub signs or reproduction photos of the Tuscan countryside, the walls and ceiling were covered with dollar bills decorated by three generations of patrons. Money was even laminated on the tabletops. Love notes, autographs, political statements, cartoons, and genuine art covered the bills in markers of every color of the rainbow. Adam guessed over ten thousand dollars covered every square inch of flat surface in the room.

When the bell over the door rang, Adam and every other man in the place looked up and stared at the woman who had just entered. Sarah hadn't described herself, but told Adam she would be carrying a large red leather briefcase. It was easy to see why she didn't give him more detail about how she looked. It would have been awkward for her to describe herself as "wow." She had a short reddish blond hair, a striking smile and moved with the grace of an athlete. When she looked his way, Adam stood and waved her over.

As she approached Adam's table he saw that her fair skin was lustrous, smooth and blemish free except for light sprinkle of freckles across her nose and cheeks. Before Adam could speak, Sarah grabbed a waiter's arm and said, "Dewers, rocks, a double!" She then collapsed into his booth. She looked exhausted and wired at the same time.

A straight scotch drinker! I like her already, Adam thought.

Without the formality of an introduction she said, "I didn't think I was going to make it over the pass. I was certain I was going to miss a turn and go plummeting down the side of the mountain or that a crazed trucker hurtling down the hill was going to take me out. I had too many near misses to count. I was traveling only about twenty miles an hour when I skidded on a turn, slid side ways, and smashed into a snow bank. After I stopped shaking, I got out of the car and saw that both wheels on the right side were off the road. Fortunately, an SUV with five young men stopped and rocked the car off the snowdrift."

Adam smiled as he patiently waited for a gap in her narrative. Sarah was talking so rapidly she was almost hyperventilating. Her scotch arrived and she took a large gulp, coughed, and continued, "That road is crazy, Mr. Faulkner, ..."

"Please, call me Adam."

"At the top of another turn I almost rear-ended a guy that decided to get out of his car and take photos of the aftermath of the snow slide. And I almost hit a freaking moose. Can you believe it? This is November, for God sake. What's this place like in March?"

"Worse," Adam admitted trying to hide a smile.

They talked about the weather, Winter Park, Sarah's job at the boutique bookstore, and Adam's love of the mountains. They shared information about their families, hobbies, and reading interests. They loved the Packers, hated the Yankees, loved Woody Allan movies and the Colbert Report, and didn't think curling was a sport. Their friendship was sealed when they discovered they were both avid skiers. After ordering a second round drinks and ordering a plain cheese pizza, the conversation turned to the reason for Sarah's trip.

"First, Sarah, even without knowing the details I understand that what Shepherd did to you was horrible. I doubt that anyone who hasn't been molested can ever truly understand, but I've worked with scores of women who have been raped and abused by someone they trusted. Each of these survivors is a hero, to me. I hope you know how proud you should be of yourself," Adam said.

Sarah lowered her eyes. "I don't feel like a hero. I pretended it didn't happen for so long. Now that I'm facing it, it's like it happened yesterday. In order for me to heal I have to find him."

"Why is it so important that you find Shepherd, after all these years?"

"Adam, It's not just what he did to me. I think I am going to be okay with that. But I feel so guilty knowing that if I said something when Mr. Shepherd molested me, maybe Molly would be alive. He may be out there right now molesting other children possibly killing them. If I would have told someone what he did to me, he might have been stopped. Who knows how many children have been hurt and maybe killed because of me? I'll never find peace until I know he's not out there molesting children. Haven't you ever felt guilty about anything? It's an awful feeling."

"Actually, I know exactly what you mean. Did Monica tell you what happened to my Julie?"

"Yes, she did, Adam. That's why we both thought you might want to help me."

"Even if we find him, it'll be very difficult for us to prove he molested you or that he killed Julie or Molly all those years ago. There's no statute of limitations on murder, but despite what you see on television, cold cases are pretty difficult to prove."

"Adam, I need to face him and show him I survived. But more importantly, we have to get him away from kids," Sarah said.

Adam studied Sarah's face for a moment. It was a blend of pain and horror tinged with hope. "We'll start tomorrow," Adam said, punctuating his resolve by setting his glass down hard on the table. He glanced out the window, "Weather's still threatening. Clearly, you can't drive back to Denver tonight. We're in between tourist seasons, and I would guess there are hotel rooms available. Listen, I have an extra room at my cabin if you want to save some money and would feel comfortable staying there."

No way, Julie thought to herself. He's probably safe, but being alone in a cabin with a strange man in the middle of nowhere is the last thing I'm going to do. "Thanks, Adam. I think I would prefer the hotel, if that's okay."

Stupid. Stupid, Adam thought. Aloud he said, "Absolutely. I know the owner of a small inn and I'm sure she'll give you a good rate."

Sarah got in her car and followed Adam through town. Ski and ride shops, bistros and condo rental agencies lined the main road. She was pleased to notice that there were no tee shirt shops to be seen. The new snow had highlighted the ski runs on the mountain. She wondered if she would ever have a chance to ski Winter Park. She followed Adam as he turned off at a lane marked with a tasteful sign for Doc Susie's Inn. Nestled in the woods along a scenic creek was a beautiful three-story Victorian home with turrets, dormers, turned posts, and decorative railings. The northeast corner of the house sported a shingled tower with angled bay windows, which allowed breathtaking views of Fraser Valley.

Adam and Sarah stamped the snow off their boots and entered a cozy reception area that smelled of strong coffee and freshly baked brownies. A note on the registration desk read, "Please ring bell." Adam tapped the solid brass Victorian desk bell and a surprisingly loud ring reverberated down the hallway. As they waited, Sarah read the plaque under the photo of Doctor Susie Anderson. It noted that the Inn was named in honor of Doc Susie, a high country physician who had graduated from the University of Michigan Medical School in 1897 and moved to the Fraser Valley. There she encountered avalanches, heavy snowdrifts, and prejudice because women doctors were rare. She and her little dog settled in a shack east of the tracks and provided medical care to the people in this small lumber camp. She died on April 16, 1960.

Sarah liked the fact that she was staying in a place named for a strong woman who had also graduated from the University of Michigan. Maybe this was a good omen. She knew they would need some luck to find Shepherd. Sarah turned at the sound of a woman's voice saying, "Well if it isn't the Sheriff from Ohio. Where've you been, Adam?"

Adam smiled and lifted Callie Sutherland off her feet and hugged her for several seconds. Clearly they're good friends, Sarah thought. Adam put Callie down, turned to Sarah and made introductions, "This is Callie. She owns Doc Susie's. Callie, this is Sarah Abbott."

Adam winked at Callie, "I told Sarah that this was the best inn in Colorado, and that you might be persuaded to give her a special off-season rate."

"You did, did you?" Callie pretended to be upset then broke into a smile again. "Well, sure. Any friend of yours will get special treatment." Callie took both of Sarah's hands in hers, "Hello Sarah. Welcome to Doc Susie's."

After checking in and putting her luggage in her room, Sarah met Adam in the large sitting room. Adam motioned her to the window. "Sarah, quick, come over here. You've got to see this, and it only lasts for a couple of minutes." Sarah rushed to the bay window. The sky, which had been overcast all day, was now clear. It had stopped snowing and the sun was just setting over Long's Peak. A glowing red horizontal band cut across Indian Peaks to the east then turned to deep purple.

"Wow, what is that?" Sarah gasped.

"It's called Alpenglow," Adam explained. "It's caused by the moisture from the snow receiving the scattered light from the setting sun."

"I've never seen anything like it. It's beautiful."

Callie stood in the doorway and wistfully watched them, wondering if Adam was going to spend the night with Sarah. She hoped not. They looked good together, but she doubted that Adam would ever settle down. She brought them a tray with two glasses, one ice filled and the other empty, and a bottle of Glenfiddich that she kept especially for his visits then left them to enjoy the fire. Adam put a log on the dying embers and sat in the leather chair next to Sarah's. By firelight, she reminded him of Lara from Dr. Zhivago.

"A little more scotch?" he asked.

"Sure, I'm still trying to mellow out after today's drive. Or after the past four months, for that matter," she added rather mournfully.

They sat quietly watching the fire for several minutes when Sarah startled Adam by blurting out "It makes me so freaking angry that this is part of who I am!"

After a few seconds of silence Adam gently asked, "What do you mean?"

"Well, Shepherd really messed me up. Until my counseling sessions I didn't know what was wrong with me, but I knew I wasn't like other women. I knew I wasn't gay, but I also knew I had almost no interest in men. I've had occasional first dates, but very few second dates." Sarah surprised herself by admitting such intimate information to a man she'd known for only a few hours.

Adam couldn't remember how many sexually abused boys and girls and men and women he had spoken with. The details of their stories were all unique but the result of their experience was exactly the same. A trusted adult took their innocence and their trust. No matter how many stories he heard, he was always moved by the impact the abuse had on victims. Regardless of the way the exploiter described the relationship, after it ended the youngsters were always damaged in some way. Adam understood what Sarah was saying but had no idea how to respond.

Sarah paused, waiting for a response. After a moment she added, "I haven't told this to anyone, but in therapy, after I really understood what Shepherd did to me, I fantasized about finding him and hurting him. Now I'm sort of afraid of what I might do to him when we find him."

Get in line, Adam thought grimly.

They watched the fire for a little longer, finished their drinks, and Sarah said she was sleepy and went to her room. Callie had turned down the feather comforter on the large canopied bed, laid out a luxurious spa robe, and lit the gas fireplace. Sarah thought the room was lovely. On the counter in the bath were a seaweed mineral bath pouch, a cranberry facial wash, a cucumber hair drench, and a rosemary honey hair conditioner. Sarah felt like she had been transported to an exclusive spa. As she slid into the hydro massaging tub, she felt herself relaxing for the first time in weeks.

Chapter 10

TUPICO FLATS, NEVADA

Lizzie was both frightened and excited to begin middle school. She looked forward to changing classes and having different teachers. As she neared the music room, she began thinking about Mr. Schafer. She felt lucky to be in his beginning band class. The girls agreed he was the most amazing teacher in the school.

The music room was freshly painted, and the built-in risers were glossy with fresh black enamel. Jim loved the risers. These girls were so naïve few of them kept their legs together when they were playing. I have the best job in the world, he thought.

Schafer had learned over the years that he had to break his girls down and destroy their self-confidence before he could begin making them dependent on him. He targeted only girls that he knew wouldn't report his behavior. He knew that when he started being nice to Lizzie she would be so grateful she would do anything to please him. When he had one of his girls totally brainwashed, the age difference no longer mattered.

The beginning band class consisted of eighteen girls and seven boys. Five of the boys said they were drummers. Most of the girls were carrying cases containing clarinets or flutes. It was late in the day and the smell of teenage boys and girls who dodged the shower routine in P.E. hung over the room. Schafer talked about his goals for the class and said, "There is nowhere in the world I'd rather be than right here in Tupico Flats, teaching the greatest kids in the world." He ended his introduction by having all his students stand in a circle, clasp hands and shout the mantra, "Goooooo spider band!" After handing out sheet music for the first piece they were going to learn he visited with the students to determine their musical experience. A number of the students had some private lessons behind them. However, most were starting from ground zero. The bell rang, and the students began filing out of the room.

As Lizzie was leaving the band room after the third week of class, Schafer called out to her, "Lizzie, stay for a minute, will you please?"

Lizzie was shocked, but pleased. She didn't think Mr. Schafer even knew her name. She wondered what he could want. She smiled to herself as she noticed several of her classmates eying her jealously as they filed out of the room.

She walked to the front of the room and stood before Mr. Shepherd's desk. It was cluttered with stacks of books and sheet music, and two antique metronomes. An old-fashioned silver picture frame held a photo of a woman and a girl who Lizzie supposed must be Mr. Schafer's family. A perfect family, she thought. A dozen or so photos of junior high school girls were pressed like butterflies under the large piece of glass that covered the desktop. Lizzie didn't recognize any of them. They stared up at her, forever thirteen years old.

Mr. Schafer continued to shuffle through some papers as Lizzie stood there looking at the photos. After a few minutes, when the other students had all left the room, he looked up and glared at her, neither smiling nor frowning. "What do you think you're doing in this class?" He continued without waiting for Lizzie's response. "Who told you, you could play the clarinet? You're the worst student in the class. Your playing sounds like a cat being pulled through a fence." He paused and then added, "Hell, you may be the worst student I've ever had."

Lizzie stood astonished, too stunned to move. She felt lightheaded, her vision blurred, and she heard a ringing in her ears. She thought she was going to faint. She grasped the desktop to steady herself. Despite her shock she knew she didn't want Mr. Shepherd to see her cry, so when tears started to sting her eyes, she turned and ran from the room. She didn't stop running until she was in the park across the street from the school. She sat on a park bench and tried to make sense of what had just happened. I'm just a beginner. What does he expect of me? She wondered.

At breakfast the next morning Lizzie said, "Mom, I don't feel well. I think I should stay home from school today."

Mrs. Sutton felt Lizzie's forehead. "You don't have a fever. Your color is good. I can't stay home with you today. Go to school. If you don't get to feeling better, go to the nurse's room and ask the nurse to call me at work."

"Mom, I don't like band. I want to drop it."

Mrs. Sutton was losing her patience. She was already late for work. "Lizzie, don't be silly. You've only had a couple of classes. If you still don't like band at the end of the term you can drop it."

"But Mr. Shepherd is a jerk."

Mrs. Sutton had seen her share of jerks. She was sorry that Lizzie was learning about men so soon. "Lizzie, there are a lot of jerks in the world. You just have to learn to deal with them. Just ignore him."

Lizzie went to school but couldn't concentrate in any of her morning classes. She kept thinking about what Mr. Schafer had said to her. She was petrified at the thought of going back into the music room. When band time came she was grateful that Mr. Schafer ignored her. He continued to ignore her every day for the next week while lavishing praise upon almost every other student. She couldn't take her eyes off of him. As she became more and more nervous her clarinet playing became worse and worse.

A few weeks later Schafer again called Lizzie up to his desk after class. Lizzie froze. She wanted to get up and run away but he was her teacher she knew she had to go to him. Again he made her wait. Maybe he is going to say he's sorry, Lizzie hoped. Schafer finally looked up and hissed, "You are too ugly to sit in the front row. Go to the back of the room, where I don't have to look at you."

Again, Lizzie's breath left her in a rush. Her mouth filled with an acrid taste. She thought she was going to throw up. As tears welled up into her eyes for the second time in two weeks she ran out of the room. This time she didn't stop running until she was home. Lizzie went to her room, closed the door, curled up on the bed, and cried herself to sleep.

Schafer had done his research on Lizzie. She was unhappy at home. Her parents had divorced when Lizzie was eight years old. She now lived with her mother. Mrs. Sutton seemed to be a nice person who was over worked and stressed out. Schafer had never seen Lizzie with any girlfriends. She seemed to be a loner. Some of Schafer's previous victims had come from two parent families, but he'd learned that it was easier to groom and seduce girls who weren't close to friends or family. He made a point of talking with Lizzie's mom at the open house the first week of school. Schafer was pretty confident that Lizzie wouldn't tell anyone what was happening in music class. He knew there were always risks, but he was confident he could talk his way out of any problem.

A few days later as Lizzie was walking down the hall, she looked up to see Mr. Schafer standing directly in front of her. She had to stop to avoid running right into him. As she started to walk around Schafer, he stepped in front of her and whispered, "With a face like yours, you'd have to put a bag over your head if you ever wanted to get asked on a date."

Lizzie felt like she had been punched in the stomach. She stood in the hall long after it had cleared of other students and teachers. Her skin was clammy and she couldn't seem to remember how to walk. She was too bewildered to form a thought. She simply was not equipped to deal with what was happening to her. She went to the nurse's office and truthfully said she had a stomachache.

Within a month Lizzie seemed to be shrinking. She missed several days of school. When she was there, she just sat in her classes staring at her desk. Her stomach ached all the time. She knew that if she had any lunch, she would throw up. In music class she sat in the back of the room and stared at her feet not even pretending to play her clarinet.

Schafer honestly didn't like this phase of the conditioning process, but he'd learned it was necessary. He knew he had to break Lizzie down completely before he could move on to the next stage. For several more weeks he surreptitiously watched Lizzie in class and in the hallway. He was relieved when it was time to progress to the next phase. When Lizzie got to class on Monday morning, Schafer caught her attention and motioned for her to come up to his desk. Lizzie felt a trickle of pee soil her panties. She knew she couldn't endure another attack. She thought about escaping, but she couldn't move. After a moment, she stood and shambled cautiously to Schafer's desk, dreading what was about to happen. When she mustered enough courage to look up, she was baffled to see a smile on his face.

"Lizzie, you really look very pretty today," Schafer said in a friendly tone, "I like the way you're wearing your hair. Why don't you sit near the front of the room from now on so I can look at you."

Lizzie was as shocked at his approval as she had been at his initial criticism. She smiled uncertainly and took a seat in the front row. Over the next few weeks Schafer alternated complimenting her appearance and completely ignoring her. She kept her eyes on him from the minute she walked into the room, never knowing what to expect. Desperately wanting his approval she practiced her clarinet as often as she could. Her stomach was still upset when she went to band class, but things were slowly changing.

At the end of Friday's class period a few weeks later, Schafer repeated his habit of asking Lizzie to wait for a minute after class. This time he smiled at her and said, "Lizzie, I think you have real potential as a musician. Your playing would really improve though, with some extra tutoring. Would you like me to give you some extra help after school?"

She smiled eagerly, "Okay."

"Now Lizzie, I'm not supposed to play favorites, so you can't tell anyone that I'm helping you. It will be our little secret. Let's start Monday right after school here in the music room. Lizzie left the classroom without tears, with a smile, a light heart, and puzzled but happy thoughts.

Lizzie thought about band class all weekend. She even dreamed about Mr. Schafer's class. On Sunday evening she tried on all her favorite school clothes. She wanted to find the perfect outfit to please Mr. Schafer. She selected her favorite pair of jeans and a new black shirt that had neon butterflies on it. She woke up early Monday morning and went into the bathroom she shared with her mother to borrow her mother's shampoo and herbal conditioner. She thought about Mr. Schafer as she showered. She brushed her teeth twice and rinsed with mouthwash before heading to the school bus stop.

After school ended on Monday Lizzie hurried to the music room and looked around for Mr. Schafer. When she saw him standing near the closet, she smiled shyly, gave him a little wave, and walked to the back of the room. Her heart was fluttering and her mouth was dry. I'm not going to be able to speak, let alone play my clarinet, she thought.

In the back of the music room there was a large closet used to store band instruments. In order to secure the instruments the door had a lock. The closet had floor to ceiling shelving on three sides. The shelves were jam-packed with tattered sheet music and dented musical instruments. Broken music stands were piled in a corner. At the far end of the room metal racks held all the band uniforms. The room smelled of musty wool and dried sweat. The room was lit with a single light bulb that swung from a cord hung from the middle of the ceiling. Before Lizzie arrived, Schafer had gone into the closet and placed two metal folding chairs side-by-side facing a single music stand.

When Lizzie arrived Schafer said, "We're going to have our lesson in here so that we won't disturb anyone who might be in one of the other classrooms." Schafer entered the room first and sat in the chair closest to the door. Lizzie tried to squeeze past him to get to the second chair. As she turned her back to him and attempted to slide by, he stood and pushed his erection against her. She kept moving and sat down next to him. She was unsure of what had just happened. She had heard girls talking about boys getting "boners," but she wasn't sure what they were. Maybe it was an accident, she thought. She tried to act like nothing had happened.

Lizzie and Schafer spent almost an hour together. When they were finished with the lesson, Lizzie packed her clarinet and started to leave. Without provocation Schafer blurted out, "Lizzie, you know no one will ever love you, don't you?"

"What?" Lizzie sputtered. She wondered if she had heard him correctly.

"I said, no one will ever love you," Schafer repeated quietly gazing into her eyes.

Lizzie choked back a sob and hurried from the room. As she walked home she asked herself why he was so mean one day and so nice the next. She wondered what she was doing wrong. She promised herself she would never go back into that room again.

By the next scheduled lesson, Lizzie had convinced herself that Mr. Schafer had bumped her accidentally, and his comment about love was just teasing. Over the next three lessons Schafer kept the atmosphere light and friendly. He even joked about how small the room was. On Friday, as Lizzie was getting ready to leave, Schafer said, "You've been practicing. Your playing has really improved."

As she was leaving after Monday's lesson, Schafer took both her hands in his, stared into her eyes for a moment, and said, "Lizzie, do you know that no one will ever love you...no one but me? You are so mature for your age, so pretty, so smart. I've never had a student like you. I think about you all the time and really look forward to our time together."

Lizzie was dumbfounded. She simply smiled, nodded, and walked away. On her way home she couldn't get Mr. Schafer's words out of her head. I think about you all the time and really look forward to our time together. Lizzie couldn't wait for her next lesson. Every day for the next week Schafer told her how special she was and how much he loved her. "It's like we are boyfriend and girlfriend, not teacher and student. I feel like we can tell each other anything," he said.

During the next several lessons Schafer's conversations got more and more personal. He told Lizzie he no longer loved his wife and they were getting a divorce. "You are prettier and sexier than my wife," he said. At one of the sessions, Schafer stood behind her as she played. He rested his hands on her shoulders and said, "Your neck and shoulders seem to get so tense when you play. Most of my students relax when I give them a little neck massage. Is it okay if I massage your neck?"

Lizzie wasn't sure how she felt about this offer, but Mr. Schafer already had his hands on her shoulders and she liked the feel of them. Schafer's hands were soft, but strong. She also liked the smell of his after-shave, English Leather. That's the same kind mom helped me pick out for daddy for Father's Day before he went away, she thought.

At each session for the next week Schafer massaged Lizzie's neck and shoulders as he softly told her how pretty she was. Finally one day while he was rubbing her back he slid his hand down under the back of her panties. Lizzie's whole body clinched as she tried to squirm away from him. She kept trying to play her clarinet without saying a word. Schafer, cupped her in his hand, and smiled to himself. His breathing sped up. I have her now. He silently exclaimed. None of my girls have ever stopped me after I got this far.

Now at each lesson Schafer put his hands under her clothing as he told her he loved her and that "No one will ever love you the way I do." Lizzie hadn't truly felt that she was loved since her father had left them. She began to believe that Schafer was in love with her. She eventually found it easy and comfortable to respond, "I love you, too."

Schafer's next step was to kiss Lizzie on the lips. He knew how important the first kiss is to a young girl. It was Lizzie's first real grown-up kiss. She had thought about what her first kiss would be like. She had even surfed the web to a site that talked about different kinds of kisses. She was mystified by the difference between friend kisses, vacuum kisses, and going for the kill kisses. Discussions about the yawn technique confused her further. She didn't really know how to kiss so she just pushed her lips against his. She was frightened when he started to breathe heavily as he touched her. She thought he might be having a heart attack.

Over the next few weeks, Schafer occasionally put his hands down the front of her pants or under her shirt as he kissed her. On other days he wouldn't touch her at all. He made sure that he smiled and told her how special she was, and gave her a hug each day as she left the music room. When he kissed her goodbye he would gently suck on her lower lip. He started to call her "Little Lizzie." At first she didn't like this name because she thought he was making fun of her tiny breasts, but he told her that people in love had "pet" names for each other.

Over the years, Schafer had learned it is very dangerous to move too fast or to use force on his girls. Other than Julie and Sarah, the only really big mistake he ever made was with Molly. Sometimes months would go by when he didn't think about

Molly. But then there were days, like today, when his stomach churned, his mouth tasted of copper, and he couldn't stop remembering what had happened at Arrowhead Lake Music Camp.

The streamside camp, nestled in four acres of pine trees, drew middle and high school music students from a five state area. Originally a sawmill and lumber camp of the M. E. Harding Lumber Company, the property was converted to vacation cottages in 1945, a church retreat in 1961, and a music camp in 1986. The view from the seventeen rustic cabins was breathtaking.

Thoughts of the camp brought back the sound of the stream trickling over the beaver dam, the sweet smell of pine, the pungent odor of Skunk Cabbage and Wapato, and the lifeless body of Molly Lincoln lying on her bunk. He tried to keep from thinking about Molly, but he couldn't ever get her completely out of his mind.

When he got the letter offering him a contract at the camp he recalls thinking that teaching at a music camp was even better than at a middle school. He would have access to the girls twenty-four hours a day. Shepherd would never have taken the job if he had known his dream job would quickly turn into a nightmare.

Although all of the campers were exceptionally bright and advanced, Molly Lincoln was truly a wunderkind. She absolutely loved the piano and practiced relentlessly. Her teachers and parents were awed by her dedication and virtuosity. Because she was shy and socially inept, she didn't spend much time with children her own age. Shepherd immediately saw her as a target of opportunity.

Because he feared a repeat of Julie's violent reaction Shepherd knew he had to figure out a method of subduing Molly while he molested her. It was his cat, Jingles, who solved his problem. Jingles was attacked by a feral cat and suffered several bites and lacerations. She developed several abscesses that needed to be lanced and surgically drained. Dr. Jones, his veterinarian, told Shepherd she would be using Ketamine to sedate Jingles. She told him the sedating effect would last 30-60 minutes. It was easy for Shepherd to distract Dr. Jones and steal a vial of Ketamine.

He patiently waited for his opportunity to use it on Molly. Finally, three weeks into the summer he got his chance. The whole camp was going on a day trip to Albany to attend a "Classical Music is Cool" concert. Shepherd took Molly aside the night before the concert and told her she needed extra practice if she was going to be ready for the camp recital.

"You can go to a concert anytime. Tell your counselor that you're having menstrual cramps and need to stay in bed. When the other campers are gone we can practice together." he told her.

"I don't know. I don't want to get in trouble."

"Don't worry," Shepherd assured her. "No one will know. You really do need the extra practice."

The next day he poured the Ketamine into a can of soda pop and continued walking to Molly's cabin. Molly opened the cabin door when he knocked.

"Hi, Molly. Before we go over to the practice room I want to go over the score you are going to use in the recital. You're having problems in several places. It's really hot out there. I brought you a cold Tab."

Shepherd put his hand on her shoulder as they walked toward her bunk. She didn't resist as he sat down beside her. He planned on performing oral sex on her after the Ketamine knocked her out. After a few sips of the Tab she became groggy and disoriented. Shepherd stroked her back as she lost consciousness. As he pulled down her pants, she started vomiting. He tried to wake her up but she went into convulsions and stopped breathing. Shepherd panicked. He'd previously told everyone he had a family emergency and was going to go home for a day. He picked up the Tab can and ran from the room. Three hours later he was pulling into his driveway in Summer Haven.

When Mrs. Polaski, the camp nurse, checked on Molly and found her body, it was clear that Molly had been dead for several hours. The police were summoned and they called the county coroner. After Molly's parents told the coroner that their daughter suffered from cyclical vomiting syndrome he ruled her death was the result of a previous medical condition.

Shepherd spent the next two weeks after Molly's death in absolute terror. He was certain he was going to be discovered and arrested. Then they will find out about Julie, he thought. The tales he had heard about the fate of child molesters at the hands of fellow prisoners haunted his waking hours. He slowly came to the realization that should he be discovered it would be better to kill himself than to go to prison. When the coroner ruled Molly's death accidental Shepherd was overcome with relief. I will never, ever touch a girl again, he vowed. But two months later he was at a new school scoping out a new batch of fourteen-year-old girls.

Chapter 11

SUMMER HAVEN, PENNSYLVANIA

Two weeks after Sarah visited Adam at Winter Park she waited for him in the baggage area of Lehigh Valley International Airport. Lehigh, Pennsylvania had the closest airport to Summer Haven. She'd flown in from Boston and Adam was arriving from Denver. Sarah's previous visit to Summer Haven and several subsequent phone calls by Adam had failed to uncover where Shepherd went after he left town. Adam had agreed to travel with Sarah's to her old school and see if they could find any clues to Shepherd's whereabouts. With almost four hundred arrests to his credit Adam knew that most of these vipers were unrepentant, manipulative and dangerous. They were also compulsive and couldn't stop even if they wanted to. If he's still out there, I'll find him, Adam thought.

Adam couldn't wait to get started. As a child he read and reread all of the Sherlock Holmes mysteries. He sometimes thought of himself as a modern day Holmes. Adam was confident he would pick up the thread that would lead them to Shepherd. The game's afoot. Release the hounds, he mumbled to himself as he waved to Sarah as he stepped off the escalator. Knowing better than to hug a sexual abuse survivor, he waited for her to reach out to shake his hand. He was again impressed by her firm grip and pleased to see her friendly smile. They picked up their bags, signed for the rental car, and headed for the parking lot.

Sarah walked slightly ahead of Adam as they walked to the parking lot. When they found their car they both went to the driver's side. Sarah got there first and got behind the wheel. Adam ended up standing outside the driver's side looking in at her. He shrugged, smiled, walked around the car and got in the passenger side.

"It will be easier if I drive," Sarah explained. "I know where we're going. Besides, I don't much like riding in the passenger seat."

As they drove toward Summer Haven, they talked about their strategy for finding Shepherd. Adam knew that no one could disappear without leaving any trace. He also knew that someone in Summer Haven could tell them where Shepherd went. The trick was going to be finding that someone.

As they drove, Sarah said, "This is Pennsylvania Dutch country. Do you like Pennsylvania Dutch food?"

"I pretty.much like any food." Adam said surreptitiously sucking in his stomach. He wasn't quite fat but knew he was only a few Twinkies away from the husky department.

"Great! You'll love the Blue Boar Inn."

After driving for about forty minutes they rounded a bend and came upon a signboard for the Blue Boar Inn. They drove up the cobblestone lane to a charming Bavarian cottage that looked as though it had been there for a hundred years. Adam was surprised to see that the parking lot was almost full. A young woman wearing what Adam assumed was supposed to be traditional German dress met them at the door. Oom-pah band music played in the background as they entered the little dining room. After they were seated, they discussed the colorful murals painted on the walls and ceiling. The scenes depicted everything from the birth of Christ to Neil Armstrong's walk on the moon. When their waiter arrived wearing lederhosen Adam felt he was at Disney's Epcot Theme Park. Because he sensed that the restaurant was special for Sarah, he refrained from asking when the laser light show would begin.

Adam looked confused as he read over the menu, which included such items as Chow chow, shoofly pie, schnitz and knepp, chicken pot pie, dried corn, and whoopie pies.

"This sounds like cartoon food. What is all this stuff?" he asked.

Sarah happily provided him with details about the food. "Chow Chow is a relish. Originally at the end of the canning season Amish cooks often had small quantities of carrots, onions, cauliflower, cucumbers, cabbage, celery, corn, peppers, and assorted beans. Everything goes into Chow Chow. Be prepared for a sour taste."

"Sounds delightful," he said sarcastically. "I think I'll pass."

Sarah was not discouraged. "I promise that you'll like Schnitz and Knepp. Schnitz is dried apple slices. Knepp is a kind of dumpling"

Adam grimaced, "This keeps getting better and better."

"Okay, but no matter what you get for an entree, you must have the most famous Amish desert, a slice of shoofly pie. It is similar to coffeecake with the addition of a gooey molasses bottom."

"I'll bite," Adam ventured. "How did it get its name?"

"I was afraid you wouldn't ask, Sarah smiled. It's pretty straightforward. The sweet ingredients attracted flies when the pies were cooling. The cooks had to "shoo" the flies away."

Sarah convinced Adam to try one of the house specialties, Hasenpfeffer, German rabbit stew.

Several Spaten Pils later they both agreed that the stew was a great choice.

Adam asked, "Shoofly pie?"

"No, I don't think so."

"What? I thought it was your favorite."

"No. I have saved the best for last. My favorite dessert of all is the whoopie pie."

"You're making this up."

"My dad and I would always get a half a dozen whoopie pies to take home. They're not really pies. There more like Hostess Ho Ho Cakes, on steroids. Dad and I would take them home and mom would freeze them. We'd eat them like an ice cream sandwich."

By now they were both relaxed and enjoying the evening. Adam couldn't remember when he'd enjoyed anyone's company as much as he did Sarah's. It seemed they had known each other for years. As their third pilsners arrived, Sarah smiled and asked, "Adam, may I ask you a personal question?"

Adam looked surprised. "I guess so, sure."

"Why do you shave your head?"

Adam laughed. "You are the oldest person to ever ask me that question."

Sarah was not sure if she has just been insulted or if Adam was embarrassed. "I'm sorry if I said something I shouldn't have."

"No, no, not at all. I shaved my head long before Michael Jordan and Bruce Willis shaved theirs. "When I was a cop in Ohio, neighborhood kids would ask me that all the time. I would make a game of it and have them guess the reason. Want to play?"

"No, I don't think so. I'm already a little gun shy."

"Okay, then don't tell me what you think. Guess the answers the kids gave."

"Only if you promise you won't get upset," Sarah said cautiously.

"Promise."

"Will you tell me if I guess the right answer?"

"Absolutely".

"Biker?"

"No."

"Skin Head?"

"No."

"Pro Wrestler?"

"No."

"Neo Nazi?"

"God, no."

"Cancer?"

"No."

"Religious order?"

"No."

"Going bald?"

"Partial credit."

"Vanity?"

"Bingo! I looked in the mirror one day and saw the receding hairline and thought I would look better, handsomer, with a shaved head. What do you think?"

"I love it."

"Sorry, that was a shameless effort to get a compliment."

"I think it's a great look for you." Sarah couldn't believe what she said next. "I've always wondered what a shaved head felt like."

Adam smiled nervously and tilted his head forward. "Don't let me stop you."

Sarah leaned forward, placed both of her hands on Adam's head, and briefly caressed it. He was startled at the electric shock that coursed through his body. He had long known that most men have a sexual arousal compartment and a romance compartment and there was often no communication between the two. He wondered if his arousal was from having an attractive woman caressing his head, or if he was starting to fall for Sarah.

His musing was interrupted when the server brought their desserts.

They lingered over steaming cups of Kronng coffee and talked until the manager told them he wanted to close the restaurant. They drove to their hotel in Breinigsville.

As Sarah opened the door to her room she turned and smiled at Adam. She felt really comfortable around him. For the first time in a long time she felt comfortable being around a man. She smiled as she said good night and slowly closed the door.

When Adam got to his room he considered calling Sarah and asking if she wanted company. He picked up the phone several times before he got the bottle of Glennfiddich from his bag and poured himself a hefty nightcap.

As he faded in and out of sleep he thought of all the women he'd ever loved. There were just two: Julie and Judith. As he drifted off to sleep erotic thoughts about Sarah mingled with memories of his four-year marriage to Judith.

Adam had met Judith during his investigation of a particularly gruesome child abuse case. She was the teacher who reported the physical and sexual abuse of one of her third grade boys. Adam was the SVU detective in charge of the case. The initial attraction was mutual admiration of each other's commitment to children. After getting to know one another during the investigation and trial they began dating. They saw each other exclusively for over a year and then got married in the shadow of the Matterhorn at Zermatt, Switzerland.

The first year of their marriage was one long honeymoon filled with laughter and adventure. Adam had accumulated a ton of vacation time, which allowed them to take skiing vacations to Aspen, Vail, Snowbird, and Alta. Their friends said they had the kind of marriage that would last forever. It didn't.

They had been married a little over four years the night Adam pulled his unmarked department car to the curb in front of their house at three in the morning. He just sat there, physically exhausted and mentally drained, unable to get out of the car. Jimmy was probably killed within a few hours of being abducted, but it had taken three months to find his decaying body in a shallow grave behind an abandoned schoolhouse. Adam spent the last hour sitting with six-year-old Jimmy Jones' parents. When he told them he had found Jimmy's body Mrs. Jones collapsed into her husband's arms. Mr. Jones gasped as if he had been punched in the chest. Adam never got used to this part of the job. Even after all these years each time he had to report a child's death his own emotions bubbled to the surface. Each time a body was recovered he relived the day that he heard that they had found Julie's remains.

Adam had been wearing the same clothes for two days and hadn't showered or shaved in over thirty hours. His shirt smelled of cigarette smoke, spilled coffee, sweat, and death. He planned on sleeping until about seven in the morning and then getting back on the trail of the bastard who killed Jimmy. Because he never had the satisfaction of seeing Julie's murderer caught and punished, he understood how much Jimmy's parents needed some closure. This was the first night in three days that he'd been able to come home to sleep. He felt a tremendous relief at being home.

When he opened the front door, he was surprised to see Judith sitting in the living room waiting for him. She was wearing black slacks and the powder blue sweater Adam bought her for her last birthday. The reading light behind her gave her blond hair a soft angelic glow. Each time Adam saw her she took his breath away. He said a silent prayer of thanks that he had found her and they had fallen in love. She really turned him on in that sweater yet he wondered briefly why she wasn't in her pajamas. As tired as he was, he hoped that maybe after a shower they could spend some time together before they went to sleep, but when he saw the pensive, subdued look on Judith's face, all thoughts of romance faded. He knew something was terribly wrong. His first thoughts were of Judith's mother who had been suffering from dementia for several years.

Adam quickly closed the front door and walked toward Judith ready to kiss her hello.

"Hi Hon, what are you doing up so late? Has something happened to your mom?

"No, Mom is fine. We need to talk, Adam," she said solemnly as she deflected his embrace.

"It must be something serious if you waited up this late."

"Something's happened to us."

"What do you mean?"

"Adam, I've tried, but I can't take this any more."

"Hon, what are you talking about? You can't take what anymore?

"Our marriage," she said softly.

"What's wrong? We have a great marriage."

She was silent for a few seconds. Then her voice cracked and she murmured, "The fact that you think so is a big part of the problem."

Adam sank down on the large leather couch and motioned for her to join him. He thought all she needed was a little assurance.

She sat across from him on the ottoman.

There was a catch in his voice when he spoke. "Have I done something wrong? Whatever it is, I can fix it."

"How can you fix a problem you can't admit exists?"

The room seemed to be closing in on him. The stale smell coffee wafted in from the breakfast nook. The living room was dark except for the reading light by Judith's chair. There was no music playing. That was odd. Judith loved jazz and was always playing Monk or Brubeck.

Judith continued. Her words came in a rush. "I won't live like this any more, Adam. I never know when you're coming home, or if you are coming home. I jump at each phone call, thinking it will be a cop telling me you've been hurt or killed. It is not just the fear. When you are home you're not really here. You live, eat, and sleep sexual abuse, kidnapping, rape, and murder. It's like you're drunk on the thrill of the chase. It is a compulsion with you. I'm so sick of hearing about your cases I could scream."

"Judith, you knew there were risks with my job. We talked about this before we were married. You knew what you were getting in to. Besides, now that I'm with SVU, I'm seldom in any real danger. I know I bring too much of my work home with me. I'm sorry. This has been a tough year. I'll do better. I'll leave my work at the office. I promise."

"Bull shit." Judith exploded. "Honestly, Adam, how many times have we had this conversation? I admire your dedication to helping children. I know you are great at your job and are doing really important work. I just need more in my life than you're capable of giving me. I love my work, too, but it is not my life."

Adam's mind was reeling as he tried to make sense of what Judith was saying. There had to be more to this than his dedication to his work. He asked weakly, "Is there someone else?"

Judith was quick to answer. "No, there is no one else. But, honestly, I've decided that I want there to be someone else. I need to know I'm the most important person in someone's life. When you're on a case, all of your passion and attention is diverted from me."

Adam's body went cold. He knew Judith was right. He'd tried to put his work in perspective. Sometimes, for months at a time, he would be home for dinner most nights. They would go to the movies or go out for dinner. They had even taken a few trips out of town. But eventually another case involving an abducted or raped child would consume his time and his thoughts. He couldn't help himself.

Judith and Adam talked all night. They both cried. In the end they decided, or Judith decided and Adam accepted, that their marriage was over. That night was seven years ago. Two years after the divorce, Adam was shot and left the force. By then Judith had moved to Florida and gotten remarried.

Reliving his marriage finally exhausted Adam and he fell into a fitful sleep.

Chapter 12

Early the next morning Adam and Sarah drove the last few hours to Summer Haven. Adam smiled and shook his head at the signboard as they entered the city limits, "Summer Haven, One E away from Heaven." Although Sarah had already been there, Adam wanted to look around and ask some questions. Just as Adam predicted, they ran into a lot of dead ends. Ron Thomas, Sarah's principal, had retired to someplace in the South. His secretary had Alzheimer's and was in a nursing home in Michigan. The superintendent of schools died two years ago. Most of the other teachers who had been at the school when Sarah was a student had retired, left teaching, or simply disappeared.

Adam decided to try another approach. He had handbills printed that displayed Sarah's photo taken from her middle school yearbook. The copy on the handbills read, "A young girl was molested by a Summer Haven teacher in 1985. If you have any information that might help her, please call 303.555.2115," Adam's cell phone number.

The day after the first poster went up, Adam received a call from Nancy Allen.

"Mr. Faulkner, I saw your flier at the grocery store this morning. I might be able to help you. I'm not sure. All I really know is that my daughter was molested by a teacher around the same time mentioned in your notice. Mindy, that's my daughter, wouldn't let me press charges. I've always regretted not filing a police report against this guy. His name was Tony Shepherd. He was the band teacher. I have no proof but I suspect he could also be responsible for a girl's death. Do you think we could be talking about the same guy?" The voice on the other end of the line was suddenly choked with emotion.

The hair stood up on the back of Adam's arms. Could it be this easy? He wondered. "Mrs. Allen," Adam began. He was striving to keep his voice calm and professional. As he talked he put her address into his GPS. "I'm just twenty minutes away. May we come to your house and speak with you?"

"Yes, I'll be home all evening."

Adam and Sarah walked to Mrs. Allen's front door and Adam rang the bell.

Mrs. Allen answered immediately. The Allan home was a nice ranch house that sat on what once was a well-maintained yard but was now dry and brown. A hollow cheeked matronly woman with gaunt eyes introduced herself as Nancy Allen. She looked to be about sixty years old and had an unhealthy pallor. When she saw Sarah she immediately said, "I know you. You're the Abbott girl. I used to play bridge with your aunt. Did Shepherd hurt you too?"

"Yes, Mrs. Allen, I'm Sarah Abbott. This is my colleague, Adam Faulkner. Thank you for agreeing to talk with us."

They were ushered into a comfortable living room decorated with family photographs. The dominant photos were of a beautiful young girl. Mrs. Allen invited them to sit down. "Can I get you something to drink?"

Sarah and Adam asked for coffee and studied the photographs while they waited for Mrs. Allen to return from the kitchen.

"I remember Mindy" Sarah told Mrs. Allen upon her return to the living room. "She was a few years younger than me. Is she okay? Where is she now?"

Mrs. Allen hesitated then said softly, "Mindy's had a rough time. She dropped out of school in the tenth grade and ran away. She can't seem to hold a job or a husband. She's been divorced twice and has been in counseling off and on for years. For the past year she's been living in Texas. We've just recently reconnected, but she still hasn't forgiven me or her father."

"Forgiven you for what?" Adam asked gently.

"Well, I noticed that Mindy was changing early in the seventh grade. She seemed depressed. She started having a sick stomach in the mornings. She didn't want to go to school most days. Her teachers told me that she had almost stopped talking in class and didn't seem to care about her schoolwork. We took her to our family physician and he said she was exhibiting symptoms similar to traumatic stress disorder. We were at our wit's end."

Adam realized that this information was valuable. "Excuse me, Mrs. Allen," Adam interrupted, "do you mind if I record our conversation?"

"If it will help catch that somabitch."

Adam got out his digital recorder and turned it on.

Ms. Allen continued, "Mindy said Mr. Shepherd made her stay after school for private music lessons."

`Sarah almost stopped breathing. She leaned toward Mrs. Allen and asked, "What did Mindy tell you Mr. Shepherd did to her?"

`"At first she told us he just made her feel uncomfortable. She said he would stare at her chest, brush against her body, and touch her hair, stuff like that. We asked her if he had touched her private parts. She said "no." She said they hadn't had sex, but she was afraid that was going to be next. When we asked her what she meant, she said all her friends knew that Mr. Shepherd was having sex with an older girl."

Sarah's body went cold and her heart raced. She thought she was going vomit. She looked at Adam and mouthed, "There are others." Then she stood up and rushed out the front door and onto the front porch. Sarah's unexpected outburst pushed Mrs. Allen over the edge and she began to weep.

Adam started to go out and try to comfort Sarah, but stopped when he realized that he couldn't think of anything helpful to say. After a few moments Sarah returned and sat back down. When Mrs. Allen regained her composure Adam continued the interview. "Mrs. Allen, what did you and your husband do when Mindy told you what Mr. Shepherd did to her?"

"We complained about Mr. Shepherd to the principal, and the superintendent, and even to the police. No one believed us because Mindy denied it ever happened to her and couldn't or wouldn't give us the names of any of the other girls she suspected were being molested."

Sarah was stunned. "It was me! I was one of the girls he molested, " she said.

Tears welled up again in Mrs. Allen's, "Oh Sarah, I'm so sorry that happened to you, too. They let Shepherd resign and leave town. The summer after he left, Mindy finally told us that Mr. Shepherd was having oral sex with her. You can't imagine what this type of information does to a parent."

Sarah said, "Do you mean he was molesting Mindy at the same time he molesed me?"

"Of course, we didn't know about you, then, but yes. After what you have told me, I guess he molesed several girls. We thought she was at music class. She finally told us he kept taking her to a little cabin outside of town and made her have oral sex with him. She said he told her he would hurt her dad and me if she told anyone. He really knew how to intimidate children. Mindy told us that when he drove her to the cabin he would pretend to talk into a head set and say things like. "Yes, I'm with Mindy now. Are you watching her mother? You know what to do to Mindy's mother if Mindy ever tells anyone? Yes, shoot her." Mindy said she was so frightened that when he did things to her she would go away in her mind and later couldn't remember what happened."

Sarah chocked back a sob. "I feel so guilty. If I'd told someone, maybe Mindy wouldn't have been hurt. I'm responsible for all of this. I should have said something."

"Don't blame yourself, honey, Mrs. Allen comforted. We told everyone and no one helped us. No one tried to stop him. But I know what guilt can do to a person. When we learned what happened, Mindy's father, David, went berserk. He confronted Shepherd and attacked him. If Shepherd had brought charges, David would have gone to jail. I guess Shepherd knew that his secret would come out if he took us to court. After Mindy ran away, David was never the same. He was overcome by his failure to protect his daughter. We divorced a few years later."

Adam didn't say anything for a few moments. Then he said, "Mrs. Allen, you mentioned on the phone that you suspected Shepherd was responsible for a girl's death. Who was she?"

"Molly Lincoln."

Instead of being pleased, Nancy Allen's confirmation of her suspicion made Sarah more despondent.

"Do you know the details of her death?"

Mrs. Allen shrugged, "Not really. Molly and some other Summer Haven kids were campers at a music camp in Sarasota, New York. About half way through the summer the local newspaper reported that Molly died while she was at the camp. The paper didn't mention it, but some of the parents knew Shepherd was a teacher at the camp!"

Sarah asked, "Did the New York doctors conduct an autopsy?"

"I guess so. Several weeks later another news story said the results of the autopsy indicated Molly had the flu and suffered from some kind of vomiting problem. The coroner said she drowned in her own vomit. The article said the only thing that was unusual was that Molly's brain was swollen a little. They never reported why."

Adam asked, "Did the police investigate Shepherd?"

"I don't really know. The rumor mill had it that there was no reason to suspect Shepherd of foul play. A friend told me that she heard that when Shepherd was interviewed he said he wasn't at the camp when she died. From what I could tell, no real investigation took place."

"What do you think happened? Sarah asked.

"He killed Molly. I knew it then and I know it now. I don't know how he did it, but I know he did it. Have you seen Molly's photo? She looks just like Mindy. Actually, now that I've seen you school photo, you, Mindy, and Molly look like you could be sisters. I think Shepherd poisoned Molly, but what could I do about it. He threatened to sue us for defamation of character when we asked questions about him and Mindy. We were afraid to say anything about Molly."

Adam stood and took Mrs. Allen's hand. "Thanks for your time Mrs. Allen. You've really been a big help. One final question, do you have any idea where Mr. Shepherd lived when he was in Summer Haven?"

"1000 Hillcrest Drive in the Orchard Manor addition, south of town. My husband drove me by his house a few nights before he attacked Shepherd. The house number was easy to remember."

Sarah hugged Mrs. Allen.

"You let me know," Mrs. Allen's voice cracked. "You'll let me know what you find out? I've waited for years for someway to avenge what he did to my daughter."

On the drive back to their hotel Sarah again became morose. "If only I'd told someone, Mindy and the others might not have been molested. Molly might be alive. I am so ashamed. He's made me his accomplice."

"Stop beating yourself up," Adam said. "You were just a little girl. The school should have protected you and Mindy. You were a child without the experience or tools to stop him. Sarah, I promise you. We're going to get this guy."

Chapter 13

TUPICO FLATS, NEVADA

During the school day Schafer regularly gave Lizzie a hall pass to go to the band room. He gradually began spending more and more time with her. Schafer had no training in mind control, yet he intuitively understood that by assaulting her identity and isolating her from her peers, she would become increasingly dependent on him for affirmation.

One day he saw Lizzie talking with Billy Green, one of her classmates. When she got to the music room, he told her that boys her age are way too immature for her and she shouldn't make friends with any boys. As she became more and more dependent on Schafer he knew it would be more and more difficult for Lizzie to tell anyone about what they were doing. She was completely in love with him. He had succeeded in convincing her that he loved her, too. He promised her that in only two more years, when she turned sixteen, they would get married. He told her she would be a beautiful bride. At one of their sessions in the band closet he gave her a copy of "Bride Magazine" and showed her a photo of the wedding gown he said he was going to buy for her. He told her to look through the magazines to get some ideas about the wedding cake she wanted. She could hardly wait until she was sixteen.

Soon Schafer moved on to the next step, the most dangerous stage. He knew he had to be very careful. While he was caressing her bare bottom he slid his finger between her legs. Lizzie froze. "Please don't do that, Mr. Schafer." She knew what he was doing was really bad, but she felt powerless to stop him.

Schafer kept his hand where it was. "Lizzie, I'm only human. You're so beautiful and sexy. I can't control myself. This is all your fault," he whispered. Schafer knew that he had to make Lizzie feel responsible for what they did in the band closet. He wanted her to feel a sense of shame, but at the same time understand she needed to please him. She was very distressed with the way he was touching her, but Schafer explained to her that this is what people who were in love did. She was confused by her conflicting feelings; on the one hand, she knew she was doing something wrong. However, on the other hand, she felt the natural pleasure of being caressed and told she was beautiful.

The next time they were together he pushed his finger inside of her, just a little at first. Lizzie started to pull away, but she knew that would make Mr. Schafer angry. She wanted to plead for him to stop, but she was silent. She whimpered softly.

Schafer knew only too well how to handle her response. He immediately removed his finger, moved in front of her and let her see the crocodile tears running down his cheeks. He whispered softly, "Don't you love me? Don't you want to make me happy?" When Lizzie began to nod, he added, "Don't you know how much I'm risking for you? I love you so much. I'll lose my job if anyone ever finds out what we do together. I'm risking everything for you." After that day, Lizzie never complained again.

By now Lizzie and Schafer didn't even pretend to practice when they met in the music closet. Lizzie would come into the room, take off her clothes, and allow Schafer to touch her. This is what people who are in love do, she told herself.

Schafer continued molesting Lizzie almost every afternoon. He had a close call late one afternoon. Lizzie was naked and sitting on his lap in the locked music closet. They heard a key turn in the lock. Schafer pushed Lizzie behind the door and quickly stepped out of the closet.

As he closed and locked the door behind him he came face-to-face with Mr. James, the custodian, who was standing outside the door. James was over six feet tall and looked like a college linebacker. Schafer had never really spoken to him, nothing more than a nod as James emptied the wastebaskets or mopped the floor. Truthfully, James frightened him. He was one of those guys whose muscles seemed ready to burst out of his shirt. There were rumors that he had a violent temper and had been reprimanded for frightening the school bullies if he saw them bothering students.

James stood his ground, looking at Schafer with a quizzical expression.

"Hi." Schafer said, trying to sound casual. "I was just putting a microphone head in the storeroom."

"I was just checking to be sure the door was locked," James said.

Stepping past him, Schafer said, "I just locked it, it's okay."

James paused, cocked his head to the side, and stared hard at Schafer. He then turned and left the music room. As he continued to make his rounds of the other classrooms he tried to make sense of what he thought he just saw. He asked himself if he really saw a pair of girl's underpants on the floor. He thought about going back to be sure, but the mess he had to clean up in the art room consumed the rest of his time and energy.

Charles James worked as a janitor since he returned from serving in Iraq. He never thought his life would turn out like this. When he got back he was expecting to pick up right where he left off, but it didn't turn out that way. Everything was fine for several months after he got home, but then the flashbacks and nightmares started. He had trouble concentrating, seemed to be in a bad mood all the time, and sometimes had difficulty remembering simple things. He was told that there was counseling available for vets suffering from post traumatic stress disorder, but he couldn't stand being around anyone that reminded him of Iraq.

Over the course of the year the flashbacks seemed to be coming more frequently. He kept seeing himself perched at the open door of his Black Hawke helicopter as it made a strike on houses near the Tigris River. He saw himself holding a M60 machine gun as the chopper swung in low over a long caravan of trucks. Suddenly a red ball of fire hit the chopper. One minute all nine crewmembers were alive, the next minute six were dead. After being evacuated he spent the next six months in hospitals. Now, honorably discharged and safe at home his sleep was still interrupted by the cries and screams of his buddies. During the day a sound or a smell could bring it all back to him.

James saw everything, but no one ever acknowledged him. Teachers and students walked past him as if he were invisible. They walked right over the wet floor that he'd just mopped. If they only knew how easy it was to kill someone. If they only knew how many people he had killed, they would show him some respect.

As James sat alone in his apartment that night, thoughts of the music room were a welcome distraction from the usual horrendous memories of war. What was Mr. Schafer doing in that locked closet? Were those girl's panties on the floor? James finally decided that he was probably mistaken.

Chapter 14

Every night that wasn't filled with a band concert or another school related event Schafer went home to his wife, Grace. They had married shortly after he left Summer Haven and changed his name. The marriage had settled into a predictable pattern. He would get home. She would have dinner ready. They would generally eat in silence. When he was finished he would disappear in his study for the rest of the evening.

Grace had stopped wondering what he did all night, locked in his study. Before they were married he seemed only mildly interested in sex, but she assumed he was just shy. Over the next year Schafer grew more and more distant. About a year after they were married he started buying Grace clothing that was too young for her. He made her call him Mr. Schafer and pretend she was a schoolgirl. When they had sex he forced her to put on knee socks and a short skirt. It was then that she began to think she'd made a terrible mistake.

Their frequent moves kept Grace isolated from her family and limited her ability to build strong friendships. Grace hoped having a child would bring them closer. Ashley was now eight years old, but Grace's marriage was still empty. She couldn't remember the last time she and Jim made love nor could she understand why she had lost her ability to arouse him. She honestly tried to appraise herself in the mirror from time to time and always concluded that, for her age, she was still attractive. Her body was well toned due to playing tennis once or twice a week. Jim asked her to keep her hair short, the way she wore it when they first met. When she smiled her nose crinkled, and she still had a sprinkling of freckles across her nose and cheeks. She had always been self-conscious of her tiny breasts. She thought that Jim might be more attracted to her if they were larger. When she suggested having breast augmentation surgery Jim said, "Big breasts are gross. I'll leave if you do anything to your breasts."

One afternoon as she was reorganizing their walk-in closet, Grace was thinking about Rick. He was the tennis coach at the club. He flirted shamelessly with her every time he gave her a lesson. He often leaned up against her as he corrected her backhand. The last time he did that, she pushed back against him. Last week they met for lunch and he made it clear that he was interested in more than her backhand. She was seriously considering having an affair with him.

Perched on a step stool she was absentmindedly taking down old shoeboxes that were stacked on the closet shelf. In the back corner of the shelf, hidden behind a stack of Tupico Flats yearbooks, was a cigar box. That seemed odd, Jim didn't smoke cigars.

Grace took the box down and opened it to find a stack of papers. The top sheet was a collage of photographs. At first she couldn't make her mind understand what she was looking at. The page contained four photographs of men and women having oral and anal sex. If that was all there was to the photos, Grace might have been able forgive Jim. But faces of Jim's middle school students had been morphed on the bodies of the women and photos of Jim's face replaced the men's faces.

Fifteen minutes later Grace was still sitting on the edge of her bed staring at the wall. Tears were streaming down her face as she tried to make sense of what she just found. Her first thought was to burn the photos. Next, she considered putting them back where she found them and pretending she hadn't seen them. Finally, she decided to confront Jim when he got home from school.

Dozens of questions tumbled through her brain. What had Jim done? Was Ashley in danger? Was this why they didn't have sex? She picked up the phone several times to call the police, but each time she hung up. She moved through the rest of the day in a daze. Routine helped her manage to clean the kitchen, get the mail, and start dinner. When Ashley got home from school, Grace sent her to a friend's house to spend the night. As was often the case, Jim got home late. As soon as he closed the front door behind him Grace flung the stack of photos in his face.

"What are these?" she shrieked, her voice out of control.

Jim's mind scrambled as he stared at the photos strewn across the carpet. He cursed himself for keeping them. His mind raced to come up with something to say or do.

"Answer me!" Grace screamed,

Jim faked remorse and said, "It's not what you think. I'm so sorry."

"I don't know what to think." Grace said staring hard at Jim. "So start explaining."

"You've found my dark place," Jim murmured. "Give them to me and I'll burn them. I promise I'll never to do this again."

"Is this why you don't touch me anymore? Can you only get off by looking at photos of children? Have you taken any photos of our Ashley? Have you touched her, hurt her?"

"No! No, of course not. I love Ashley."

"I want you out of this house. I don't even know who you are. This is sick, Jim. You're really, really sick."

"Let me spend the night on the sofa. I'll find a place tomorrow."

It was only later, after Grace had calmed down, that she realized she couldn't afford to kick Jim out. She admitted she loved the nice house, the cars, and the knowledge that Ashley's college education was secure. She knew she could never face her family if this got out. She didn't know what to do. How would she support herself? Jim had never allowed her to work outside the home. Her degree in music history was over fifteen years old. She didn't have any marketable skills, certainly none that would allow her to live in this house, belong to the tennis club, and drive a new Accord every three years. She didn't know what would happen to Ashley if she divorced him.

The next morning Grace got up early, went to her computer, and got on line. First, she read all that she could find about pedophiles. Next, she looked through the phone directory of Millersburg, a nearby town, until she found the name of a psychiatrist who treated deviant sexual behaviors. She called Dr. Steven Motice's office and made an appointment for them both for the next day.

She started to go into the living room several times before she mustered her courage enough to confront him. She didn't know how she would feel when she saw him. When Jim heard her come in he sat up but looked at the floor. He had no idea what to say.

"Jim, you need to get help. You need to go to a counselor." With her heart in her throat, she asked quietly, "Jim, swear that you haven't done anything to Ashley or any of these girls. You haven't, have you?"

"I swear. I just like to look at their photos. It is my private fantasy world. I'd never touch a student. But you're right,

Grace, I need help." Jim managed to say this in a defeated, embarrassed tone, but he was long past wanting to stop. He was in full-fledged damage control as his mind scrambled to come up with something that would satisfy Grace.

Jim tried to stop so many times. Each time he started at a new school he promised himself he wouldn't do it again. Yet, each time he fell back into his old habits within a few months.

Jim was afraid that if he didn't agree to go to counseling, Grace was going to turn him in to the police. A prison term was sure to follow. Jim knew he couldn't go to prison.

During the first half hour of the drive to Millersburg they were both silent. Sarah stared out the passenger window deep in thought. She wondered how she could be so stupid, so clueless? How long had this been going on? Was Ashley in danger? Grace fought against the voice inside her head that was telling her to turn the car around, pack up Ashley, and get far away from Jim.

As Jim drove he stared straight ahead. He knew this was going to be tricky. He had to be careful not to let the doctor know what his real perversion was. He knew he had to get the doctor to assure Grace that he was cured. His mind scurried to develop a plan. His only hope was that Dr. Motice was inexperienced enough to be fooled. Jim became more confident as he remembered how good he was at deception. He just needed to do what he always did, charm his way out of this situation.

Jim was relieved to see that Dr. Motice's office was in a rundown shopping plaza with half the stores boarded up. As they left the parking lot and walked to the office, they passed the Tender Trap strip club and the Duk Su Noh Korean nail salon. Jim became even more confident when they entered an empty waiting room, stepped on a welcome mat, and heard a buzzer sound in another room. Dr. Motice came out of his office when he heard the buzzer. His apparent attempt to grow a beard, probably to look older, wasn't working. He looked like he was about eighteen.

At their first session Grace and Jim each told Dr. Motice what caused them to make an appointment. Jim was very passive and looked and sounded contrite. Grace didn't take her eyes off him as he talked with the doctor. Jim seemed genuinely ashamed and remorseful. After Grace told Motice about the photos, Motice asked Jim, what the photos meant to him.

"I don't know. I like to look at sexy photos. I know it is illegal to buy child porn. One day I was just fooling around and started making my own, Jim said.

Grace started to rock back and forth and wept soundlessly.

Jim turned to her and said, "I am so sorry, Grace. Please forgive me. I love you."

"But why did you want to use photos of little girls? Do you want to have sex with little girls?" She asked.

"No, of course not. It was just sort of a whim. I don't know why I did it. I put the pictures on the shelf last year. Honey, I haven't looked at them in months. I honestly forgot they were there."

Grace tried to regain her composure and looked at the floor in silence. She really wanted to believe him, but on some level she knew she always suspected he was not right sexually. The creeping panic she experienced last night reappeared.

For the rest of the appointment Dr. Motice talked with them about their marriage and their sex life. Grace told him about Jim's early insistence that she role play with him. She said it made her uncomfortable pretending to be a young girl, but she went along because she wanted to make Jim happy.

As the fifty-minute appointment drew to a close Dr. Motice told them he thought Jim could benefit from therapy. "Generally, we will need twenty to fifty sessions, two or three times week. I need to be very clear that these sessions will not help unless you are willing and committed to attending every session until we mutually decide that we are finished."

Jim scheduled his first private visit for later in the week. As they were leaving Dr. Motice put his hand on Jim's shoulder, "You're lucky that Grace insisted that you come here, Jim. People with sexual perversions seldom seek treatment unless induced by an arrest or discovery by a family member. You were lucky it was Grace and not the police who discovered those photos."

At the next session Dr. Motice attempted to discover Jim's true motives. "Jim, sexual perversions are conditions in which sexual excitement or orgasm is associated with acts or imagery that society considers abnormal. On the other hand, sexual fantasy that heightens sexual excitement and leads to legal acts can be a healthy part of a relationship. "

"I know that Dr. Motice. I'm not stupid!" Jim was aware his defensiveness was not going to serve him well. In a more contrite tone he added. "I know what I did is wrong. I don't know why I did it."

"Jim, if our sessions are going to be helpful, you need to be honest with me. Is this photo college really a one time thing?"

Jim hesitated. He wasn't sure how truthful he needed to be. "No. I have always liked younger looking women. I've tried to stop. I just can't."

After every session Motice would consult his textbooks and journals. After several more sessions, Dr. Motice lectured,

"Jim, you have a sexual impulse disorder characterized by intensely arousing, recurrent sexual fantasies about young girls. Generally these feelings result in guilt, depression, shame, isolation, and impairment in the capacity for normal social and sexual relationships. Grace said you two don't have a satisfying sex life. Do you agree with her?"

Here we go, Jim thought. "Yes, she's right. I have trouble getting hard with her unless I fantasize about young girls. Then I feel like I'm cheating on her, so I avoid having sex with her."

"That's a great insight." Dr. Motice leaned forward and said, "Jim. I would like to spend some time in our next sessions talking about your childhood and your first memories of having sexual thoughts."

Now we are getting some place. I'll just tell this guy some stories and then agree with whatever he tells me, Jim thought.

As Motice talked Jim recalled events from his past. Of course, he remembered the day at David's house. He could still feel the heat of the attic and the smell of the moldy quilts. Debbie's panties were pale green; her friend's were pink with little red hearts. Both girls smelled like vanilla. Memories of that day still gave him an erection. Of course he didn't dare share any of this with Dr. Motice.

Dr. Motice asked, "Have you ever had an embarrassing or humiliating experience with females your own age?"

Jim had no trouble remembering his humiliations. Most of his contacts with girls or women who were his age were failures. "One day when I was in my high school algebra class I was standing at the chalkboard working a math problem when I got a huge erection."

"That's not unusual for a healthy teenage boy," Motice said.

"I put my hand in my pocket and tried to push it back in place with no luck. I tried to go back to my seat, but the teacher wouldn't let me. She said I had to stay at the board until I solved the math problem. My pants bulged out in a way that everyone could see. One at a time, the girls in the front of the room noticed my erection and started to point and laugh at me. When some boys noticed what the girls were looking at, they joined in the laughter. In a stage whisper one boy said, "Getting turned on by math, are we?" Finally, the teacher noticed what was happening and allowed me to return to my seat. By then my erection had subsided, but I was totally humiliated."

Dr. Motice leaned back in his chair and smiled reassuringly. "Most boys have an embarrassing story about a poorly timed erection." He then again leaned forward in his chair and continued, "These memories of negative experiences you have had with girls your own age are really important, Jim. A leading psychoanalytic theory holds that your fixation on young girls may really be an expression of hostility you had toward girls your own age. What we will be trying to do is erase the underlying traumas."

Twenty years ago Jim might have been profoundly affected by Dr. Motice's explanation. Today he was only half listening as Dr. Motice rambled on. Jim was trying to figure out the best way of conning him.

After several weeks of appointments, Dr. Motice decided to try aversion imagery. He paired images that Jim found arousing with images of a frightening or unpleasant nature, such as being arrested, fired, or divorced. He then showed Jim some photos of young girls. While Jim was looking at the photos,

Dr. Motice told him what happens to child molesters in prison. He told him the story of a convicted child molester who was imprisoned in Indiana. "Within his first week of confinement two prisoners restrained him while another tattooed the name of the molested child on his forehead. The prisoner was placed in solitary for his own protection. Soon after he was released from solitary back into the general prison population, he was repeatedly sodomized and eventually murdered."

Although Jim was frightened by the story, he told Dr. Motice there was no change in his obsession. He intuitively knew that he shouldn't recover too quickly.

Dr. Motice then tried desensitization procedures in an attempt to neutralize the anxiety-provoking aspects of having a sexual relationship with adult women by having Jim view video images of attractive adult women while introducing a series of relaxation procedures aimed at reducing Jim's anxiety.

Jim considered telling the doctor that the therapy was working, but decided to wait.

After another six sessions Dr. Motice introduced the possibility of drug therapy. "Drugs are sometimes prescribed to treat sexual dysfunctional behaviors, Jim. We could try an antiandrogen that would temporarily lower your testosterone levels, or we could go with a serotonergic that would boost your levels of serotonin. Either of these strategies may help you."

When Dr. Motice started talking about drug therapy, Jim knew it was time to fake his healing. No way am I going to take any drugs. During the next session Jim told Dr. Motice that their sessions together had been helping. "I've been spending more time with Grace. I think things are getting better." Jim said.

When Dr. Motice met with Grace she confirmed that Jim was very attentive and had begun buying her flowers and little gifts. She said he was acting like he couldn't resist her in the bedroom.

Several sessions later Jim turned to Dr. Motice and said, "From what you told me, I guess my problem could have gotten more serious. I am so grateful that you were here to help me. I think you saved our marriage." Jim could see that Dr. Motice had been completely fooled. Jim thought he was probably thinking about the article he would write about his success.

Jim was worried that Grace was going to be paying more attention to all of his actions. Having a wife and daughter had given him cover from suspicion in the past. He knew he was going to have to be very careful until he was sure Grace trusted him again.

By now Jim was regularly performing oral sex on fourteen-year-old Lizzie Sutton.

Chapter 15

SUMMER HAVEN, PENNSYLVANIA

Adam punched 1000 Hillcrest Drive into his GPS and Sarah followed the turn-by-turn directions to Shepherd's old house. When Sarah rang the bell a young mother answered the door. Two young children peeked out from behind her skirt. "Hello, my name is Sarah Abbott. This is Adam Faulkner." Adam knelt down to try and shake the little boy's hand, causing the child to turn and scamper down the hallway. Sarah smiled and continued, "We're trying to locate a man who once lived in your house. We are looking for Tony Shepherd. Do you know him?"

While she was trying to pry her daughter's hand from her skirt her son returned and gave Adam a stuffed rabbit. The woman replied, "No, I don't think so. We've only lived here for two years. The Schislers lived here before us."

"Have you ever received any mail addressed to him? Sarah asked.

"No. I don't believe so. When we first moved in, Blue, the man across the street, told my husband that he once played in a rock band with a guy who used to live in our house. I don't know if he's the guy you are looking for."

Adam and Sarah thanked her, walked across the street, and knocked on the door at 1005. After the third knock they were about to leave when the door was jerked open by a fifty year old man who looked like a roadie for the Grateful Dead. He was sixty pounds over-weight, was wearing a green Team Garcia ball cap and a vintage Skeleton Jester tee shirt that stopped four inches above his belt. He kept one hand on the door and the other held a can of beer. From the glazed look of his eyes Adam suspected he'd been stoned since Garcia died in 1995.

Adam said, "Hello, sir. My name is Adam Faulkner and this is Sarah Abbott. What's your name?"

"Blue."

"Is that your first name or last name?'

"It's just Blue."

"Mr. Blue. We're looking for Tony Shepherd. We understand you played in a band with him. Is that correct?"

"What's it to ya?"

"As I said, this is Ms. Abbott, one of Shepherd's former students. We're trying to locate him."

"Haven't seen him since he quit the band. We had a sweet sound. It really pissed us off when he disappeared. He was great on the keyboard. Actually, he could play any instrument."

"What do you mean disappeared?" Adam asked.

"Just what I said. One weekend we had a gig at The Icehouse. After we broke down and loaded our gear he said good by and we never saw him again."

"You have no idea where he went?" Sarah asked.

"Heard that he moved to Montana, or Missouri, or Mississippi. Some "M" place." What do ya want with him?"

"He is an old teacher of mine, Sarah repeated. "Has he ever called you on the phone?"

"Naw."

"Have you ever received any mail from him?" Adam asked.

He stared into space for a few moments and said, "From who?"

Sarah stepped closer to Blue and raised her voice, "Tony Shepherd! Tony Shepherd! Do you know where he is?"

"Naw. A few months after he disappeared I think he sent me a postcard with that big honking arch on it."

Sarah continued with her interview, "What do you mean you think he sent you a card? Was the picture on the card the St. Louis Arch?"

"Whatever," Blue muttered as he turned and slammed the door closed.

They stared at each other for a moment then they left the porch and walked to their car. Adam said, "Shepherd may have made his first mistake."

"Even if he's in Missouri or even St. Louis, how will we find him?" Sarah asked.

"I'm not sure," Adam said wearily. Lets get something to eat and think things over."

As Adam drove toward town Sarah pointed out the window and said, "There! Stop there! This was my favorite restaurant when I was a girl." Adam couldn't believe what he was seeing. He had to force himself to turn into the parking lot of the Cozy Corner Diner. When Adam didn't turn off the ignition or make any move to get out of the car, Sarah reached over and put her hand on his arm. "What is it Adam?"

"This is really getting spooky. This is the second déjà vu moment I have had on this case." He hadn't told Sarah how much she looked like Julie.

"What do you mean?"

"This diner looks just like the one Julie and I used to go to every Saturday morning when we were kids in Deer Falls. It brings back lots of memories," he said with a catch in his voice.

"Bad memories?"

Adam didn't answer her. "Let's go inside," he said.

Adam felt like he had stepped out of a time machine after traveling back to the week before Julie disappeared. The classic stainless steel diner of the 1950's was the twin of the one where Julie and he went for Hamburgers and a chocolate shake every Saturday morning after her gymnastic class. As he moved through the vestibule entrance he was bombarded with the sights and smells of his youth. The stainless steel exhaust hood was not quite able to eliminate the smell of onions, peppers and frying beef patties. He led Sarah across the black and white checkered tiles to a booth. Tears formed in the corner of his eyes as he watched Sarah settle herself across from him.

"Adam, what's the matter? Are you ill?" Sarah asked.

Adam smiled ruefully, "Everything's fine. I went on a little trip, but I'm back."

"Adam what did you mean when you said this was the second déjà vu experience on this case?"

"Nothing, really. I was just babbling."

"I don't think so. You meant something. Tell me."

Somewhat reluctantly Adam told Sarah about Julie and what she has meant to him. He told her about their love and his loss. He told her how much it hurt him every time he found the dead body of an abducted child and how he seemed to lose a little more of himself with every case. When he finished, Sarah was silent for a moment then asked softly, "Adam, why did you agree to help me?"

"Sarah, honestly, I wasn't going to tell you this. When you walked into Antonio's I thought you were Julie, for a second. Your resemblance to her is uncanny. I felt like if I turned you down, I would be abandoning Julie again." He stopped short of adding that he wanted to find Shepherd so he could kill him.

Sarah was a little disturbed by this turn of events, but her concern didn't outweigh her deep desire to find Shepherd. Before she could respond the waitress appeared at their table. They ordered burgers and fries. They talked about the case as they waited for their food to arrive. Adam leaned back in the booth and pondered their next step.

"I have an hunch. Let's draw a fifty-mile circle around St. Louis and start contacting music stores in the area. We have his photo from the yearbook. If he's in the area, maybe someone who sells and rents band instruments will recognize him."

Chapter 16

TUPICO FLATS, NEVADA

Jim never tired of the rhythmic motion of seduction. He enjoyed the step-by-step dance of grooming. He remembered every detail of each girl he tutored after school. By the second week of December, Schafer was performing oral sex on Lizzie several times a week. No one had ever talked with Lizzie about her sexuality. She had no idea what was normal for a girl her age. Schafer told her that sex was a way that two people showed their love for one another. He had her believing that sex equaled love.

At first she was embarrassed when he put his face in her private area. She would pretend she was somewhere else. She closed her eyes and counted the seconds until he would stop. Gradually she began enjoying the warm tingling sensations. She didn't have orgasms but her body began feeling sexual pleasure and her mind associated that pleasure with Schafer.

Schafer never got undressed or had her touch him. He learned from the experience with Sarah that he must not rush things.

Soon after he left college Schafer began collecting child pornography, mostly books, magazines, and movies. He then moved to dial in bulletin boards and the Internet. With the advent of digital imaging and file sharing he was amazed by how easy it was to access and trade pornographic material. He spent countless hours surfing Web sites, chat rooms, and newsgroups and ultimately came across peer-to-peer technology. His purchase of a popular peer-to-peer file-sharing program opened up a whole new world. Now he could initiate direct communication with other men who loved children the way he did.

Although he knew that others, who didn't understand, would call him a pedophile he was comforted to learn that there were others out there who loved young girls. He had found a community of hundreds of men who enjoyed having sex with young girls or watching men having sex with them. At first he was afraid to buy a membership, but his compulsion got the better of him. Soon he belonged to five sites that provided illegal photos and movies of adults having sex with underage children.

While he was preparing to mail his bank draft to subscribe to yet another "child love" site, he began to calculate how much money the owners of these sites were making. Child porn had a seemingly inexhaustible worldwide market. Schafer estimated that if he started his own site he could reasonably expect to make almost a hundred thousand tax-free dollars during its first year.

Schafer knew Lizzie would be the perfect debutant for his website. He knew his members would go crazy watching a video of Lizzie's first sexual encounter.

The network of like-minded people he tapped into amazed Schafer. It was like going to graduate school and majoring in child molestation. As he gained the trust of other pedophiles, he learned new techniques to seduce children. He also learned strategies to avoid detection. As Schafer began accessing child porn photos and movies, he lived in constant fear that Grace would discover his stash. Although his computer was password protected, and he kept his study padlocked ever since Grace had found the collages, he worried that she would find a way to get into his study.

Schafer quickly learned that people who frequented these "member only" chat rooms were very suspicious. It took him months before he was trusted as a comrade rather than a spy. One evening he was in a chat room where the members were discussing ways to use other people's computers to access and store photographs and movies. Schafer entered the conversation, "I'm not too computer savvy. How does this all work?"

Comments began popping up on his screen.

Joe: "The vast majority of personal computers have immensely more memory than the owner will ever use. This unused memory is like a warehouse waiting to be filled."

Bill: "I've just developed a virus that allows me to store and view my collection of photos and movies on other people's computers with little chance of being detected."

Sam: "I just purchased a virus that hacks into a target computer and programs it to visit as many as fifty child love sites per minute."

Schafer was fascinated "Wow. How does this work? Tell me more about this."

Sam: "I just log on to the host computer while the owner is asleep and view and download our special material all night. When I'm ready to leave, I store my material on the host computer and log out."

Bill: "The beauty of this program is that unless the computer owner is looking for a virus, it's unlikely he will know his computer is infected."

Sam laughed: "Yeah, he won't know until the police knock on his door and arrest him for having child pornography!"

Bill: "Not sure if this is an urban legend or not, but I heard that one of our friends got the charges against him dropped when he convinced the district attorney that a virus was to blame for the pictures he had on his computer."

Schafer also learned there were groups of men who met to trade and sell photographs and videos. It was rumored that some even traded children. He wondered how that worked. The conclaves were incredibly secret and their location changed with each meeting. At first Schafer was afraid to attend a meeting, but eventually a mutual trust developed between Schafer and someone using the name David, an on-line contact. David told Schafer that there was going to be a meeting the next week in St. George, California. Schafer knew it would be stupid for him to go, but like so many of his urges, he was powerless to control his need to attend. The location would allow him to drive there and get back before school on Monday.

He told Grace he was going to attend a band director's conference in northern Nevada. He left for California right after school on Friday. Because the meeting took place in another state, and was almost three hundred miles from Tupico Flats, Schafer didn't expect to recognize anyone or be recognized. He met David at a local watering hole. After a few drinks David drove them to the meeting. The meeting was held in a small bungalow in a quiet suburban neighborhood. When he entered the house he saw about a dozen middle-aged men drinking beer and talking. He was shocked when he saw someone he recognized from Tupico Flats. His first instinct was to turn and run. However, he quickly realized that he didn't have as much to lose as his fellow traveler.

Chapter 17

RILEY, MISSOURI

Adam and Sarah had been calling music stores for a week. Finally, they got lucky with a music store in Riley, Missouri. When they told Steve, the owner of Max's Music Store, they were investigating a possible child molestation case and described Shepherd, Steve said he once he had a customer that fit Shepherd's description. Upon arrival at the music store they showed Steve a photo of Shepherd and waited anxiously for his reaction.

"Yes, I know him. But his names' not Shepherd. It's Schafer," Steve said.

Sarah and Adam started speaking at the same time. "Where is he?" Sarah asked breathlessly.

"When did you see him last? Is he still in town?" Adam asked.

"I think he left town. He used to teach at Riley Middle School. He was there for three or four years."

Sarah sighed, unable to contain her disappointment.

"Can you get us a list of the female students who bought or rented band instruments from you while Schafer was in town?" Adam asked. "We're willing to pay you for your time."

"It will take me a little time to put a list together, but yes, I can get you the names. Come back at five o'clock."

When Sarah and Adam returned that evening, Steve gave them a list with over two hundred names.

"Wow! This is going to take a long time," Sarah said.

As they were about to leave Steve said. "You know, putting this list together got me to thinking. There was one girl that abruptly stopped taking lessons in the middle of the semester. She was actually quite good, and I was surprised when her mom brought her clarinet back and asked me if I could try and sell it for her."

Sarah glanced hopefully at Adam. "Do you remember her name?" She asked.

"Let me take another look at the list." After perusing the list for several minutes, Steve pointed to the name Gretchen Cocan. "Yes, here it is."

"Do you know why she quit band?" Sarah asked.

"Please, don't quote me on this, but I seem to remember that that there were rumors about Mr. Schafer. Someone told me that Mrs. Cocan filed some type of complaint against him. He left town shortly after Gretchen quit the band."

"You've really been a big help," Sarah said as she shook Steve's hand. Adam wasn't willing to give up on Steve's assistance. "Is there anything else that you remember?"

"You really should talk with Randy Wilson. I think he was the superintendent of schools when Gretchen was a student," Steve replied.

Randy Wilson was not listed in the phone book. Several people told Adam that they thought Wilson had died. Others thought he was in a nursing home somewhere out of town. After some false starts they learned that Randy Wilson's daughter's married name was Janet Evans. After a few phone calls, Adam and Sarah finally located her. She told them Mr. Wilson was a resident of St. Catherine of Siena Senior Village, located in a town forty miles to the south.

"Would you please call your father and ask him if he will speak with us?" Sarah asked.

"Sure. I'm happy to do that. He doesn't get many visitors. Although I'm sure he'll enjoy your visit, he's in early Alzheimer's," Mrs. Evans said sadly.

Their excitement grew as Sarah and Adam drove to the nursing home. As they entered the reception area of the three-story brick building, they were impressed by how spacious and attractive it was. Audubon print decorated the walls; fresh flowers graced the tables, and a roaring gas fire glowed in the stone fireplace. A gray-haired woman was playing Mozart on the grand piano. She smiled at them as they entered the foyer. Pretty cool. I wouldn't mind living here, Adam thought, as they waited to be escorted to Mr. Wilson's room.

Five minutes later Adam realized that first impressions are often deceiving. From the reception area they walked through a fire door and entered a long hallway. Cadaverous pasty-faced old men and women were slouched in wheelchairs on either side of the hall. Some were held in their chairs by straps around their chests. Gaunt red-rimmed eyes stared into space. Some of the residents were facing the wall mumbling to themselves. As they passed a tall, frail man, he looked up at them beseechingly and softly asked, "Are you here to visit me?" The smell of disinfectant didn't quite mask the smell of urine and feces.

Just as they reached room 203, the door opened and two teenage girls came out carrying two beagle puppies.

"Are you relatives of Mr. Wilson?" Sarah inquired.

"No, we're volunteers from St. Catherine Church. Many of the residents really enjoy petting and holding the puppies, so once a week we volunteer to visit the residents who want us to stop by. Mr. Wilson is really a nice man. It is to bad he doesn't get many visitors."

Adam reached out and scratched a puppy behind the ears, the place where Bronco liked to be scratched. When the girls cleared the doorway, Adam rapped on the door. A frail voice called out, "Come in."

Mr. Wilson's daughter told Adam her father was seventy years old, but he looked ten years older. He probably weighed less than a hundred pounds. He was wearing a suit that must have fit him fifty pounds ago. His white shirt was adorned with food stains. A floral tie was knotted loosely under his chin. Mr. Wilson smiled at them as they entered his room. "Hello, do I know you?"

"Your daughter, Janet, said you agreed to talk with us." Sarah said extending her hand. "I'm Sarah Abbott, and this is Adam Faulkner. We've come to speak with you about a teacher who taught in the district when you were the superintendent."

Mr. Watson smiled sadly, "I'm not so good with names. I hope I can remember."

"I know what you mean." Adam grinned. "I'm not very good at remembering names either." Mr. Wilson looked relieved. Sarah asked, "Do you remember James Schafer?"

Mr. Watson stared out the window for a moment repeating the name under his breath. "I don't think so. I had my stroke in November and was never able to go back to work. I've been in here since I got out of the hospital. I thought I was going to get better...but I didn't. I never figured I'd end up like this."

Adam wasn't sure what to say to show Mr. Watson that he sympathized with his plight. He paused and said, "It must be difficult living away from your family. But, this seems like a pretty nice place."

"Yes. The staff is friendly and they do a good job, and I have some friends. We are going to a ball game tomorrow."

"Great. I wish I could join you. When you were the superintendent there was a music teacher named Jim Schaefer. Do you remember anything about him?"

"He was the music teacher. Is that right?"

"Yes, he was the band teacher. Do you remember anything else about him?"

"There was some sort of complaint. Is that right?"

"Do you remember what the complaint was about?"

"If I remember right, a student said he did something to her. There wasn't any evidence. We thought it would be better for the child if things were handled quietly."

Sarah made an effort to control herself. Leaning toward Mr. Wilson and forcing a smile she asked, "What do you mean you didn't have any evidence? You had Mrs. Cocan's statement, didn't you?"

Wilson looked frightened. "Did I say something wrong?"

"No, Mr. Wilson," Sarah said soothingly. "I'm sorry I raised my voice. You didn't say anything wrong. Do you remember Gretchen Cocan?"

"I don't think so."

"That's the little girl's name. Do you remember what her mother said happened?"

Mr. Watson was clearly getting more and more confused. "What could we do? What could we do?"

"What happened to Schafer?"

"What do you mean? Did something happen to him?"

"He left Riley," Adam said. "Do you know where he went?"

"My memory is not so good since my stroke. I had a stroke when I was superintendent. It was in November. I think."

"Mr. Wilson, do you know where he went?" Adam asked.

"I think he just sort of disappeared. Is that right?"

Sarah looked at Adam and shook her head. There was no point in upsetting Mr. Wilson any further. They thanked him for his time and said good-bye. They decided to call Gretchen's mother, Sally Cocan.

Chapter 18

As they sat in their rental car in St. Catherine's parking lot, Adam flipped open his cell and called Mrs. Cocan. "Hello, Mrs. Cocan. My name is Adam Faulkner. I'm a private investigator working for Ms. Sarah Abbott. Is Gretchen Cocan your daughter?"

"Yes. What is this about?"

"We would like to talk with you about one of Gretchen's middle school teachers. May we come out to your home and talk with you?"

Mrs. Cocan was silent for a few moments before telling Adam they could come the next afternoon. She hung up the phone and slumped in her chair. She knew they would ask her about Jim Schafer.

That night Sally Cocan relived the day she learned that Mr. Schafer had molested her oldest daughter. At first her memories evaporated and eluded her grasp before coming back to her in fragments. She had been in the kitchen when she heard Gretchen coming up the front steps crying. Through her sobs, Gretchen begged Sally not to let her little sister, Gayle, enroll in Mr. Schafer's music class or in the band.

Sally had protested. "You loved being in the band. You know Gayle idolizes you. She wants to be just like you."

"Mom, don't you remember? I quit the band! I never told you why. I quit because Mr. Schafer messed with me. He put his hands inside my pants and pushed his fingers inside of me."

Sally had tried to appear calm as Gretchen told the story of what Mr. Schafer had done. She had almost passed out from trying to control her outrage.

At eight o'clock the next morning Mrs. Cocan and her husband had gone to the superintendent's office and demanded a complete investigation. They also demanded that Mr. Wilson remove Schafer from all contact with children.

Superintendent Wilson refused to remove Schafer from the classroom, but he did promise to conduct an investigation. Several days later Sally went with Gretchen when Gretchen was asked to tell her story. When Gretchen and her parents entered the conference room, they were shocked to see Mr. Schafer was present. "Why is he here?" Mr. Cocan demanded. Wilson said soothingly, "Well, the accused has a right to confront his accuser." Schaefer smiled at Gretchen and then stared at her throughout the questioning. When she was asked to tell the hearing committee what happened she began to cry. After several attempts to get her to talk, the superintendent said she could leave the room. Three of Gretchen's classmates were interviewed one by one; none admitted to having seen anything inappropriate. Several teachers were interviewed; no one admitted to suspecting that Mr. Schafer had done anything wrong.

When Schafer was interviewed, he calmly explained that Gretchen was an overly emotional child who must have misunderstood his actions. "Yes, I was alone with her in the band room, but I never touched her. I don't know why she's making up this crazy story."

Sally had called the superintendent every other day to ask about the investigation. After about two weeks the superintendent informed her that the results of the investigation were inconclusive. Wilson offered to pay to transport Gretchen' little sister, Gayle, to the high school if she wanted to continue in the band. Ms. Cocan told him Gayle was not interested. Sally called the president of the school board and was told that the board supported the superintendent's decision. Sitting in her living room years later, reliving the nightmare, Sally shuddered remembering that she was barely able to talk her husband out of going to Schafer's house and assaulting him.

When Adam and Sarah arrived at the Cocan house they were invited into the front room. Before they were seated Ms. Cocan said, "The teacher your asking about is Jim Schafer, isn't it?"

"Yes," Sarah admitted. She paused to contemplate how direct to be. Mrs. Cocan's facial expression told Sarah that she needn't sugar coat her words. "He molested me and we think he may also have molested Gretchen as well as many other girls. He may still be doing it. We're looking for clues to help us find him."

"We've traced him to Riley," Adam interjected. "We believe Schafer molested your daughter. Can you tell us what happened with Gretchen?"

Mrs. Cocan hadn't ever spoken with a private investigator and was a little nervous. She sat rigidly twisting the wedding band on her left hand. Finally, she lowered her eyes and began her story. "Gretchen told us Mr. Schafer put his hands in her underwear and touched her private parts. At first, I believed Gretchen. My husband and I went to the school and demanded an investigation. We demanded that Mr. Schafer be removed from contact with kids. I'm ashamed to say that when

Gretchen wouldn't tell the school what Schafer had done; I began to think she made up the story. We knew Mr. Schafer was married and had a daughter. He was a very popular teacher. Nobody could believe such a sweet guy would molest a child. When Gretchen continued to refuse to talk about what happened we just sort of let it go."

"It's understandable that you didn't suspect him. You're not alone. But let me assure you. He did molest me and he probably molested Gretchen," Sarah said.

"Mrs. Cocan, we think he is still teaching and still molesting children. Do you know where he went after he left Riley?" Adam asked.

"I don't. Maybe Gretchen does."

"Would you call her?"

"Ok. She lives in Bakersfield, California. She's single and working as a hostess at a restaurant. Her relationship with me hasn't been good since middle school. Excuse me. I want to call her from the other room."

Ten minutes after Sally left the room, she returned. "I didn't think Gretchen would want to dredge up this part of her past, but she said she knows where Schafer is. She's even spied on him. She just told me she has often fantasized about getting a gun and shooting him." Mrs. Cocan handed them a scrap of paper with an address and phone number and said, "Gretchen has agreed to meet with you at this address in Bakersfield. Call her and let her know when you can get there. Take this photo. It is the most recent one I have."

Chapter 19

BAKERSFIELD, CALIFORNIA

A week later, Sarah and Adam pulled into the parking lot of Hog's Breath, a biker bar on the outskirts of Bakersfield. Gretchen had agreed to meet them after her shift ended at eleven o'clock that evening. Hog's Breath was a whitewashed cinderblock building with bars on all the windows, and a doorman that looked like an extra for a Hell's Angels movie. "I wonder what a hostess does in this place?" Sarah asked Adam. Adam had a pretty good idea about what Gretchen did. Adam had been in plenty of dives like this over the years and wasn't sure it was safe for Sarah to go in. Sarah, however, was out of the car and heading for the door before he could stop her. The doorman looked them over but didn't interfere as they went inside. Once inside they had to stop to allow their eyes to adjust to the darkness. Every guy in the room turned to look at Sarah. It was clear that they didn't get many female customers. The front half of the room consisted of a bar and several booths. A few dozen chairs surrounded a raised stage with a pole extending up to the ceiling in the back of the room.

Sarah and Adam took a booth near the bar, ordered beers, and waited for Gretchen. As they waited the lights dimmed and "Seventeen" by Ladytron started pulsating through the huge speakers. Most of the two-dozen men who had been nursing beers at booths or tables got up and moved to the chairs that surrounded the stage. The lights dimmed even further and a young woman wearing a string satin bikini and a garter came out from behind a curtain and started to gyrate her body to the music.

Adam thought Sarah looked embarrassed. He knew he was uncomfortable. They both tried to keep from staring at the girl on the stage. The dancer took off her bra after the first song and the bikini bottom at the end of the second song. During the third song she moved around the stage squatting in front of each man encouraging him to put money in her red lace garter. Adam had to suppress a laugh when he saw an old man pull out a small flashlight and shine it between the dancer's legs. At the end of the third song the dancer collected the dollar bills that had been tossed on the stage and then, still nude, walked around the room asking if anyone wanted a lap dance. When she got to their booth, she smiled and shook her breasts at Adam. Adam smiled, put a five-dollar bill in her garter and said, "No, thanks." The dancer turned to Sarah, smiled and said, "How about you, honey?" Sarah blushed and shook her head.

A few minutes later the dancer, wearing a short leather skirt and the bikini top, came back to their table and introduced her self. "Hi. I'm Gretchen. You're the folks my mom told me about, right?"

She smelled of sweat and cheap perfume. Butterfly and flower tattoos covered her arms from her wrists to her shoulders and she had a small angel wing on either side of her neck. Her face alone would keep her from getting through an airport metal detector. Eyebrows, nostrils, septum, lips, and ears were adorned with rings, barbells, and studs. Adam didn't want to think about what else might be pierced. Sarah was mesmerized as she watched Gretchen slide a pearl tongue ball back and forth across her lower lip.

Gretchen couldn't be recognized as the innocent girl in Mrs. Cocan's photo. The first word that came to mind Adam was "damaged."

Sarah scooted over in the booth to allow Gretchen to sit down. Gretchen ignored her, slid up against Adam, and signaled for the waiter. She smiled at Adam and asked, "Buy a girl a drink?" Adam said, "Sure." She ordered a double Jose Cuervo Black with a beer chaser.

Adam immediately recognized her red bloodshot eyes, runny nose, and frequent sniffing as strong indications that Gretchen was a cocaine addict. He sighed. He'd seen these signs many times before. He knew that victims of childhood sexual abuse often made very poor witnesses. It was not uncommon for victims of abuse to begin abusing drugs or alcohol. They often take on the persona of a very anti-social person, and because they often have difficulty developing normal romantic relationships, they often become sexually promiscuous. By the time they're asked to testify at a trial they often don't look anything like the innocent child who was abused.

As Sarah told Gretchen what they knew about Schafer, Gretchen stared at the table and picked at the cuticles of her fingers until they bled. Beneath her tattoos Adam noticed scars on her wrists that could be signs of cutting or worse. He didn't think that one incidence of Schafer touching her vagina would have unhinged her enough to cause the symptoms he was seeing. "Gretchen would you tell us what you know about Mr. Schafer?" Adam asked carefully.

Gretchen was silent for a few moments and then said, "I told my best friend about him but she promised she would never tell. I've never told anyone everything he did to me. My mother freaked out when I tried to tell her what happened. At first my father acted like he was going to kill Schafer, then he stopped looking at me. He made me feel like I'd done something wrong. I was afraid to tell anyone what really happened. I still have nightmares of being in a car with him and of going out to a little cottage outside of town. No one knows what he did to me there."

Sarah and Adam waited for Gretchen to continue, but she seemed lost in thought, eyes downcast. After a few moments Sarah said, "Schafer molested me when I was the same age as you were when he molested you. I understand much of your pain. I want him to pay for what he's done to me and you and dozens of other young girls through the years. Gretchen, he took me in his car and forced me to give him head. Its taken me until now to face what happened. Can you help us get him?"

Gretchen's face softened and looked at Sarah and then at Adam. They could both see the innocent girl hidden under the effects of her abuse. Gretchen took a deep breath and continued, "Okay. I'll tell you. It started so slowly that I really didn't understand what was happening. He was just so nice to me. He made me feel so special. All the other girls in my music class were envious of me. They all wanted Mr. Schafer to tutor them. It started in school, in the music room during my private lessons. He started touching me, and then he made me touch him. Eventually he would take me to a little house outside of town. We would go there two or three times a week. One of the bedrooms was decorated all in pink, the perfect little girl's room. Honestly, it was nicer than my room at home. There were stuffed animals and posters of rock groups tacked on the walls. He had a small cassette player and he played all the most popular songs. As soon as we'd get there he'd tell me to get undressed. Then he made me masturbate while he watched. I didn't even know what I was doing. He had to show me what he wanted. He made me do everything you can do with a woman. Except, I wasn't a woman. I was scared out of my mind all the time, and I blamed myself. It usually ended with him forcing me to blow him. I was only fourteen years old! I felt like I was living in a horrible nightmare and couldn't wake up. He showed me guns he kept in the trunk of his car and told me he would kill me if I told anyone what he did. I went on for a year and then one day he just told me he didn't want to see me anymore. I noticed he started spending time with another girl. I kept quiet for two years. Then when my little sister wanted to sign up for band, I had to tell. I couldn't let the same thing happen to her. But when I told, no one stopped him."

Gretchen sat silently again, then with a choked voice volunteered, "He's still alive and he's still teaching. I saw him a few weeks ago."

Sarah's heart skipped a beat. "You really saw him? Where is he?"

Gretchen said, "He's in Tupico Flats, Nevada. I found him by accident. I was depressed. I'm mostly depressed. My boyfriend, Rob, suggested we hop on his chopper and ride to Reno for a long weekend. At first I didn't want to go. I'd never had much money so I don't gamble. But Rob insisted that it would be fun so we went. The hotel where we stayed was hosting the Junior Teen Miss Nevada Beauty Pageant that weekend. When we went into the lobby to register, we were surrounded by dozens of Britney Spears wantabes.

"To escape the mob of teenage girls Rob hit the craps tables and I headed for the bar. The son-of-a-bitch was in the bar."

Gretchen voice hardened. "He was sitting alone at a table in the back surreptitiously watching the young girls walk by. I was so angry that I began to shake. I turned around and hurried back into the lobby, before he could notice me. Rob was still at the craps tables. I waited for Schafer to come out of the bar and then followed him into the parking garage. As he drove away, I saw a 'Tupico Flats Fighting Black Widow Band' sticker on the rear bumper of his SUV.

"When we got back home, I told Rob I wanted a gun. To tell him I was going use it to kill my middle school music teacher, probably would have been a mistake, so I told him I wanted it for personal protection. He took me to a shooting range where I shot a bunch of pistols. A Smith & Wesson revolver fit my hand the best. It's lightweight and is very accurate. So Rob bought me a used one. I went to the range every day until I was a pretty good shot.

"Two weeks after I saw him in Reno I packed up my gun and drove to Tupico Flats. I followed Schafer home from school. He has a wife and daughter. I spied on him for two days, but after I saw he had a family I couldn't pull the trigger."

Sarah slid out of the booth, stood up and said, "Let's go Adam. We've got him!" Adam put his hand on her shoulder. "Wait a second, Sarah. We need more information."

Adam took out a notebook. "Gretchen, what's his address? What kind of car does he drive? What did you learn about his schedule, hobbies, favorite restaurants?"

After she had answered all of Adam's questions Gretchen asked them to keep her informed. They promised to do everything possible to catch him. They thanked her for her time and the information. Adam ordered another tequila for Gretchen, paid for the drinks, left a generous tip, and followed Sarah to their car.

As they drove away from the bar, Adam said, "She's really been damaged. I think she's capable of doing anything. If Schafer doesn't go to jail, he'd better be on the lookout for her."

"He'd better go to jail," Sarah responded.

Chapter 20

TUPICO FLATS, NEVADA

For the third time this week Lizzie and her mom were screaming at each other. Mrs. Sutton was at her wits end. She'd heard the teenage years were difficult times for moms and teenaged daughters, but nothing had prepared her for the daily warfare that she was experiencing.

Mrs. Sutton tried to control her voice, "Okay, if that's the way you want it, your room is yours. From now on it's your responsibility to keep it clean. I'm sick of cleaning up after you. If you want to live in a pig sty, that's your business."

"Great! It is my room! And these are my things! Just stay out!" Lizzie shouted as she slammed her bedroom door. The room, like Lizzie, was in a state of transition from little girl to teenager. When Lizzie was born she came home to a room out of a storybook. A painted moon and stick-on glow-in-the-dark stars highlighted a midnight blue ceiling. The bedspread and curtains were of moon and star fabric. A moon and stars were cut out in the headboard. A net had been strung in a corner to hold the dozens of stuffed animals she would collect.

Lizzie was doing her best to extinguish all signs of her childhood. She had plastered her walls with posters of singers: Justin Bieber, Jason Derulo, Miley Cyrus, Black Eyed Peas and and New Boyz. On the inside of her door she had taped a poster of her favorite song and group, Thnks Fr Th Mmrs by Fall Out Boy. Her stuffed animals had been exiled to some boxes under the stairs in the basement.

Despite her promise to stay out of Lizzie's room, Mrs. Sutton opened the door a week later to see if there was any improvement. Mrs. Sutton couldn't believe that other teenager's rooms looked like this. Dirty laundry and clean clothes lay jumbled together on the floor. Plates of half eaten food were shoved under the bed. A jumbo-sized cardboard drink cup had leaked through and warped the top of the dresser. Tears came to Mrs. Sutton's eyes as she saw evidence of Lizzie's carelessness and disregard for property. It had taken her six months to save enough money to buy Lizzie this bedroom set. She looked at the posters taped to the walls and ceiling and didn't recognize the names of any of the groups sharing the room with Lizzie. Since Mrs. Sutton bought Lizzie and i-pod she had no idea what kind of music her daughter listened to. Mrs. Sutton closed the door, shook her head, and slowly walked back downstairs.

Mrs. Sutton assumed Lizzie would eventually become disgusted with the squalor and decide to clean her room. Weeks later, it was obvious Mrs. Sutton's plan wasn't working. At first, Mrs. Sutton avoided looking into Lizzie's room. Finally, she gave up and decided to clean the room herself. She grabbed a handful of paper towels and started to sop up the pool of pop on the dresser top when she noticed it had leaked into the top drawer and soaked through a stack of t-shirts. She sighed at the thought of more laundry. As she emptied the drawer a small red notebook fell onto the floor.

Mrs. Sutton picked it up and saw that "Mrs. Lizzie Schafer" and "Mr. and Mrs. James R. Schafer" were written dozens of times on the front cover. Hearts surrounded each inscription. She smiled as she remembered the sweet crushes she had when she was Lizzie's age. Her smile faded with the realization that James Schafer was Lizzie's band teacher. She was immediately suspicious. She needed to know what Lizzie was writing about her teacher.

Fifteen minutes later Mrs. Sutton was shaking and her stomach was roiling as she sat on the edge of Lizzie's bed. It took her fifteen minutes more to will herself to think straight. If what she had just read was true, Lizzie's teacher was molesting her. She wondered how this could be possible. She thought she surely would have noticed something if it were true. She thought about going up to the school and confronting Mr. Schafer. She considered calling the police, ultimately she decided to wait and talk with Lizzie when she got home from school.

Time stood still as Mrs. Sutton waited for Lizzie to get home. When Lizzie finally entered the house, Mrs. Sutton rushed toward her waving the notebook. "What's the meaning of this?" Mrs. Sutton demanded struggling to keep her voice under control. Lizzie's expression of shock, fear, and embarrassment told Mrs. Sutton all she needed to know.

"Has Mr. Schafer done anything to you? Have you had sex with him?" Mrs. Sutton asked.

"What are you doing with my diary?" Lizzie shouted as she snatched it from her mother's hand. Mrs. Sutton was shocked at the fury that Lizzie unleashed on her. She barely yanked the diary back out of Lizzie's hands.

"Answer me. Are you having sex with your teacher?"

"You promised to stay out of my room! You're a liar!" Lizzie screamed, as she pushed past Mrs. Sutton and ran up to her room.

Mrs. Sutton rushed after her. "We have to talk about what you wrote, Lizzie."

Lizzie sat stiffly on the edge of the bed. "I just made it up, Mom. None of this is true. Mr. Schafer is my favorite teacher, that's all."

"Some of the things in here are pretty specific and very sexual, Lizzie," Mrs. Sutton persisted. "If you aren't doing these things, how do you know about this kind of stuff?"

"Mom, you are so old school," Lizzie replied petulantly, flopping on her back on the bed.

"I don't even know what that means," Mrs. Sutton said helplessly.

"Kid's today know a lot more about sex than you think. Judy Wright's father has a drawer full of porn DVD's, and you can find anything you want on the Web."

Mrs. Sutton thought this reaction over for a moment. She decided not to let it divert the conversation away from what was really important to her, to Lizzie. She took a deep breath. "Lizzie, this is very important. Swear to me that you are not having sex with your teacher, or anyone else, for that matter."

"Mom, I already told you. This is made up stuff I write in my journal. You wouldn't be so freaked out if you'd kept your promise to stay out of my room."

By now they were both crying. Mrs. Sutton tried again. "Lizzie, swear that you are not doing anything with Mr. Schafer."

"Okay, Okay. I swear."

"Why are you being so difficult? Lizzie, I don't even know who you are. Show me some respect."

"If dad were here things would be so different. You drove him away. You don't deserve respect! You're a rotten mother!"

Mrs. Sutton felt like she was slapped in the face. She wanted to tell Lizzie that her father was a drunk and an adulterer but once again, she willed herself to keep that secret. "You're going to stay in your room until you apologize and until you tell me the truth about you and Mr. Schafer, " Mrs. Sutton said as she backed out of Lizzie's room.

"Fine!" Lizzie hollered as she slammed the door.

Mrs. Sutton stood in the hallway staring at the closed door. She was shaking so badly that she had to put her hands on the wall to steady herself. Finally she staggered to her bedroom and collapsed on the bed. She knew she spent too much time working. She almost wished Lizzie's father were here. She didn't know what to do.

Several hours later, Lizzie came into Mrs. Sutton's bedroom and lay down on the bed beside her. She put her head on Mrs. Sutton's chest and looked up into her eyes. "I'm sorry, Mommy. I'm so sorry. I didn't mean what I said. Honest, Mom, I haven't done anything bad. I love you, Mommy."

Tears welled in Mrs. Sutton's eyes. "I love you too, Lizzie, more than you'll ever know." They hugged for several minutes then Lizzie went back to her room. Mrs. Sutton desperately wanted to believe her.

It was about this time that Schafer began text-messaging Lizzie late at night. Sometimes they would instant message for hours, long after her mom thought she was asleep. He always told her that he couldn't sleep because he couldn't stop thinking about her and what they did together.

One night he was bold enough to text her, "hav u eva thought bout having sex wid me?"

She hesitated before answering, and then replied, "Of course I've thought bout it, I'm nt a baby u no."

"That's all dat I thnk bout," he responded. "I thnk bout u every time I fuk wid ma wife. I also thnk bout u wen I masturbate. Do u eva masturbate?"

Lizzie closed her phone. She didn't know how to answer him. She knew Schafer would be disappointed in her if she said no.

A few weeks later Schafer bought disposable cell phones for Lizzie and himself. He told her to keep the phone a secret and to use it only to call him. A few nights after she got the phone he texted, "u c the camera on ur cell phone?"

"Yes." She heard her mother outside her door. "I've GTG. ma Mom iz coming up da stairs," she replied.

Lizzie slept with her phone under her pillow. The next night the phone vibrated at three in the morning. It was Schafer texting Lizzie and telling her to call him. He knew better than to take the chance of her mother hearing her phone ring.

When she called him he said, "Lizzie, I've a little favor to ask of you that will make me very happy. I want you to take off all of your clothes and use your new phone to take some photos of yourself in the mirror and send them to me. Would you do that for me?" Schafer asked.

Intuitively, Lizzie knew this would be a big mistake. "No! I can't do that." she replied and abruptly closed her phone.

Schafer sent her thirty text messages during that night, each asking her to send him some photographs. She didn't answer. He didn't mention the photos again for a week. Then as she was leaving her private lesson he used another one of his tactics, "If you don't send me the photos I've asked for, I'll know you really don't love me. Schafer then told her exactly how he wanted her to pose when she took the photos. It took another week of pleading, but Schafer finally got an e-mail attachment with three explicit nude photos of Lizzie.

Schafer loved looking at the photos of Lizzie. One day, several weeks later, Lizzie tried to pull away when Schafer started to fondle her. Schafer held her face in his hand and said, "I have the photos you sent me. Do you want me to send them to your mom? Maybe I should e-mail them to every student in school. Everyone will think you are a slut. What do you think your mom and your friends will do when they find out what the kind of girl you are?" Lizzie stopped resisting and allowed Schafer to do what he wanted.

Now Schafer had the first photos to post on his "Little Miss Debutant" web site. Within two weeks of posting the three nude photos of Lizzie he had almost one hundred one-week trial subscriptions to his new web site. He knew that in order to convert these subscribers into full year subscribers, he would have to up the anti. He bought a Super low light flat pinhole lens camera and a portable DVR, for five hundred dollars, and installed the camera in the air duct of the music storage room.

At their next tutoring session Lizzie followed the routine that they had established. She came into the closet, got undressed, sat on the folding chair, and waited for Schafer's instructions. By now her emotions were so confused she really didn't know if he loved her, but she was helpless to stay away.

As Lizzie looked at him expectantly Schafer said, "Lizzie, today I just want to look at you. Turn your chair so that you're facing me. Lizzie hesitated then did as she was told. He waited a few moments, "Now spread your legs and touch yourself for me."

Again Lizzie hesitated before doing as she was told. After a few minutes Schafer said, Thank you, Lizzie. You are so beautiful. Now please get dressed and leave." She was relieved and disappointed at the same time. As soon as he was alone he retrieved the DVR, attached it to his laptop, and uploaded the movie to his web site. Within an hour he received an encrypted message from one of his subscribers.

"Hello, I have an American client who lives in Mexico City. He has authorized me to offer you fifty thousand dollars for the girl in your recent video. If you are interested contact me at the enclosed secure address."

Schafer was dumfounded. He didn't know if this was a joke, a police trap or a legitimate offer. He decided to ignore the message. But, by the next evening his compulsive personality forced him to reply. "How do I know you are who you say you are?"

"If you agree, I will wire you an m-payment in the amount of twenty five thousand dollars."

"What's an m-payment," Schaefer asked.

"It's a cheap, swift, mostly untraceable money transfer. I can send one from anywhere, anytime as long as I have a mobile phone."

"Okay. I'm in."

"I will call you in a few weeks for the girl's route home from school. Be sure to have witnesses that see her leave the school and can provide you with an alibi. My friends and I will get her in our van, be in Reno in two hours, LA that night, and Mexico City the next morning."

Schafer was becoming bored with Lizzie. A new girl had recently moved into the school district he thought she was much cuter than Lizzie. It might be time to get rid of Lizzie, he thought. Usually he just stopped tutoring his girls when he was finished with them. However, he was worried that Lizzie might cause trouble if he suddenly dropped her. Getting her out of town had some real appeal.

Chapter 22

Adam and Sarah sat in their rental car in the parking lot of Tupico Flats Middle School. Neither of them spoke. Sarah was having difficulty breathing. She took several deep breaths through her nose. "We've found him, Shepherd, or Schafer or whatever he is calling himself now. He's in there right now. Let's go in and get him," Sarah said grimly.

"Take it easy," Adam cautioned, we don't want to scare him off before we can make him pay for what he's done. Statutes of limitation will protect him against past rape charges. The murders of Julie and Molly will be incredibly difficult to prove after so many years. First, we have to find out if he is still molesting children. If he is we have to get him for what he's doing now. Then we'll see if we can make him pay for all the other stuff."

Sarah took another deep breath. "Okay," she acquiesced. "What's the plan?"

"Sarah, we've talked about this before." Adam's voice was calm and patient. "Our first step is to visit with the principal and see if we can find out if there are any suspicions about Shepherd. Our job will be a lot easier if we can get the principal on board."

Sarah and Adam entered the school and followed the signs and the red line painted on the floor that directed them to the principal's office. As they walked down the hall, Sarah scanned the face of every male teacher they passed. She knew she'd know Schafer if she saw him, even fifteen years after he molested her. She also looked at the face of every girl, looking for herself.

A short walk brought them to a glass enclosed office. A chest-high counter separated a waiting area from the school secretary's desk. They didn't have an appointment so they hoped that the principal was in his office and could see them immediately.

The secretary stuck her head into the principal's office and told him he had visitors. A minute later the principal bounded out of the office. "Hello, I'm Bill Boyken. Everyone calls me Bull, he said as he extended his hand. My secretary said you had important business with me. What can I do for you?" Boyken was a giant of a man, at least six foot six and probably three hundred pounds. Even Adam was a little intimidated. He tried not to flinch as his fingers were crushed in a vise-like grip.

"Hello Mr. Boyken, I'm Adam Faulkner...

"Call me Bull," Boyken interrupted.

"I'm a private investigator, and this is Sarah Abbott," Adam continued as he flexed his fingers and massaged the spot where Bill's huge ring had bruised into his hand.

Please come into my office, Bill said cordially. The office was a shrine to "Big Bull" Boyken and Nebraska football. Framed jerseys, authentic helmets, miniature helmets, autographed footballs and several magazine covers displaying photos of Bull Boyken adorned the walls. A replica of the Outland Trophy, awarded to the best interior lineman by the Football Writers Association of America, held the obvious place of honor in an alcove below a front window.

There was no way to begin a conversation without mentioning football. Before Adam could speak, Bill jumped in and said, "You're a pretty big guy. Play ball?"

"Played in high school. Blew out my knee during my freshman year at Ohio State," Adam said casually.

"The Buckeyes are 2-0 against us," Bill laughed, "But, I won't hold that against you."

"Thanks," Adam smiled.

"Hell, I had ACL, medial meniscus, lateral meniscus, MCL, LCL, and PCL surgeries and still managed to play three years in the NFL and six in Canada." As he talked, he pulled both pants legs up over his knees to show a road map of red and purple scars. He smiled slyly at Adam and said, "Must not grow them so tough back east in Ohio."

Adam resisted telling Bill that he had always thought of Nebraska football players as Corn Fed Lard Asses. He stifled a laugh as he thought of a scene from "Forrest Gump" and shot back, "Glad you weren't shot in the buttocks."

Boyken was obviously not a Tom Hanks movie buff. He stared blankly at Adam. After a short pause Boyken launched into a football story that he had clearly told hundreds of times. It was something about him being put in as a running back and scoring the winning touchdown against Oklahoma.

Helpless to stop him, Sarah and Adam sat in two Nebraska red leather chairs and tried to be patient as they waited for a chance to tell Bill why they'd come. Ten minutes later they knew more about Bill and Nebraska football than any non-Husker should ever want to know.

Bill waited expectantly for compliments and follow up questions. Hearing none and obviously disappointed, he finally asked, "So, what can I do for you?"

"It's pretty difficult to know where to begin," Adam said. "So I guess I'll come right out and say it. "Sarah was molested by a teacher when she was in middle school, and we believe the teacher who molested her is teaching at this school." Adam was careful not to say "your school" or give away the teacher's name or subject area.

Bill's face turned red. He clenched and unclenched his fists and sat silently for a moment. When he spoke his voice had lost its previous warmth. "That's a pretty serious charge. I don't know where you got your information, but it's wrong. I hand picked every teacher in this school. I stand behind every one of them. Who are you talking about? I need a name"

"Jim Schafer," Adam said, his eyes directly meeting Boyken's gaze.

"Your crazy. Jim's one of the best teachers I've got. The students and parents love him."

"So you're saying you haven't had any complaints or suspicions regarding Mr. Schafer."

"Damn straight. That's exactly what I'm saying."

"Do you mind if we talk with some of your teachers and students?"

"Of course I mind," Boyken growled." He stood up and moved around his desk in one quick motion. "I think it would be best if you left now."

It was clear the meeting was over. Sarah was speechless as they left the office and retraced their steps out of the building.

Sarah was shaking as they reached the parking lot. She was so angry she could hardly speak. "He has to know how serious teacher-student abuse is. He's hiding something?"

"I don't know. Shepherd has fooled a lot of people. I guess if your looking the wrong way you might miss abuse."

"Don't you dare take his side, Adam," she said as she slammed the car door shut. They sat in the parking lot for a few minutes. Sarah sat silently. Finally, she asked flatly, "Sorry, Adam. What's plan B?"

"Well luckily I have one," Adam said, trying to sound cheerful. "I want to get a look at Shepherd in action. As we were waiting for 'The Bull,' I noticed an announcement for a band concert on Monday night. I think we should nose around town over the weekend, see what else we can turn up, and go to the concert on Monday evening."

As Boyken was leaving the building at the end of the day, Jim Schafer fell into step along side of him. Schafer knew the answer to the question before he asked, "Any plans for the weekend, Bull?"

"Just got my HD big screen TV installed," Boyken boasted. I'll be watching Big Red football. It's the Big 12 Championship. We're going to cream Texas." He paused to saver the thought then continued, I remember the last game I played against the Longhorns..."

Shepherd smiled to himself. He knew how to get Boyken going and enjoyed manipulating him into one of his 'back in the day' stories. By the time they got to their cars Boyken had finished his story and asked, "What about you, Jim? What are you and that pretty wife of yours going to do this weekend?"

"I'll probably spend the whole weekend rehearsing my band. You know our big concert's on Monday."

As Boyken got in his car his demeanor changed abruptly. "Jim," he said seriously. "I had a weird conversation in my office this afternoon."

Schafer immediately tensed. "Really? With whom?"

"Well, a private investigator and a woman stopped by. They think one of my teachers is a child molester. I told them to get the hell out town."

A knot formed in Schafer's stomach. He felt like turning and running to his car. He forced himself to keep his voice calm. "Who are they accusing?"

"That's the crazy thing." Bill said shaking his head in disbelief. "They said it was you."

Schafer forced himself to breathe and keep smiling.

His throat was so dry he felt like he was being strangled. He knew he had to say something. "That is crazy," he said with sincere dismay. "That kind of false accusation could ruin a guy's reputation. Do you think I should file a defamation suit against them?"

Bill started the ignition. "Let's wait until next week and see what happens. They may just leave town."

When Schafer got into his car his hand was shaking so badly he couldn't put the key in the ignition. He leaned against the steering wheel, his mind racing to find a way out. No one had ever been this close before. He wondered how long he had before they found him. He thought about Grace and Ashley and what they would think if he were exposed. When he finally started the car, he sat there for ten minutes before he was able to drive. Questions tumbled through his mind: How did they find me? Who have they talked to? Who was the woman? Should I call Lizzie?

Chapter 23

Monday evening the Tupico Flats Middle School auditorium was packed with proud parents and relatives of band members. The atmosphere was festive. Athletic banners hung from the ceiling, student artwork was displayed on dividers set up along each wall. The band kids looked great in white shirts and black slacks. Sarah and Adam had made sure they arrived early in order to get seats close enough to be able to clearly see the face of each child. Sarah was surprised her stomach felt queasy as she climbed the bleachers to find a seat. She had been nervous months ago when she visited her old middle school. She didn't understand why, but tonight she felt worse.

While Adam and Sarah were selecting their seats, Jim Schafer was throwing up in the band room. He'd been in a state of panic since his conversation with Boyken on Friday afternoon. On the drive home his heart had started racing and he had felt weak and dizzy. He thought he was having a heart attack and pulled his car to the side of the road. He opened his cell phone, ready to call 911. His sense of terror and impending doom was overwhelming. He took several deep breaths and calmed down enough to continue driving, but nausea and dizziness returned before he had driven five blocks. At the intersection where he needed to make a right turn and continue to his house, he felt an overwhelming need to escape. He slowed the car and considered turning left and driving until he was in Canada. He had tried never to let himself think about what would happen if he were ever caught. Now, disjointed nightmarish thoughts of humiliation, arrest, a trial, and prison tumbled through his head. Questions pierced his panic. Who is this detective? Does he know about Julie and Molly? Are the police going to come here and arrest me? He had spent Saturday and Sunday locked in his study. When Grace knocked on the door, he told her he was working on the score for the concert. He was actually scrubbing his computer files and shredding everything incriminating. Sunday morning he collected all the prescription drugs in the house. He was pretty sure he had enough to kill himself. I can just float off to sleep. He comforted himself. I have an out if I need one.

When no one came for him by Monday morning, Shepherd told himself Boyken was wrong. Still, he'd have to be on his guard. As he left for school he swallowed two of Grace's Xanax and put the half full bottle in his briefcase.

After the student musicians took their places, the lights dimmed, and Jim Schafer strode to the podium. Sarah gasped and dug her fingernails into Adam's arm. "It's him!" she whispered. Then the band struck up Frank Erickson's *Air for Band*. When the clarinet section was featured, Sarah's palms began to sweat and she started to hyperventilate. Thoughts of being in the car with Mr. Shepherd came rushing back to her. She crossed her arms over her chest and rocked back and forth, trying to remain calm. This was the same piece Shepherd made her play the day he molested her. She tried to remain seated, but she couldn't. Oh, God. I'm going to be sick, she thought as she hastily excused herself, and bolted from the auditorium.

Several minutes later, Adam found Sarah outside the girl's restroom.

Adam was not surprised by Sarah's reaction. He'd seen other women panic when they confronted the man who raped them. "Sarah, are you going to be okay?"

Sarah nodded. "Adam, I honestly thought I could do this. Now, I don't know if I can. One minute I was fine, and the next minute I couldn't get enough air and felt like I was going to throw up."

Adam put his hand lightly on Sarah's shoulder. "Sarah, it's the shock of seeing him again. You can wait out here. I'll check him out and we can meet after the concert."

"No. I'm okay now. I'm going back inside," Sarah spoke with renewed confidence.

Five minutes after they returned to their seats Sarah whispered to Adam, "I see her. Second row, short blond hair. Playing the clarinet."

Adam scanned the faces until he found the girl Sarah had indicated. "How do you know it's her?" he asked.

Sarah was quiet for a moment and then whispered, "I'm looking at myself fifteen years ago. Look at how she's watching him. She hasn't taken her eyes off of him since he walked on stage. That poor baby, she looks like a frightened little rabbit."

Schafer was the quintessential showman, nearly bounding off the podium with every crescendo, exaggerating every stroke of the baton. One moment he was leaping like Baryshnikov, the next jabbing his baton like a matador's sword. He left the stage between selections and returned wearing a white fright wig. The parents and kids roared with laughter and applause.

Over the years Shepherd had learned that parents in the audience were interested only in their own children. He'd begun the tradition of having students stand and announce his or her name after their selection. Adam and Sarah anxiously waited for the blond clarinetist to stand. She stood ands said in a soft, sweet voice "I'm Lizzie, Lizzie Sutton."

As they walked to their car after the concert Sarah persuaded Adam to go for broke and try to visit Lizzie's home that night. Adam used his PDA to get the Sutton's address and phone number. They called Mrs. Sutton and told her they wanted to talk with her about the school's music program. At first she was reluctant.

"Its nine o'clock. Can't this wait until tomorrow?" she asked.

Adam didn't want to use the phone to tell her the real reason for the call. They agreed to meet at the Sutton house the next day after Mrs. Sutton got off of work.

Sarah and Adam arrived at 3012 Barton Drive early and waited for Mrs. Sutton to get home. They gave her a few moments after she entered the house before they knocked. Mrs. Sutton opened the front door and looked at them suspiciously.

"Hello, Mrs. Sutton. Thank you so much for agreeing to see us. I am Adam Faulkner and this is Sarah Abbott. Adam showed her his identification and said, "We are looking for a man that molested Sarah when she was in middle school. We think he is teaching at Lizzie's school. May we come in?"

Mrs. Sutton paled and reached for the door jam to steady herself. She whispered, "Oh My God. It's true. Is it Mr. Schafer? It's Mr. Schafer, isn't it?"

Sarah and Adam exchanged glances and then turned their attention back to Mrs. Sutton. She was wringing her hands and rocking back and fourth.

"Please let us come in. I think we have a lot to talk about," Sarah said.

When they were settled in the sparsely furnished living room, Mrs. Sutton asked if she could get them something to drink.

Neither Sarah nor Adam was thirsty and they wanted to get on with it, but they understood that sharing food and drink often helped people to relax.

"Coffee would be great," Sarah said. "Me too," echoed Adam.

Mrs. Sutton excused herself and went into the kitchen.

Sarah and Adam looked around the room. The furniture was clean but old and threadbare. There were no books or newspapers in sight. The sofa and two chairs were facing the television and there was significant wear on the carpet in front of each chair. Several reproductions of Paris street scenes hung over the sofa. What appeared to be a recent school photograph of Lizzie sat on the television.

When Mrs. Sutton returned she demanded, "Tell me what you know about Mr. Schafer. Is Lizzie in danger?"

Over the months they had worked together, Sarah and Adam had become adept at deciding who should take the lead during interviews. Sarah took a deep breath and began. "Mrs. Sutton, We believe his real name is Tony Shepherd. We believe he is a child molester."

"It's him. I know it's him. I read Lizzie's journal. She wrote that Schafer had been having oral sex with her in the music room. When I confronted her, she denied everything and said she had just written about her fantasies. I want to believe her, but I don't. Not really. Is Mr. Schafer molesting my daughter? He is isn't he?" Mrs. Sutton's sentences ran together. "He seems like a great teacher and person. He has a lovely wife and a beautiful daughter. What would make him even want to have sex with a child?"

"Because nobody stops him!" Sarah replied bluntly.

Adam shot her a look of warning and attempted to smooth over her harsh statement. "From what I've read, most psychologists don't believe people choose to be pedophiles," he volunteered gently.

Sarah realized her error and jumped in to add more information. "Generally, this disorder begins in adolescence and is usually chronic. Some never go beyond fantasizing about children. Others abuse their own children. Schafer is an example of the type who becomes employed in a place where he can gain unsupervised access to children. His marriage is probably a cover to avoid suspicion. "

Sarah waited for Mrs. Sutton to absorb this information then she spoke quietly. "I was one of his first victims. He's taught in five school districts since he molested me. We believe he molested several children in each of these districts."

Mrs. Sutton was incredulous. "If you know all of this, why isn't he in jail?"

"It is a long and complicated story," Adam admitted.

They explained why Sarah's case could not be won and how most of the time Schafer left school districts before he was suspected.

"But with Lizzie's testimony and her diary, I think we can put him in prison." Sarah said.

"But, Lizzie says it never happened. She says she made up the stuff she wrote in the journal, " Mrs. Sutton said hopefully.

"Lizzie may be in love with Schafer, or she may be afraid of him, or she may be too embarrassed to tell the truth. Schafer really messes with children's minds. Can we see the diary? It's going to be a really big help," Adam said.

Mrs. Sutton sat rigidly in her chair and gazed at Lizzie's photo. Finally, she spoke with grim determination. "If you're sure of what you say you know, and if he's hurting my little girl, then I'm willing to help you. I don't know about Lizzie, though." Mrs. Sutton retrieved Lizzie's journal from her desk and handed it to Sarah.

Sarah opened the journal and she and Adam began reading. It broke Sarah's heart to read Lizzie's most secret thoughts. It was clear that Shepherd was the heartthrob of every seventh grade girl. Lizzie's entries were a perfect account of the classic grooming process. What chance does a child have against this predator Sarah thought as she slammed the journal shut.

"Do you mind if we stay here and wait for Lizzie to get home from school?" Adam asked.

"Okay," She said meekly.

As they waited for Lizzie Sarah and Adam took turns reading Lizzie's journal. When they had finished they exchanged quite glances of victory.

Chapter 24

When Lizzie got home from school she found her mother sitting in the living room with two people she didn't know. She could tell by the way they looked at her when she entered the room that they had been talking about her. Mrs. Sutton greeted her, "Hi, Honey. Please come here a minute. I want you to meet these people."

Sarah smiled warmly and extended her hand. "Hello, Lizzie, I'm Sarah Abbott and this is my friend, Adam Faulkner. We're really pleased to meet you." Sarah could see the fear in Lizzie's eyes. It was clear that Lizzie didn't know what was happening, but she intuitively knew it wasn't good.

"How was school today, Lizzie," Sarah asked politely.

"Okay, I guess." Lizzie murmured, glancing from Sarah, to Adam, to her mother.

"We were at your concert last night. Your orchestra is really good," Adam said.

Lizzie ignored the complement, turned to her mother, and asked, "Why are they here, mom?"

"Lizzie," Mrs. Sutton began, "Mr. Faulkner and Miss Abbott are here about Mr. Schafer. I let them read your journal..."

Lizzie jumped to her feet, white-faced, and fists clinched "What? Mother! How could you do this? You know that's private. I told you it was just made up stuff."

Mrs. Sutton struggled to control her voice. "These people say that Mr. Schafer has molested other middle school girls. They think he should be arrested."

Lizzie, who had been on her way out of the room, whirled and faced Adam and Sarah, "No, Mr. Schafer never did anything to me. He's the best teacher in the school. Ask anyone. He wouldn't do what you say he did."

Her mother grabbed her and hugged her. "Honey, sit here with me for a minute and listen to what these people have to say."

Lizzie plopped down on the sofa, arms crossed, eyes downcast.

"Lizzie," Sarah began, "I want you to know I understand how you are feeling. You think Mr. Schafer loves you. He tricked you to make you feel that way. I know this is really embarrassing. I was embarrassed too. I was so embarrassed by what he did to me that I didn't tell anyone. It is because of me that he was able to go on and hurt other girls. It is because of me that he was able to hurt you. I am so sorry. Schafer molested me when I was your age and he's molested several girls in every school district he has worked in. He tricked us just like he tricked you. We have to stop him or he will molest other girls."

Lizzie considered what Sarah had told her. She knew Mr. Schafer loved her and would never lie to her. "No, that's not true. I've never had sex with anybody. Mom, make them go away." With that, Lizzie stood and raced from the room.

Mrs. Sutton remained seated, closed her eyes, and took a deep breath. Then she raised her head with a look of determination. "Let's wait for her to calm down. I'll go up and get her in a little while. We can try to talk with her some more."

As soon as Lizzie got to her room she grabbed her cell phone out of her backpack and called Schafer.

He answered her call immediately. Lizzie was frantic. "Mr. S., there are people at my house who are saying bad things about you."

Schafer's hands started to tingle. He felt the sweat pour down his chest and back. "What? What? Who's there? What are they saying?" These are the people who were at the school, he thought.

"They asked me questions about you and me. They're saying you've had sex with other girls at other schools. That's not true, is it?"

Schafer couldn't speak. This time he was sure he was having a heart attack. He reached in his pocket, opened the pill bottle, and dry swallowed two Xanax.

"Mr. S., why are they saying these things about you?"

Schafer paused, before answering. He tried unsuccessfully to slow his breathing. He knew that what he said in the next few seconds would likely set the direction for the rest of his life. "I don't know. You know you're the only one I have ever been in love with," Schafer said. "You didn't tell them anything did you? Unless you tell them about us, they'll never be able to prove anything happened. " The twenty-five dollar investment in the two disposable phones was a God send, he thought.

"The lady said you had sex with her when she was my age. She is saying they're going to get you arrested. What's going on?"

Schafer's knees gave out and he flopped into his chair. It seemed that the classroom was spinning. He felt the blood rushing from his head. His mind was careening as he tried to think who could be in Lizzie's house."

Schafer was losing control. "Shit! Shit! Shit! Listen, Lizzie. I don't know these people. I don't know why they are lying about me, but if you don't tell them anything they can't arrest me. Just stick with your story. Remember, we never did anything. I love you Lizzie."

"I love you, too. What should I do? They're still downstairs with my mom."

"Tell them they're crazy. Just don't admit to anything."

Lizzie hesitated and then said in a soft voice, "My mom found my diary and gave it to them."

A diary! A diary! "Holy fuck, you kept a diary? How stupid are you? What have you done to me? What did you write?"

Lizzie was shocked and frightened by how angry Schafer was. She hesitated and then said, "Mostly I told my diary about how much I love you and how much I love to be with you."

"You didn't tell them about what we did in the band room or on the band trip did you?"

Lizzie didn't answer.

"Lizzie, please. Tell me. What did you write?"

Lizzie didn't know what to do or say. Finally she said, "Well, I told my diary that the band room was our special place and that we kissed each other and the other stuff we did."

"Lizzie, you have to tell them you made that all up, that it was just your way of wishful thinking about me. Tell them it's not true." Then a thought struck him. "No one is listening to this call are they?"

"No. I told you, they're downstairs talking with my mom."

Schafer didn't know what to do. He knew this was bad. This was real bad. He wanted to threaten Lizzie, but he was afraid that might backfire. He considered telling her what would happen to her if her friends found out about her. But, that could also backfire and cause her to panic. He decided the best approach was to pull her in as tight as he could. A plausible plan gradually entered his mind. He remembered one of his former girls had used Wikipedia to research marriageable age laws. A marriage proposal might work. Hell, he had to do something.

"Listen, Lizzie. You know I love you more than anything. Let's not wait to get married. Girls can get married at fourteen in Paraguay. I'll divorce my wife and we can get married right away. You know I love you, don't you? I'll see you in school tomorrow, honey. I love you."

Lizzie didn't answer.

As soon as soon as he hung up, Schafer got the phone directory and placed a call to the man from Tupico Flats he had recognized at his club meeting. There was a firm rule that prohibited any contact with others outside the meeting, but he was desperate.

The phone was answered on the third ring. Schafer said, "Hello, this is Schafer. You know, from our meeting in California."

At first the line was silent, then in a quiet controlled voice the man said, "What are you doing calling me? You know we're never to contact each other."

"Please don't hang up," Schafer begged. "A private investigator is in town and he is onto me. I don't know how much he knows about us. He may just be after me. He may be after all of us. I don't know. He says he is going to put me in jail. You've got to help me."

"Schafer, I can't do anything to help you. Never call me again"

"Wait! Listen, you'd better help me. You've got a lot more to lose than I do. I'm not going to jail alone. If I have to name names in order to stay out of jail, I will."

The man was silent for a moment. Then in a tight voice he said, "Okay. I'll look into what you've said and see what I can do. Don't call me again. I'll call you."

Schafer thanked him and hung up the phone. Maybe there is a way out of this, yet. He thought.

Mrs. Sutton, Sarah, and Adam sat in a tense silence after Lizzie left the room. "It's been almost twenty minutes, I'm going to go up and see if she's calmed down. If she has, I'll bring her back down," Mrs. Sutton said.

A few minutes later Mrs. Sutton returned with Lizzie. It was clear that they had both been crying. Mrs. Sutton sat beside Lizzie on the sofa and held both of her hands. Lizzie looked scared and vulnerable.

"Lizzie," Sarah began. Believe me I know how upsetting this is. Please let me tell you what I know and you make up your own mind about Mr. Schafer. She pulled a manila envelope from her briefcase and took out a photograph. She handed it to Lizzie. This is a photo of Julie Romano. We think this is the first girl that Mr. Schafer molested."

Lizzie tried not to look at the photo, but she peeked at it as Sarah talked.

Sarah took out a second photo. "This is me when I was in middle school. I was in Mr. Schafer's music class and the band. I guess I kind of fell under his spell, too. My mom and dad were dead. Mr. Schafer was really nice to me. His name was Shepherd then. He made me feel very special. Then he took advantage of me including touching me in my private areas. I was afraid but I never told anybody."

By now both Mrs. Sutton and Sarah were leaning toward the coffee table and looking at the photos. Sarah took another photo from the envelope. "This is Molly Lincoln. She was another of Mr. Schafer's students. She died while attending a band camp where Mr. Schafer was teaching."

Mrs. Sutton interrupted. "She died? Are you saying that Mr. Schafer killed someone?"

"He was never arrested, but yes, we believe Schafer killed Molly and Julie."

Sarah pulled out the next photo and handed it to Lizzie.

"This is Mindy Allen. Mr. Schafer was her band teacher. He molested her. She ended up dropping out of school."

Lizzie and her mother were now both paying close attention.

Sarah showed Lizzie another photo. "This is Gretchen Cocan. She was also in Mr. Schafer's music class. Mr. Schafer kept her after school to give her private music lessons. Mr. Schafer molested this girl, too. Today she is abusing drugs and working as a striper in a biker bar."

Lizzie and her mother stared silently at the array of photographs now laid out on the coffee table. Adam broke their contemplation. "Mr. Schafer has molested many girls like you, Lizzie. He leaves town before he gets caught and starts again in a new school."

Lizzie got up and looked out the window. She wasn't listening to Adam. She was listening to a voice in her head. *"I'll divorce my wife and we can get married right away. You know I love you, don't you? I'll see you in school tomorrow, honey. I love you. Don't tell them anything."*

"Lizzie," Sarah said, gently putting her arm on Lizzie's shoulder and guiding her back to the sofa, "the last photo is the most important of all. It is the young girl who has the chance to stop Mr. Schafer from hurting anyone else," Sarah then placed Lizzie's school photo on the table. Pausing only briefly and giving Lizzie a gentle hug, Sarah asked fervently, "Will you help us?"

Chapter 25

Adam made an appointment with the Washington County Attorney for the next morning. Sarah and Adam talked about their strategy as they drove to his office. The courthouse dominated the head of Rhyolite Street, as it had for more than one hundred years. Like a medieval cathedral, it expressed the hopes of the people of Tupico Flats. The early mining industry built it as a symbol of stability and prosperity. Representing evil caught in the web of law, a dragon-like creature captured in a net was carved on the triangle pediment above the main door. A stone tablet with the Ten Commandments carved in relief, donated by the local VFW, flanked the steep flight of steps on the right. A mountain howitzer that had been carried over the Sierra Nevada Mountains in pursuit of Manifest Destiny guarded the left side of the building.

As they found a parking place in front of the courthouse Sarah was almost jubilant, "I can hardly believe it. We've got him."

"Let's not jump the gun," Adam cautioned. "With any luck at all Schafer is going to jail, but we've to get the county attorney on board."

"What do you mean, get him on board? He has to prosecute this case."

Adam nodded, "In a perfect world that would be true. However, each county only has so much money in its budget. County attorneys have a great deal of discretion about which cases they prosecute. Budget is always paramount in these small towns, and money isn't the only issue. Politics is every bit as important. County attorneys usually don't take cases unless they believe there is a reasonable chance of a victory. They need to have a good batting average when they run in the next election."

Sarah was giving Adam's comments some thought as he opened the courthouse door for her. The driver's license bureau, county commissioners offices, election office, park and recreation department, and county attorney shared the building. The inside of the building was dark and uninviting. The building directory indicated that the county attorney's office was on the third floor.

After walking up the three flights of stairs and past a rabbit warren of cubicles they reached a door at the end of the hall. The lettering on the frosted glass window announced "Lawrence R. Sail, County Attorney."

The receptionist, Mrs. Evans looked like she had been in the building since it was built. Her blue dress perfectly matched the color of her hair. Her face glowed with a thick coating of makeup; her lipstick, the color of tomato sauce, looked like it was put on by a four-year-old futilely trying to color within the lines. She had no pores.

"She looks like Kabuki actress," Sarah whispered to Adam when Mrs. Evans turned to answer the phone.

"A red nose away from clown school," Adam grinned back.

Mrs. Evans continued talking on the phone without looking up from her computer screen. After a few more minutes she replaced the receiver in the cradle and directed her attention to Sarah and Adam.

"Hello, I'm Adam Faulkner and this is Sarah Abbott, we have a nine o'clock appointment with Mr. Sail." Adam said.

Mrs. Evens smiled as she stood and led them to Sail's office. "He's running a little late. Please wait for him in his office. Can I get you some coffee?"

"That would be great," Adam, said. "Two black, please."

The county attorney's office was large and brightly lit. The desk was clear except for a phone and a laptop. The wall was plastered with photos of Sail shaking hands with senators, law enforcement officers, community members, and national party leaders. The place of honor on the power wall was a photo of Sail shaking hands with the sitting president. Another wall had award plaques of every shape and descriptions. Mrs. Evans returned with coffee just as Sail entered his office. He was well over six feet tall and very lean. He had a protruding Adams apple, deep-set brown eyes, a long hooked nose, and was nearly bald. A modern Ichabod Crane, Sarah thought.

Sail extended his hand first to Sarah, then Adam. "Hello. Sorry I'm a few minutes late. As he sat down behind his desk Mrs. Evans brought him a cup of coffee. "Your message was somewhat vague, Mr. Faulkner, something about a child having been molested in our town?"

Adam nodded, "We are confident that there is a girl at Red Rock Middle School who is being molested by a teacher."

"We've talked to the child's mother, and she's ready to file a complaint," Sarah added.

Sail tilted his head, looked at them quizzically for a moment, and then asked, "Tell me again who you are and what your interest is in this matter. Why aren't the girl and her mother here talking with me?"

Adam presented his credentials as a retired law enforcement officer. "I was a detective with the Columbus, Ohio, Special Victims Unit and have over fifteen years experience tracking down child abusers. We have visited with the child and her mother. We all thought it would be better if Sarah and I met with you first and gave you some important background information. You see, this same teacher molested Sarah when she was in middle school in Pennsylvania. Adam nodded toward Sarah. We've confirmed five other children he abused and believe there are more. We have strong evidence that he's currently molesting Lizzie Sutton."

Sail didn't show any emotion, "Lizzie Sutton," he said thoughtfully. "I know her. I was her T-ball coach when she was in the first grade. Who's the teacher?"

"Now he calls himself Jim Schafer. He changed his name from Tony Shepherd. The fact he changed his name shows he's trying to hide something," Sarah said.

"When you beat him over the head with the circumstances surrounding his name change, Schafer's defense will collapse like a house of cards," Adam said.

Again, Sail didn't show any emotion. "Well, we'll have to see about that. I've never met Schafer, but I've heard the name. From what I hear he is a pretty popular teacher," Sail continued.

Sarah and Adam looked at each other knowingly. They'd heard this response many times. "Mr. Sail, that is exactly how he gets away with it," Sarah explained. "You know that teachers who molest children don't wear trench coats, or hang around playgrounds and drag little kids into the woods. They get away with their crimes precisely because they're often the last person anyone would suspect."

Sail, remained silent and seemed unconvinced. "I think he's married. Why would he want to have sex with a child?"

"As I am sure you know, molestation is a very complex issue. It is very common for child molesters to have families, go to church and appear to be pillars of the community," Adam said. "We understand your skepticism. This is exactly why Sarah and I came to speak with you before you talk with

Mrs. Sutton and Lizzie Sutton," Adam interjected. "Parents of abused children are reluctant to come forward because of the embarrassment attached. It is even more difficult when people in authority don't believe them. You can understand why they are afraid they will have no chance against one of the most popular people in town."

Sail had been directing all of his comments to Adam. He turned to Sarah and said rather harshly, "You might start by telling me why you didn't file a complaint against him."

Sarah was taken aback. Her voice cracked. "I was just a little girl when it happened. I was afraid and too embarrassed to tell anyone. I tried to pretend that nothing happened. Now, the statute of limitations prevents me from doing anything."

Sail continued sitting quietly, his face impassive. In a disinterested voice he said, "Well, show me what you've got."

Adam opened his briefcase and took out the chronology of Shepherd's victims. "These documents provide evidence of what we're saying. We've visited each school where Shepherd was employed. We have convincing evidence that he molested at least one girl in every school."

After Sarah and Adam reviewed all of the documentation with Sail, Sarah opened her briefcase and withdrew Lizzie's journal. "Lizzie has written in her journal every day since she was in second grade. Look at the entries she made when she first enrolled in Shepherd's, I mean Shafer's, band class," She opened the book to a marked page and handed it to Sail.

As Sail read page after page, his face lost its indifference and he began to look uncomfortable. "Okay, if this stuff is the real deal, you've convinced me that Schafer may have molested students in the past. You know there's nothing I can do about that now. The diary is another matter. I need to talk with

Mrs. Sutton and Lizzie. I've got to tell you, I don't think this is a case we are going to want to try. I don't think we can convict Jim Schafer unless Lizzie is pretty damned compelling."

"Mr. Sail, Lizzie has been raped by a serial molester who has molested other children. You can't just ignore it," Sarah said.

Sail stared at Sarah for a moment and then forcefully said, "Miss Abbott, I know what my job is! Of course, I'll take this matter seriously. However, I also have a fiscal obligation to the taxpayers of my county." Sail stood up making it clear that the meeting was over. "Bring Lizzie and her mother by at one o'clock tomorrow."

As they walked to the car Sarah noticed the look on Adam's face. "That's an odd expression, Adam. What's wrong?"

"I really don't know, Sarah. Sail just seems a little hinky to me. Generally county attorneys love cases like ours, tons of publicity. Win or lose they get credit for fighting the good fight. I expected him to jump on it rather than discourage us. I'm wondering why he is so reluctant to pursue such a serious allegation."

Chapter 26

Sarah and Adam ushered Lizzie and her mother into Mr. Sail's office at precisely one o'clock the next afternoon. They were surprised to see another man sitting beside Sail's desk. Sail rose from his chair and greeted them formally. "I'd like you to meet Gordon Johnson. He's our newest Assistant County Attorney. Please sit down and make yourselves comfortable," he urged. "I'm about to go to trial with another case and won't be able to give your case the attention it deserves. Mr. Johnson will be working with you."

Johnson looked to be about twenty-five, with a pasty complexion, and thinning blond hair. Adam started to protest, then thought better of it and shook Mr. Johnson's hand. Johnson's handshake was weak and he didn't look Adam in the eyes.

Sail stood, put his hand on the doorknob, and said, "I've walked Gordon through all the material you left with me and caught him up on our conversation. I'm sorry. I'm going to have to excuse myself. I have to leave town unexpectedly to attend a meeting this afternoon in Las Vegas. Mr. Johnson will take you down the hall to his office." He smiled as he ushered them out of his office and closed the door behind them.

As they followed Johnson down the hall and into his small, cluttered office Adam's "Bull Shit" detector was going off. Something's not right here, he thought. Sail is the boss. He has a ton of trial experience. Johnson looked more like a law clerk than a lawyer. Adam had a feeling they were in trouble.

Johnson's office was furnished with antique burled oak furniture. The walls were lined with law books. The five of them stood in the middle of the room looking for a place to sit down. Every flat surface was covered with law journals, open law books, file folders, or stacks of legal documents.

Johnson cleared off four chairs for them and then he sat behind his desk. "You'll have to excuse the mess. I just started here a few weeks ago and I'm still getting settled into my office. I understand you have something to tell me about Mr. Schmidt. Is that right?"

Adam could see by Sarah's expression that she was as angry and disappointed as he was. "His name is Schafer. Jim Schafer," Adam said coldly.

"Oh, sure. Sorry. Schafer it is," Johnson apologized nonchalantly.

Mrs. Sutton glanced at Sarah, but said nothing. Adam said, "Mr. Johnson. As you can imagine, this is very difficult for Mrs. Sutton and Lizzie. You have seen all of the documentation. Has Mr. Sail told you that Schafer changed his name and has moved from district to district?"

"Yes, Mr. Sail has filled me in on all of your allegations. He said that this case would stand or fall on Lizzie's testimony."

Lizzie tightened her grasp on her mother's hand. Mrs. Sutton looked at Adam and Sarah with a look that said this is a bad idea. Get us out of here.

Adam started to tell Johnson what they had learned. Johnson interrupted, turned to Mrs. Sutton and Lizzie and said "I want to hear this from the horse's mouth."

Adam tightened his hands into fists as Mrs. Sutton said, "This is very difficult for Lizzie, for both of us. Lizzie thought Mr. Schafer was in love with her. She's just starting to come to grips with the fact that he lied to her. She isn't sure she wants to get Mr. Schafer in trouble."

Johnson leaned across his desk toward Lizzie. "Well, this is going to be a waste of everyone's time if she won't testify."

Adam and Sarah were both amazed at Johnson's lack of grace. Sarah was about to speak when Lizzie blurted out tearfully, "He said he was going to leave his wife and marry me when I turn sixteen, maybe sooner,"

"Adam, Sarah and Mrs. Sutton turned to stare at Lizzie. "Lizzie, when did Mr. Schafer tell you he wanted to marry you?" Adam asked.

Lizzie's face turned white. She saw that she had said too much. "Oh, he was just kidding around. He told all the girls he wanted to marry us. We knew he was just kidding."

"Lizzie, I've read your journal. Is what you have written true?" Johnson asked brusquely.

Adam was no longer shocked by Johnson's style. He was angry that Johnson was being so direct. The proper course would have been to build trust with Lizzie.

Lizzie ignored Johnson's question and turned to her mom. "Mom, please don't make me talk about this. I want to go home."

"Lizzie, Mr. Schafer has hurt a lot of girls and he's going to go to jail. You need to tell the truth," her mother said emphatically. In a softer tone she reiterated, "Honey, I know you're scared and hurt, but you know what happened is wrong. Tell Mr. Johnson the truth. Please."

"Lizzie, I think your diary would be considered a contemporaneous writing. It'll be very powerful evidence. Is it true that you've kept the diary since you were in the second grade and you kept a day-by-day account of what Mr. Schafer did to you in the music room and on your band trip?" Johnson asked.

Lizzie seemed to shrink into herself. She put her ring finger into her mouth and started chewing on her fingernail. She didn't answer.

Were going to get nowhere fast if this jerk continues, Adam thought. Aloud, he said, "Mr. Johnson would you mind if I asked Lizzie some background questions to sort of help us get started?"

Johnson seemed relieved. "Not at all. Go ahead."

Eventually, Lizzie admitted that she wrote in her diary every day. "What we do is okay, because we are in love," she finally blurted.

After much prodding and many tears Lizzie told them about getting undressed in the band closet and letting Mr. Schafer put his mouth on her private parts. She said he never had sex with her and never hurt her.

Johnson interrupted her and said, "What do you mean, he never had sex with you? You just told us he performed cunnilingus."

Lizzie looked mystified. "What's that?"

"Honey, the medical term for what Mr. Schafer did to you is cunnilingus," Sarah said, staring daggers at Johnson, "but that's really not important for you to know."

"Lizzie, did Mr. Schafer ever make you do these things anywhere else besides in the band room?" Johnson asked.

Johnson noticed how Sarah was staring at him. However, he seemed clueless as to the cause.

"Yes. On our band trip to Carson City," Lizzie said meekly. "He told me to say I was sick and not go to the Capitol with the rest of the band. He left with the band. He told me that after about an hour he told the others he needed to come back to the hotel to check on me."

"What happened when he came to your room," Johnson asked.

"When he came back to my room," her voice grew softer and she lowered her eyes, "we did stuff."

Johnson looked at Adam and tried to look apologetic as he continued. "Lizzie you need to tell us what he did."

"Is this really necessary?" Mrs. Sutton asked. "We all know what he did."

"If this case goes to trial Lizzie is going to have to tell the court exactly what Mr. Schafer did."

For the next twenty minutes Lizzie painfully told them how Mr. Schafer started grooming her. When she finished her story her mother and Sarah were crying and Adam was gritting his teeth. Johnson said, "Well I think I have all that I need."

After Mrs. Sutton and Lizzie left Johnson's office, Adam and Sarah stayed to try and persuade Johnson to prosecute the most popular man in Tupico Flats.

Adam said, "What we've told you, Lizzie's journal, and her testimony should have convinced you that Schafer is a serial child molester. The fact Shepherd changed his name should seal the deal."

"Yes, that's true," Johnson, admitted reluctantly. "However, the county's prosecution budget has taken some serious hits with two murder trials this year. This morning Mr. Sail told me he isn't sure he's going to approve going forward with this case. This type of litigation is very expensive. It's not unusual for such a case to cost over a hundred thousand dollars, and Mr. Sail isn't very confident it's winnable."

"You can't make your decision based only on money," Sarah argued. "Shepherd has really done a lot of damage and he's not finished. He'll hurt other girls if you don't stop him."

Johnson appeared not to have heard her, "The fact he changed his name is important. But, really, this case comes down to Lizzie's word against Mr. Schafer's. She has to be very solid when she is on the stand, and from what I've just seen, I'm not sure she can do it."

Adam couldn't stand it any longer and exploded from his chair. "You can't be serious!" He shouted. "We've done most of your work for you. We've proven he has molested at least five girls, including the woman sitting right in front of you. We tracked him down, found a current victim, told you he changed his name, and gave you all of our documentation. Don't tell me that you're going to let him get away again! Just don't tell me that."

Johnson looked pained. "Mr. Faulkner. I know how Sarah feels..."

Adam's anger was catching. "I'm right here." Sarah was almost shouting. "Don't talk about me like I'm not here. And, no! You don't know how I feel! Tony Shepherd raped me, and has molested other young girls. Each of our lives has been damaged by what he did to us. We want justice."

"Okay," Johnson admitted apologetically. "I don't know how you feel. But let me explain another weaknesses of your case. I haven't prosecuted many sexual abuse or exploitation cases, but I know from law school that juries have an expectation of what a rape victim should do. If a plaintiff doesn't confirm to these stereotypes they may not believe her."

"Then it's your job to educate the jury," Sarah said matter-of-factly.

Johnson continued, "Yes, I guess that's true. However, Lizzie's behavior may give the jury a reason to confirm their stereotypes."

"What are you talking about?" Sarah asked.

"Well first, there is what is called the 'Hue and Cry' doctrine. Juries and some judges believe that real victims complain right away. Lizzie didn't come forward for several months after she says Schafer began molesting her. In fact she didn't come forward until she was discovered and, in essence, forced to reveal her situation. Combine this with the fact that Schafer is an award winning teacher who is literally loved by all his students and their parents and it's very possible a jury will believe him and not Lizzie."

Adam and Sarah sat silent. They both knew how much truth there was in Johnson's statement.

Johnson continued, "Listen, I'm just telling it like it is. I've read about some victims of child abuse who have recanted their testimony, requested the case be dismissed, and even asked their parents to pay for the abuser's lawyer. A colleague told me about one of his cases where the victim testified for the abuser! Additionally, Schafer's attorney will likely force you to testify, Sarah."

Sarah was shocked. "Me? Why me?"

"They'll try to convince the jury that you hate Schafer and you have relentlessly pursued him. They'll stress the fact that you're seeing a counselor, and make you seem like a wacko. And if that doesn't work, they'll try to make the jury see you as someone who is manipulating Lizzie to get back at Schafer for what you say he did to you."

Adam had been watching Johnson closely throughout their conversation. He decided to act on a hunch. "Mr. Johnson, can you tell us a little bit about your background? What were you doing before you became an assistant county attorney?"

"I worked in a small law office with my dad for five years after I got out of law school. Mostly we had a general practice: wills, divorce, DWI, that sort of thing. When my dad died last year, I decided to close shop and work for Mr. Sail. He's been a long-time family friend."

"Will Mr. Sail be working with you on this case?"

"Sure. He'll supervise all my cases until I've been here for a year."

Adam couldn't conceal his frustration. "Mr. Johnson, you know what the moral and ethical thing to do is. Will you be able to live with yourself knowing that Shepherd molested young girls in the past and will continue if you don't stop him? Mr. Johnson, are you going to prosecute or not."

Johnson let out a deep sigh. "I'm going to recommend that we go forward with this. I hope I'm not making a mistake."

Sarah and Adam left Johnson's office angrier than they had been during the entire hunt. Adam said, "If Sail doesn't approve the prosecution, Shepherd will be gone before the end of the year. Something's wrong here."

"What do you mean?" Sarah asked.

"I'm not sure. I just think giving this case to Johnson was a very strange decision on Sail's part. It is obvious that Johnson has no experience and is a lightweight."

A week later a warrant was issued for James Schafer's arrest.

Chapter 27

The sun was just starting to show over the fence in Schafer's backyard. He'd been awake since 2:00 a.m. He sat in his study staring out the window thinking about the phone call he made last night. Although he was told never to call again, he called the man he'd seen at the meeting and pleaded, "You've got to help me. I can't go to jail."

"I've checked into this Faulkner guy," He replied. "He's trouble. He was a cop and now he's a PI. He seems to be a bull-dog. Once he gets on a case he doesn't stop. I don't think I can keep you from being arrested. But I think I can influence the outcome of the trial. You need to get a good lawyer and keep your mouth shut. I've done all I can. And, Schafer, seriously, don't you ever call me again."

In those sleepless early morning hours Shepherd mentally listed his options. He could pack up the family and leave town now. He could leave alone. He could see Lizzie and threaten her. He could have her kidnapped and sent to Mexico. He could kill her. He could kill himself. In the end, he decided to wait. Maybe, just maybe, he wouldn't be arrested, he prayed.

When officer Ron Skylock picked up the paperwork for the arrest, he couldn't believe the name on the warrant. James R. Schafer! He wondered if there could be two Jim Schafers in Tupico Flats. The Jim Schafer he knew was his daughter's music teacher and played on his recreation league softball team. He had a daughter and a wife who was a knock out. This man just couldn't be the man Ron knew. But when he saw the address on the warrant, he knew it was his friend.

Schafer couldn't force himself to take any action. The only thing he could do was to try carry on as if nothing was wrong. He backed his car out of his driveway and headed toward school. He'd traveled about a block when he saw red flashing lights in his rear view mirror. Before he could react, police cars pulled in front and in back of his car.

"Oh Shit! Oh Shit! Oh Shit." He started trembling. His hands went numb. He felt a choking sensation and an urgent need to urinate. The day he had been dreading for twenty years had finally arrived. Schafer heard someone calling his name. Coming out of a daze he saw his friend, Ron Skylock, standing at the driver's side window.

"Mr. James Schafer. You are under arrest for rape," Officer Skylock said.

"Ron, what's going on?" Schafer stammered. It was important, he knew, to act surprised.

"Please get out of your car slowly and put your hands on the roof."

Schafer put his head in his arms, leaned on the steering wheel and sobbed. After a second request, he stumbled out of the car and followed Skylock's directions.

"Jim, I hate to do this, but I don't have a choice. I'm sure you can get this all straightened out downtown," Skylock said sadly as read Schafer the Miranda rights.

"What's going on, Ron?"

Skylock put Schafer in handcuffs, put his hand on Jim's head and gently shoved him into the back of the police car.

When they were out of earshot of the other officer, Skylock whispered, "Jim, don't say anything until you've consulted with an attorney."

"Ron. I'm afraid. Please tell me what's going to happen to me?"

"I'll take you to the safety building where you'll be processed. They'll take your personal information, record the charges against you, and fingerprint and photograph you. Then they'll confiscate your personal property and place you in a holding cell."

Shepherd started to whimper. "Jesus! They're going to put me in jail without a trial. How do I get out?"

"For some charges there are standard bail schedules, but because of the nature of the charges against you, you'll have to appear in court and have a judge set bail. Be prepared. In cases involving alleged rape of a child, the bail may be set pretty high,"

"Rape of a child?" Shepherd feigned shock.

When he got to the safety center, Schafer was shaking so badly that an officer had to steady his hand as he signed his name. Schafer remembered the name of an attorney he had met at a bar. He had to call Grace.

With a quaking voice Schafer said, "Hi hon. I've got a problem."

"What's the matter, Jim? Are you hurt?"

"No. I'm at the Safety Center. They think I did something bad. I need you to call someone for me."

Grace was quiet for a moment.

"What have you done?"

Schafer ignored the question and said, "Right now you need to call Ron Browne." Jim asked Grace to call Ron Browne because Browne was the only lawyer he knew.

"His number is in the card file on my desk in the study. The combination to the pad lock is right 25, left past 25 to 6, and then right to 7. Tell Browne where I am. Ask him to get down here as fast as he can."

"Jim. Have you been arrested?"

"Yes."

"What have you been charged with?"

"Grace. We can talk later…"

Grace interrupted. "Tell me! What are the charges?"

"Rape of a minor."

Grace was silent, again. She then said, "Jim, I'll make the call for you. Then I'm taking Ashley to my mother's. I won't put her through this. I hope you're going to be okay," Grace said as she hung up.

Schafer was very lucky that the attorney he knew was a fraternity brother of Reggie Parker, a nationally known defense attorney from Las Vegas who loved high profile cases.

The county safety building was one of the newest buildings in Tupico Flats. Built mostly of glass, it was home to the police and fire departments and the jail. It was generally pretty quiet on weekday mornings. Not today.

Mrs. Socorro Gomez has worked as a clerk in the police department for less than a year. Prior to that she was the secretary at Tupico Flats Middle School. One of her responsibilities was logging arrest reports into the computer. Her job was usually pretty boring, but today she had entered a report that read like a police crime show on television. Jim Schafer, the most popular teacher in town, had just been arrested for raping one of his students.

When Mrs. Gomez was hired, she was warned to keep all police business strictly confidential. She agreed that the policy was a good one. However, Mr. Schafer's arrest was too hot to keep quiet. Within twenty minutes of seeing the report Mrs. Gomez had told three co-workers and each of them had told three more. Rumors were criss-crossing the building. Within an hour of Schafer's arrival everyone knew the charges against him. No one could believe it. If she could have figured out a reason to walk down to the holding cell, Mrs. Gomez would have, just to see for herself if Mr. Schafer was really there.

Although Mrs. Gomez was very aware that she could lose her job if anyone found out she had breached confidentiality, as soon as she got in her car at 11:55 a.m. she was on her cell phone to her daughter. Linda was the reason Mrs. Gomez had left her job at the middle school. As a seventh grader, Linda hated having her mother at school, as she phrased it "getting into my business."

Linda was in Mr. Schafer's music class. Mrs. Gomez had to make sure Mr. Schafer had not done anything to her. "Hi honey. How would you like to have lunch with your mom today?" Socorro was not surprised by Linda's reply.

"I'm having lunch with my friends, Mom."

"Linda I need to talk to you. It's important."

"Can't it wait until we get home tonight?"

"No, it can't. I'll pick you up by the flagpole in five minutes. Please don't keep me waiting."

Mrs. Gomez had to wait fifteen minutes before Linda got in the car, crossed her arms over her chest, and began the passive aggressive behavior that had become her pattern ever since she started middle school.

"Linda, I have something to ask you and you need to tell me the truth," Mrs. Gomez said.

Linda sat silently.

"Linda, has Mr. Schafer ever done anything that made you feel uncomfortable?"

Linda jerked her head toward her mother. "What? What are you talking about?"

"You know. Has he ever touched you in a sexual way?"

"Gross, Mom. Why are you asking me that?"

"Well, you might as well hear it from me. Mr. Schafer has been arrested and charged with molesting one of your class-mates."

Linda laughed nervously. "What are you talking about? That's crazy. Who'd they say he molested?"

"I shouldn't tell you this but it's Lizzie Sutton. You can't tell anyone or I'll lose my job."

Linda and some of her friends had wondered why Mr. Schafer spent so much time with Lizzie, but Linda wasn't about to let her mother know she had suspicions. "Mr. Schafer is a great teacher, Mom. He wouldn't do that."

"Okay, honey. I just needed to be sure you are okay. Linda, remember, you can't tell anyone what I just told you. I could get in a lot of trouble." Mrs. Gomez said.

After stopping for a hamburger on the way back to the school Linda got out of the car on a side street a block from the school. Mrs. Gomez rolled down the window and reminded Linda not to tell anyone. She rolled up the car window and headed back to work relieved that her daughter was safe.

At 1:40 p.m. Lizzie Sutton entered the second floor girls' restroom. As soon as the door closed Linda Gomez stepped in front of Lizzie and shoved her hard against the back of the door. Linda and four other girls formed a tight circle around Lizzie.

"What kind of lies are you telling about Mr. Schafer?" one of the girls demanded.

Lizzie froze. "What are you talking about?"

"My mom works at the police department. They just arrested Mr. Schafer because you said he raped you."

Lizzie panicked and tried to get out of the restroom, but her pathway was blocked. "I didn't say Mr. Schafer raped me." Lizzie made a feeble attempt to act innocent. "I don't know what you're talking about."

"At first my mom wasn't going to tell me what happened. She just started asking me about Mr. Schafer and if he ever touched me. She said she saw the police report. Your name was on it."

Lizzie tried to break free, but the girls stepped in front of her and one punched her in the face. Blood streamed from her nose as she slid to the floor and began sobbing. Linda spat on Lizzie and said, "You better not testify against Mr. Schafer. He is the best teacher in the school. If he did anything to you, you asked for it."

Lizzie got up slowly and washed her face. She dabbed at the blood on her blouse with little effect. She left restroom, walked out of school and headed for home. By 2:00 p.m. everyone in the school knew Lizzie Sutton was responsible for Mr. Schafer's arrest. When Lizzie entered her house her mother came out of the kitchen to see why she was home so early.

"Lizzie, you're bleeding! What happened to your face?"

Lizzie raised her head and stared at her mother. In a very quiet voice she said, "Mr. Schafer's been arrested, and everyone knows it's because of me. I'll never forgive you for telling everyone about my diary! I got jumped in the bathroom. Mom, my friends from band beat me up. Look at my nose. I have blood all over me." She turned and slowly climbed the stairs to her room. "I'm not going to testify and you can't make me," Lizzie said as she quietly closed the door to her room.

Mrs. Sutton followed Lizzie up the stairs and knocked on her bedroom door. There was no answer. "Lizzie, no one was supposed to know who filed the report. I don't know what happened," she called through the closed door.

Lizzie's reply was muffled. "Mom, I'm not going to testify. We have to get Mr. Schafer a lawyer. What happened is my fault. We can't let him go to jail."

Chapter 28

The morning after his arrest James R. Schafer appeared before Judge Clark B. Williams for arraignment. Williams, a district judge for almost thirty years, had a reputation for being erratic in his rulings.

Williams read the charges. "Mr. Schafer you have been charged with violating Nevada Revised Statute 200.363, rape, and Nevada Revised Statute 201.230, lewdness with a child under 14 years old. Mr. Schafer, do you have an attorney?"

Reggie Parker stood up. He was tall and lean with broad shoulders, close-cropped black hair, piercing green eyes, and a dark suntan. He was a formidable figure in his trademark black silk suit with matching shirt and tie. He moved with the grace of a jungle cat. When Reggie was not present, opposing attorneys referred to him as Darth Vader.

"Your honor, I'm Reggie Parker. I'm representing Mr. Schafer."

"How does your client plead, Mr. Parker?"

"Not guilty!"

"Your honor," Gordon Johnson intervened. "Because of the age of the victim and the heinous nature of the crime, the county asks that bond be set at one million dollars."

Reggie was ready with a protest, "Mr. Schafer is a beloved teacher and respected member of the Tupico Flats community. He has no prior criminal offenses and no ability to raise that kind of bond. He has a wife and daughter. We respectfully request that Mr. Schafer be released on his own recognizance."

Judge Williams studied Schafer's file for a few moments. "I don't think Mr. Schafer is a flight risk and he has strong ties to this community. I'm ordering him released on his own recognizance."

Sarah jumped to her feet and shouted, "You've got to be kidding. He's violated Lizzie Sutton and others. Of course, he is a threat to the community and every child who lives here."

Judge Williams stared at Sarah for a moment and then said, "Young lady, if you want to be in the courtroom you'd better show some respect. Another outburst like that and I will have you permanently removed from my courtroom.

Gordon Johnson threw a warning look at Sarah then turned his attention back to the judge. "The county disagrees your honor. We believe he is a risk. We ask that you reconsider your ruling."

Although Adam knew that half of those charged with rape were released on bail, he was still surprised by the Williams' decision.

Reggie smiled at Sarah. He mentally filed away her emotional outburst, knowing he could use it against her later.

Judge Williams was obviously not swayed by Sarah's outburst or Johnson's request said, "Mr. Schafer, you are free to leave. Trial is set for May sixteenth. Bailiff, call the next case."

Sixty days! Sarah thought. I can't wait that long.

That afternoon Johnson filed a motion for a change of venue. He argued that Jim Schafer was a well-known personality, almost a local hero, and the local newspapers had published several editorials questioning the integrity of the plaintiff, thus beginning a wave of prejudice across the community.

Judge Williams denied the motion, saying it was premature. In his decision he wrote, "A good-faith effort should be made to seat a jury in this county. I believe the defendant should be tried in the community where the alleged crime occurred. The court is aware there has been publicity generated in this case. However, much of that publicity has been supportive of the county's case. I refer you to a Sunday story in *The Tupico Flats Mercury* in which the editor of the newspaper presented a lengthy discussion of child abuse cases. The court believes Mr. Schafer can receive a fair trial in this county." He concluded, "The court will conduct the jury selection in such a way as to minimize issues relating to pre-trial publicity and prejudice. Should pre-trial publicity become an issue, the court will then entertain a new motion for a change of venue."

Chapter 29

TABERNASH, COLORADO

Sarah quit her job at a bookstore when she and Adam started their hunt for Shepherd. She was living on money from a trust fund left to her by her parents. Before she went back to Boston to await the trial, Adam invited her to Colorado. He felt they both deserved a little break before the intensity of the coming trial.

They flew to Denver and he drove them to his cabin. There was over three feet of snow on the ground and the pine trees were glistening in the sunlight. As they walked up the steps to his cabin Adam said,

"Winter in Tabernash is spectacular."

"Yes, and spectacularly cold," Sarah grumbled, as she snuggled down into her hooded ski parka.

"This area is known as the 'Ice Box of America' because the winter temperature may reach fifty degrees below zero." He unlocked the door and held it open for Sarah to enter. "I'm glad you decided to visit. The skiing is going to be great. Winter Park catches storms from every direction. Last year we had almost 400 inches."

Sarah was more appreciative of the inside of the cabin than its outer surroundings. "Your house is amazing," she said. "I've never seen anything like it."

Adam proudly rattled off the history and merits of his home. "My friend Adrian called it a rustic log cabin. It's about fifty years old. A local architect built it. She used antique beams with nail holes as well as wormholes. Most of the other materials are local. The mantel is hand-hewn from timber cut on this property. Adrian said that the beams were cut using a broad axe and simple hand tools and then aged. I love the axe marks on the beams and timbers. No two are alike."

"Did you furnish it?" Sarah asked as she walked around the room.

"I would like to say yes, but, honestly, it was completely furnished. Adrian wanted the cabin to be in harmony with nature, so she selected only earth tones. The oversize leather sofa, two buster chairs, and the ottoman are my only additions. Oh, and I also recently added the chandelier."

"Pretty unusual, what's it made of?"

"The frame is made of mule deer antlers, the diffuser is rawhide."

As Adam built a fire in the fieldstone fireplace, Sarah wandered around the cabin. "Can I check out the upstairs?"

"Sure. There's just one bedroom and a bath up there. Let me know if you want the loft or the larger bedroom on this floor."

Sarah stopped at the top of the stairway to admire a stained glass panel hanging in front of a large window. The colorful opaque design of a mountain scene took her breath away. A spectacular border of blue Columbine and Edelweiss framed a snow covered mountain peak. "You can't tell me that this stained glass was here when you bought this place."

"I fell in love with it when I saw it at last year's art festival. If you look out the window behind it you can see the top of Byers Peak, the mountain in the stained glass, off to your right. This area was hit hard by a pine beetle infestation, which killed most of the lodge pole pines. With so many of the trees gone I now have a much better view across the valley. I miss the trees, but I'm beginning to appreciate beauty that was previously hidden." Sarah thought hiding the real mountain with a reproduction of the mountain seemed sort of weird.

As they sat in front of the roaring fire that evening, each nursing a second scotch, Sarah said, "I hope I can keep up with you tomorrow. I used to ski almost every weekend, but it's been several years since I've been on the slopes."

"If you can ski the black ice of New England you won't have any problem in Colorado. The only thing you'll have to get used is our powder. Last time I was out, I was in powder up to my thighs."

"Yikes, that's pretty scary. That means it would be over my hips. What are you getting me into?" Sarah teased.

"You'll be the hottest girl on the slopes. I'll bet you'll be blasting the powder in no time," Adam assured her. Sarah wondered if Adam was flirting with her or if she was imagining things.

The next morning they were among the first in line for the chair lift. As they started up the mountain, Adam continued his chronicle of the area, "The mountain is beautiful at the base, and it only gets better from here. This is the highest six-person chair lift in the world." Jeez, why can't I shut up for two seconds, Adam thought?

"The chairs are really blowing back and forth," Sarah noted as she clutched the safety bar. "Are we safe?"

"Totally." Adam assured her. "We are above 12,000 feet, there's always a bit of turbulence. You'll love Parsenn Bowl. Gladed tree runs. Unreal powder. It looks like about a six inches of new snow. We'll be making fresh tracks."

They skied off the lift and turned to face down the run. The beauty of the surrounding peaks and the valley below stunned Sarah. Last night's snow had erased all signs of human life. The sky was a cloudless cornflower blue. A light breeze was at their backs, and the morning sun was in their faces.

"Adam, you can see forever," Sarah marveled. "This is the most beautiful place I have ever been. I feel like I'm almost in heaven."

Adam experienced a moment of gratification. "I know. I can barely keep from breaking into a John Denver song myself," he joked. Now you know why I moved out here. I'm not a church-going guy, but I feel God's presence every time I come here. When I first got here, I used to ski to tunes on my iPod. Now I prefer the total silence of the mountain." Without thinking he put his arm around her shoulder and pulled her close. She didn't pull away. They could see for miles across Fraser Valley. Adam pointed out the approximate location of his cabin. A porcupine scurried across the trail and Bohemian Waxwings, Pine Grosbeaks, and Mountain Chickadees chattered in the nearby treetops. Adam didn't want to take his arm away, but finally he asked, "Ready?"

They had taken a few runs as they worked their way across the mountain to Parsenn Bowl. As Adam demonstrated the difference between skiing on hard pack and powder, he helped Sarah develop a delicate touch and learn how to sit slightly back and distribute her weight equally on her skis. Sarah adapted quickly. The powder plumed around her head as she gained more confidence with each turn.

When they reached the top of Parsenn Bowl Adam asked, "Do you want me to lead the way or stay behind in case you need some help?"

Sarah frowned at his feeble chivalry but acquiesced to it. "I'll go first," She pushed off the cornice, dropped four feet, and hit 20 inches of virgin powder.

Adam marveled at her gracefulness. She moved as if she'd skied powder for years. He watched her glide from side to side. She's magnificent, he thought. As he watcher her trim figure negotiate the terrain, the romantic feelings he had been having turned erotic. However, he was acutely aware of the ethical temptation he faced. He was her confidant, her friend, and her advisor. Even if she were interested, it would be wrong for me to cross the line from friend to lover, he thought He pushed off and raced to catch up with her.

They skied through the lunch hour, not wanting to break the perfect harmony they had achieved. The tall Douglas Spruce trees that guarded the trails were flocked with snow. When the wind picked up, cascades of snow silently fell from the pines. They had an incredible morning skiing side-by-side, interlocking the arcs of their turns. At one o'clock they stopped for lunch at Sunspot. They huddled in front of the fireplace sharing a bottle of wine. Anyone watching them would have thought they were lovers.

After lunch they alternated following each other. The leader would decide on the course: fall line or moguls. The follower tried to stay in the exact track of the leader. The lack of oxygen, combined with Adam's bad back, and his twenty extra pounds conspired against him. He skied as far as he could and Sarah would ski down to him. After they had rested for a few moments Sarah pushed off and headed down the trail. Adam waited for her to make three or four turns, and then he followed. She caught some nice air over a cross trail, bounced through a chute of gnarly egg crate moguls, and then disappeared into the trees.

Adam's shoulders barely cleared the two lodgepoles that guarded Sarah's entrance into the trees. Seconds in, his left hand hit a low hanging limb, dumping a dollop of powder on his head as he skied past. Adam's skis clattered over the crud then sank into some powder then tried to fly out from under him as he accelerated onto a patch of hard pack. His quads began burning, his lungs quickly followed, his edges lost their precision, and his skis began to separate. Adam knew he was in trouble when he started sliding around trees rather than edging past them. He lost sight of Sarah. He hoped the light up ahead was the trail.

His body was screaming for him to stop but he knew trying to stop in the trees on this incline was a really bad idea. Adam was hoping he wasn't going to pay a price for not wearing a helmet. His right ski tip caught an exposed tree root and spun him off balance. He broke out of the trees not with the flourish he had hoped for, doing instead an imitation of the 'agony of defeat' from the Wide World of Sports. He tumbled spectacularly, leaving his sunglasses and skis to find their own way out of the trees, planted his face in the snow, and slid to a stop. To add insult to injury, he received a barrage of insulting gibes, taunts and jeers from a group of teenagers riding the lift that passed directly over his head.

Adam wiped the snow off his face to see Sarah leaning on her poles, smiling down at him.

"Are you okay?" Her voice was tinged with concern.

"Yeah," he said, sheepishly. "Please don't make me do that again," he only half joked.

After he had checked gingerly for broken bones, Adam climbed uphill into the trees to retrieve his skis and glasses and put them on.

As he skied over to Sarah, she laughed and said, "Adam, I thought we agreed. No trick skiing!" She looked back up the mountain and said, "That was fantastic. I've never skied a more exciting run."

Adam was sucking air and gritting his teeth. The pain in his thighs brought tears to his eyes. He didn't trust himself to speak. He didn't want her to see his state of utter exhaustion.

Sarah couldn't help herself. She smiled and asked, "Do you want me to go first, or stay behind in case you need my help?"

Adam's penchant for machismo almost caused him to push off. Thankfully, his survival instinct prevailed. "Let's just stay here for a few more moments enjoying the view." He took a few deep breaths and continued, "Otherwise, I'm either going to have a stroke or a heart attack. You're amazing. It kills me to admit it, but I can't keep up with you."

Sarah turned and faced him. She slid her skis between his and hugged him. "Sorry, Adam. I just got carried away. It's been so long since I felt this free or this happy. For a moment I forgot you were with me. It was just the mountain and me."

They were both tired but neither wanted the day to end. The light was getting flat and it was becoming difficult to see the moguls, so they headed to the base. On the way to the cabin they stopped at a Cajun restaurant for an early dinner. The red beans and rice and fresh baked corn bread really hit the spot. They laughed as they relived the day. Sarah spent quite a bit of time laughing as she recounted what Adam looked like as he catapulted out of the trees.

As they got out of the car at the cabin, Adam said, "If I don't hit the hot tub soon my back will tighten up. Do you want to join me?"

"Absolutely. I didn't want to stop skiing, but honestly, every muscle in my body is aching."

Adam usually soaked in the nude, but found a pair of running shorts to wear. "I'll go out and shovel a path to the tub and check the chemicals. You have to be a chemist to keep the bromine, PH, and alkaline at the right levels. In order to get the best back massage I bought a hot tub with two jet motors. Be careful when you get in, they're really powerful."

As Adam took the cover off the spa, postage-stamp sized snowflakes began falling. He checked the chemicals, turned on the jets, and slid into the tub. It was a little after six o'clock and the sun was setting over Byers Peak. Five minutes later Sarah came out. She was wearing a modest yellow one-piece bathing suit. Adam had suspected she had a great body. It was better than he imagined.

Sarah slid into the spa and the jumbo storm blaster immediately shot her across the tub and into Adam's arms. He caught her on his lap. She could feel his erection, but didn't move away. After an awkward moment, they embraced and then kissed. Adam pulled away from her and said, "Sorry."

But Sarah made no move to get off his lap. The continued closeness crumbled his resolve. Adam tentatively slipped his hand under the top of her suit and cupped her breast. She pressed against him. Moments later, they slipped off their suits, kissed, and began exploring each other's bodies. When Sarah reached between Adam's legs and pulled him toward her he grasped her wrist and again pulled away.

Her eyes registered surprise and her voice expressed hurt, "What is it Adam? What's the matter?"

"Sarah, I don't have to tell you how excited you make me. I've been fantasizing about making love to you for weeks."

"Then why did you stop me?"

"Sarah, this is really difficult for me to explain. You've been hurt so deeply by Shepherd. He polluted such a big part of your life. You've told me that you don't trust men. Now, the first man you trust is going to have sex with you? It just seems like the wrong thing for me to do."

Her voice was agitated. "Adam, that's my decision to make. Don't patronize me."

She wriggled into her suit and started to climb out of the hot tub.

"Sarah, stop. You've misunderstood me. I am trying to be an ethical person. I didn't mean to imply that you were incapable of making decisions."

"Then why did we spend the past half hour getting each other so turned on?"

"Sarah, I just told you how much I want you. God, you can clearly see how much I want you. Believe me, right now my penis thinks I'm an idiot."

Sarah smiled in spite of herself. "I better head to bed, Adam. See you in the morning."

Adam stayed in the hot tub. The temptation to follow Sarah to her room was almost overwhelming. But, in the end he knew he couldn't. He turned and pressed against the jumbo storm blaster. As he got out of the spa he hoped he would remember to put in an extra portion of bromine tomorrow.

Adam couldn't fall asleep. His thoughts were about Sarah. Today was one of the best days he could remember. They had gotten to know each other over the past months and seemed to be very compatible. However, he knew there was no future with Sarah. Mostly because he knew if Shepherd was set free, he would have to kill him for Julie.

Adam was having his second cup of coffee when Sarah came down to breakfast. She walked past him to the coffee pot and stood with her back to him. After a few moments she turned and said, "Adam, I think we need to talk about last night. We've become so close, but I'm confused by my feelings for you."

"What are you feeling now, Sarah?"

"I haven't wanted to have anyone in my life for a long time," Sarah started hesitantly. "But being with you has given me hope that I can be happy again." She reached across the table and took his hand. "Adam, you are the first man I have trusted since I was twelve years old."

"Do you remember the movie, 'When Harry Met Sally?" Adam asked.

"Sure," Sarah said.

"I guess we have to figure out if Harry was right when he told Sally '...men and women can't be friends because the sex part always gets in the way.'"

Sarah frowned, "I hope he was wrong."

Chapter 30

TUPICO FLATS, NEVADA

Sarah and Adam returned to Tupico Flats several days before the trial started. As they sat in the hotel bar, a television news anchor interrupted their conversation; "Tupico Flats middle school music teacher James R. Schafer goes on trial Monday. The 50-year old Schafer has been charged with five counts of rape and lewdness with a child under the age of 14. If convicted, he faces a lifetime prison sentence. Superintendent Richard Dalton told WKKY that Schafer has been placed on paid leave until the conclusion of the trial."

The bartender turned up the television's volume, brought them their drinks, and said, "Honesty, when I first heard about a teacher having sex with a student I was all set to get my shotgun, until I heard it was Jim Schafer that was accused of this crime. I know Jim. He didn't do it."

A guy sitting at the end of the bar chimed in, "There're stories like this all around the country. I hear that most of them are false accusations filed because the kid has a failing grade or isn't making the team, or some other bogus complaint. This is the first time I ever hoped to be called for jury duty. If they would've called me, I'd make sure Jim was set free."

The scene on the television shifted to the steps of the courthouse. Reporters were jockeying with each other for position, shouting questions and then uploading their stories to their blogs. Assistant County Attorney Johnson was being interviewed. He looked like a deer caught in the headlights of an oncoming truck and his voice betrayed the confident words he spoke. The wind was blowing his comb-over straight up in the air. He had an unhealthy pallor; "We believe we will be able to prove that Mr. Schafer violated the laws of Nevada when he had a sexual relationship with a minor in his care."

A woman sitting at a table near the bar said, "Look at that Johnson guy. Reggie is going to eat his lunch."

Sarah sighed and said, "I agree with her. Johnson's killing us."

The camera shifted to the other side of the courthouse steps where Reggie Parker was being interviewed. The news announcer opened, "Looks like we have a celebrity in town. Schafer's lawyer is Reggie Parker. He's known as the defense lawyer of the stars. He has represented defendants in high profile cases all across the country. Rumor has it that Reggie is taking this case pro bono." Reggie was saying, "I have plenty of money. Sometimes you just have to get involved when you see an injustice. Mr. Schafer is a paragon of virtue. He is perhaps the most beloved teacher in the history of Tupico Flats."

"The media is a wild card in this trial," Adam stated grimly. "It's clear that no matter what the truth is, the media has already decided that Schafer isn't guilty. Reporters don't care about facts. They just want the airtime. The trial's become the biggest spectator sport in the state."

Sarah took a gulp of her scotch, trying to drown the trepidation that was quickly falling over her. "Shepherd's going to get away again, isn't he?" she murmured sadly.

"Let's not make any quick assumptions," Adam said. "We have several advantage in this trial.

"Like what?" Sarah asked cynically.

"Well, Johnson gets to make our case first. He has a victim that has suffered genuine harm. Johnson should be able to win points when he talks about Shepherd changing his name and moving from town to town. And Lizzie is young, vulnerable, and inherently sympathetic. Johnson's main theme is going to be that Lizzie has suffered and Shepherd's responsible. Shepherd changing his name should sway the jury."

"Drop the Pollyanna act, Adam." Sarah snapped. "He's going to get away with it. I know it, and you know it. Johnson is a lightweight. Mrs. Sutton has already told us Lizzie is having second thoughts about testifying."

In his heart he too feared that Shepherd would go free. He also feared his own actions if Shepherd walked. For Sarah's sake he maintained his air of optimism.

"Sarah, we have a good chance of getting a conviction. If we don't, we at least have enough evidence to have him investigated by the state-licensing department. He won't ever teach again," Adam said.

"That's not good enough." As Sarah sipped her second scotch, she secretly vowed that if Shepherd weren't convicted, she'd keep her promise.

There weren't many places to eat in Tupico Flats. Sarah and Adam learned that locals ate at Billy's Daughter's Saloon, a semi authentic miner's bar. The building had been used as a restaurant and bar for over 100 years. They both loved the flashing neon sign that said simply, "Get in here!" The food was good and the service was fast. The dining area was decorated with black and white photos of the restaurant's previous clientele. They sat in a corner booth under a photo of two pioneer women leading a mule up the side of a mountain. A sixteen year-old server brought the couple at the next booth their breakfast.

She was wearing a nametag that said Kelly. Adam guessed she played on the high school basketball or volleyball team. She was almost six feet tall and carried herself with confidence and authority. A ubiquitous maroon and gold ribbon was pinned to her apron, an indication she was a supporter of Shepherd.

"What's with the ribbon?" her customer asked.

"This is so cool," Kelly bubbled. "A group of music students started the ribbon campaign when Mr. Schafer was arrested. It sort of means, 'Free Mr. S.'"

The couple must have been from out of town because they asked, "Whose Mr. S?"

Adam and Sarah listened with interest and a growing sense of depression as Kelly continued her story. "He's just the greatest teacher in the whole school. He's been falsely accused of having sex with a student. None of us believe it. He was my teacher when I was in middle school and he was the best teacher I ever had. He made school fun. Would you like to sign our petition? This is the fourth day in a row where all the papers and television stations have dragged his name through the mud." This last sentence was laced with bitterness.

Kelly came over to Adam and Sarah's table carrying a clipboard. "Would you like to sign our petition? It says that we believe Mr. Schafer is innocent and should be allowed back in his classroom."

Sarah opened her mouth to tell Kelly what she could do with her petition, but Adam's warning glance quieted her. "We're just passing through," Adam said. Adam paid the bill, and they left the restaurant. As they walked across the parking lot to their car two men cut them off. Adam instinctively stepped between Sarah and the two men prepared for a fight.

The taller of the two men wore a work shirt, dirty coveralls, and a Cargill Feed cap. He asked, "Are you the folks that have been helping the Sutton girl?"

"Yes," Adam said, cautiously.

The man reached out to shake Adam's hand and said, "My name is Wall Stephens, and this is my friend Jerry Stockton. We want to thank you for helping that little girl. Both of our daughters go to school with her. Our girls say Lizzie is a good kid. They know Mr. Schafer plays favorites and they believe Lizzie is telling the truth. My wife is a teacher down at the elementary school. She says a lot of the other teachers support Lizzie. If Schafer has done what he's accused of, he needs to go to jail. Teachers are supposed to be people we can all trust and look up to."

Adam's shoulders slumped with relief.

"Thank you, Wall." Sarah said warmly. "I can't tell you how much your words mean to us."

"Good luck," Wall said. Jerry just smiled and nodded. They turned and ambled back to a dust-covered pickup.

"Just when you start to think everyone's against you, a good person steps up. Let's hope there are people like those two on the jury," Sarah said.

Sarah and Adam waved goodbye to Wall and Jerry as they drove out of the lot.

Chapter 31

The large grandfather clock in the lobby of the county court-house chimed three times as Gordon Johnson walked gingerly into his office balancing a three-foot thick stack of file folders. He was tired. For the past two months Schafer's attorney had buried him under mountains of paperwork. There were motions, counter motions, and counter-counter motions. Nothing came easy. Reggie challenged the hearing process, the trial date, and tried to have Johnson's expert witness excluded. Most of Schafer's witnesses were teachers and students who said the same thing, "I've never seen Schafer do anything unprofessional. "Yes, I know I am a mandatory reporter of suspected child abuse." "Yes, I would unhesitatingly allow my child to be in Mr. Schafer's class." Each interview represented three or four hours of his life that he'd never get back.

He'd dumped the phone records from Schafer's home and cell phone and found no incriminating evidence. He'd conducted the interviews in order to be thorough, and because his boss required that he take as long as necessary to adequately prepare the case. Lots of lawyers love the drama and suspense of the courtroom. Johnson wasn't one of them. He much preferred researching the law and preparing cases for trial. His dad did most of the trial work for their firm. He'd learned that if he did the preparation well, he often didn't have to appear in court. He knew this wasn't going to be one of those cases. This case was going to trial. As he dumped the folders on his desk and turned to his secretary he was surprised to see Lizzie and her mother. They were slumped in two side chairs. Both of them looked exhausted. "Please forgive me for being late," Johnson apologized deciding not to admit he'd forgotten their 2 o'clock appointment. "Jenny Kentwood's interview took longer than I thought it would."

Lizzie didn't even look up. Mrs. Sutton tried to smile. "We understand," she said, but her tired eyes spoke silently of the stress and pain that surrounded them. "Mr. Johnson, we're exhausted. We want this to end. It seems like the whole town is against us. My boss said the bar is losing business because I work there. He's threatening to fire me. You know Lizzie's stopped going to school because of the continual harassment. I'm not sure she's even going to testify. One day she says she will. The next day she says she won't."

Johnson led them to the conference room and got them a cup of coffee and soft a drink. Adam and Sarah joined them at four o'clock and Johnson briefed them on the preparation for the trial. "The school board has stipulated that Schafer was a teacher at the time we allege he raped Lizzie. However, they argue that they had no knowledge of any inappropriate behavior. They also say that, if the accusations are true and if they had known, they would've done the right thing. We have a couple of teachers who will state that they knew Mr. Schafer met with students in the music storage room. We also have a witness who will testify that Lizzie was frequently seen riding in Mr. Schafer's car. On the other hand, Reggie will counter with dozens of teachers who will say that they worked in the same school as Mr. Schafer, and that they never saw him do anything inappropriate."

To make his point Johnson opened a file folder and pulled out a type written paper. "Here, listen to what Tara Wilson said yesterday. She was one of Schafer's students for two years.

I quote, 'Mr. Schafer gave me private lessons in the music room. He never did anything like what they are saying he did. I don't know what kind of evidence they have or anything like that, but it doesn't seem possible that he'd molest anyone. I just think it can't be true."

Mrs. Sutton reflected on the interview for a moment. She ran her hand over her face and asked wearily, "What about the principal and other teachers? It seems obvious that they knew. How can they say they didn't know?"

"Remember, this isn't a civil case against the school board," Johnson reminded her. "It's a criminal case against Jim Schafer. If it were a civil case, we would be in better shape because we could show the school administrators and staff saw behaviors that should have raised suspicions. However, the school board and most of the employees are afraid of being sued if they admit that they knew or saw anything. I have a teacher and a school custodian who will help our case. The teacher, Miss. Richmond, will say she thought Mr. Schafer gave Lizzie too many passes to get out of class and go to his room. The janitor, Mr. James, will say that he found Mr. Schafer in the locked music storage closet one day after school when he went in to clean. He says Schafer quickly closed the door and looked guilty. James thinks he saw a pair of girl's underpants on the closet floor. That's about it."

Ever since she had found Lizzie's journal, Mrs. Sutton had been reading everything she could put her hands on about teachers who sexually abused students. She even found two web sites devoted to educating people about teachers who molested students. She quickly responded with her newfound knowledge. "The school did everything wrong. They should have conducted a background check, had a specific policy prohibiting sexual abuse and exploitation, trained the staff and students about the signs of abuse, paid attention, investigated, and caught the bastard." She ticked the behaviors off on her left hand as she spoke.

"That's what you and I think, but our opinion doesn't matter to the court."

"Well, then damn it, what does matter?" Mrs. Sutton's voice was shrill.

"We have to get Lizzie's journal entered as an exhibit, and Lizzie must testify very specifically about what happened, where it happened, and when it happened."

"I don't want to testify," Lizzie said sullenly. "Can't we just stop all of this now?" Her voice turned to pleading and tears began streaming down her cheeks. Johnson exchanged glances with Adam and Sarah. They all knew they had a big problem, but were unsure how to proceed.

After a moment Sarah took Lizzie's hand and softly said, "Honey, I know how hard this is for you. You are being very brave. I promise you I will be right there with you. Your mom and Mr. Faulkner and Mr. Johnson will all be there to help you through this."

Lizzie wiped her eyes and continued staring at the floor.

It seemed to Adam that Johnson took every opportunity to frighten Lizzie, when he should have been helping her feel confident.

"How about some good news?" Johnson said with as much cheer as he could muster. You know we've had trouble finding an expert to testify for us. We've found a college professor whose willing to explain the grooming process and offer an opinion in this case. This guy was a teacher and a principal in his earlier career so he has practical experience in schools as well as a wealth of scholarly research."

"How did you find him?" Adam asked.

"My boss gave me his name. In fact, Mr. Sail was quite insistent. He said he had a friend who used Dr. Ross in several trials. I called him, told him about the case, and he said he could help us," Johnson said.

"Will we have a chance to meet him before the trial?" Sarah asked.

"I don't think so. He will be out of the country on holiday until just before the trial. I sent him everything we've obtained during discovery last week and asked him to review the material and call me to discuss his testimony. I talked with him this morning. It's just what we need. He labeled Schafer a classic pedophile and mobile molester. I can't wait to get him on the stand. His testimony will be an important factor in the trial."

Adam and Sarah had spent many hours with Lizzie. When Lizzie was with them she seemed ready to testify. When she was at home she was a mess. She hadn't been to school since she was assaulted. The school was sending a teacher to the house, but Lizzie would only see her about half the time. Lizzie couldn't sleep. She was tired all the time and was losing weight. She thought she was losing her mind. Some days she believed what Sarah had told her and even believed that Schafer was abusing her. Other days she missed Schafer and believed he loved her."

Mrs. Sutton was also having trouble. On the one hand, she was very appreciative of a group of parents who had banded together to support her and Lizzie. They brought food to the house and stopped by to be sure that everything was okay. They told her that they would be at the trial to support her.

One even started a blog to keep everyone up to date on the progress of the trial. On the other hand, people were accosting her at the grocery store. Reporters were hounding her day and night. She became more depressed with each insult.

"I can't understand why so many parents can support a child molester," Mrs. Sutton complained.

"I think some of them are in denial. If they believed Schafer molested Lizzie they would have to wonder if the same thing had happened to their child. Hell, for years I couldn't face what happened to me." Sarah said.

"Jury selection starts tomorrow. Let's get some rest," Adam said, as he stood and headed for the door.

Chapter 32

Before jury selection began, Johnson filed a motion to exclude television from the courtroom. Judge Williams scheduled a hearing on the motion for eight o'clock the morning that jury selection was set to begin.

Johnson presented his argument in the calm of Judge Williams' chambers. "Judge Williams, I respectfully submit that public exposure through a televised trial is almost certain to create an undue level of anxiety in Lizzie Sutton. This increased anxiety could render this fragile child, who is now competent to testify, unable to function. Having cameras in the courtroom would present a clear and present danger to the administration of justice."

Judge Williams leaned back in his leather chair and pondered Johnson's plea. "It's the court's responsibility to prevent distractions, ensure decorum, and see to the fair administration of justice, but I just don't think cameras are that intrusive. When cameras were bulky and noisy you would have had a point. Today, in my opinion, television isn't that intrusive." Leaning forward he focused on Reggie Parker. "Generally, the defense requests that electronic media be barred. What's your position, Mr. Parker?"

"Judge Williams, Mr. Schafer and I have no secrets." Reggie replied. "We have no objection to allowing the electronic media in the courtroom."

Johnson tried again, "Judge Williams you have the option of allowing Lizzie to testify on closed-circuit TV to avoid having to face Mr. Schafer. This child has already been traumatized enough. We're seeking justice, not marketing Lizzie as the poster child for preventing child abuse. If you are going to allow cameras in the courtroom, please allow Lizzie to testify from another room."

Judge Williams nodded, "I understand your point, Mr. Johnson. However, allowing cameras in my courtroom is not inherently a denial of due process. You haven't adequately demonstrated that allowing the cameras would have a sufficiently adverse impact on Ms. Sutton. This case is important and of interest to the community. I want people to see what happens." He paused and stared at both attorneys. "I want to make it very clear that I won't tolerate theatrics and flamboyance in my courtroom," he warned.

Johnson tried a third time, "Judge Williams, I respectfully ask that you reconsider your ruling in light of Lizzie Sutton's age and the immensurable distress and that the media will cause her."

"Your points are noted for the record," the judge said curtly. "On balance there is more to be gained than lost. The clerk will deliver a copy of my ruling. He rose from his chair – a sure sign of dismissal. "Gentlemen, I will see you in court this afternoon." Mrs. Sutton, Sarah, Lizzie, and Adam were waiting in Johnson's office. When he confessed he'd been unsuccessful at barring media coverage Mrs. Johnson put her head in her hands. "I feel like we are in a car speeding toward a cliff. It seems like nothing is going right for us. Lizzie isn't going to get justice, is she?"

"We will do the best we can. We're just going to have to trust the system." Johnson said. No one in the room was very optimistic. After Johnson and Mrs. Sutton left them, Adam admitted, "I know what Mrs. Sutton means. I'm also concerned about today's ruling. I can't figure out if Johnson is just inexperienced or if he is intentionally blowing this case."

"I know what you mean, he really seems unsure of himself." Sarah said.

"I can't figure out how the judge could ignore case law that clearly indicates young children should be protected from publicity when they testify. It is common practice for courts to protect children by having them testify before a camera in a separate room."

That afternoon Judge Williams met with the prospective jurors and explained the procedures and told them they must complete a 30-page, 125 questionnaire made up of questions from both the prosecution and defense. Williams also asked them to complete a one-page hardship questionnaire that was designed to determine who had legitimate reasons to be excused from jury duty. As Williams continued giving his directions some of the potential jurors began reading the questionnaires. Several could be heard muttering objections to the personal nature of some of the questions. Joann Black, juror number 14, turned to Nancy Fairchild, juror number 2, and in a stage whisper asked, "How dare they ask me if I ever looked at pornography?" Nancy blushed and nodded her agreement. Others seemed upset at some of the questions.

Judge Williams then explained the voir dire process. "Each of you will be asked to take a seat at the conference table. Lawyers for both sides and Ms. Shafer and her mother will also be seated at the table. Each side has a number of preemptory challenges that can be used to exclude a juror for almost any reason. Any juror who gives an answer that indicates that they have already judged the case may be excluded for cause.

Sarah, Adam, Johnson and Johnson's assistants had a working lunch in Johnson's cramped office before jury selection began. Three walls were covered floor to ceiling with the photos of the one hundred and ten people in the jury pool. For weeks the team had been trying to figure out who they wanted on the jury. Under each photo was a brief biography of each person. Scribbled notes covered the rest of the bio page. Some names had stars beside them others had a crude skull and cross bones.

"Selecting jurors is like the game 'Where's Waldo'," Johnson said. "We've identified everyone who has a personal friendship with Schafer. We will try to get rid of them. We also have quite a few potential jurors who've had some contact with child sexual abuse in their family or among their friends. We need to keep as many of these people as we can."

Sarah looked at the photos with the stars and skulls. "That still leaves about two thirds of the people. How do you decide who else you want or don't want?"

"I have to find and reject the weirdoes. Some lawyers reject people who smile too much; others reject knitters. My father looked at their shoes, found out what they read, if they read," Johnson said cynically. "He told me he sometimes rejected jurors just because they creeped him out."

"What possible difference do clothing, books, and your sensibilities have on a person's suitability?" Sarah asked over her roast beef sandwich.

"Lots," Johnson replied, "My job is to get a conviction. My dad used to say 'jurors who read self-help books tend to believe everyone has a good side.' They may have a hard time accepting evil. He used to like the guys wearing cowboy boots and bolo ties. He said they tend to be law and order types, and aren't afraid to convict. I don't want college professors, counselors, or social workers. They have a tendency to want to help offenders rather than convict them. Some lawyers think people who read Harlequin novels tend to be too sympathetic."

"Aren't you discriminating against people just because of their personal tastes?" Sarah argued.

"Of course I am. I'm not trying to create a list of people I'd like to have a drink with after work. I'm trying to put together group of people that I can convince to convict Jim Schafer. I know these are gross generalizations," he said, apologetically. "Research has shown that personal preferences are important predictors of jurors behavior in court decisions."

As Adam listened to Johnson he once again wished Johnson's father were conducting the trial. "I was involved in a trial once where during a break in the selection process a prospective juror got out his cell phone and started screaming at his wife. He was rejected. It is critical that we get a jury that has a strong sense of justice."

Johnson smiled, "Yeah, I have a friend who is a county attorney in California. He rejects anyone who is carrying a mystery novel. He says he doesn't want any armchair detectives. I'm worried about getting a jury that will be unaffected by the goings on in this town. Have you seen the petitions to get Schafer back in the classroom and the 'Free Mr. S.' signs posted all around town?"

Sarah and Adam nodded solemnly. "Can't you try again to get a change of venue?" Sarah asked.

"The judge told me I couldn't even submit a petition until we see how the selection process goes. He seems to think we can seat an unbiased jury from this county. I'm not so sure. I'll try to eliminate anyone who has personal beliefs that are not sympathetic to Lizzie. But we have to remember that Reggie is trying to do exactly the opposite."

Across town in a suite of offices Reggie Parker had rented, his defenses team was studying the same faces that were on Johnson's wall. Gilbert Martinez, Parker's jury consultant, coordinated the massive data that had been collected on each jury finalist. In addition to their answers to the two surveys, they had collected data from public records, had bird's-eye satellite views of each prospective jurors' home, notations about observations of body language, dress, and general demeanor. Martinez entered all of this material into a computer program that ranked each juror according to his or her likely sympathy to Jim Schafer.

Chapter 33

Just inside the front door of the hundred-year-old courthouse a graceful three-story walnut staircase spiraled upward. A beautiful gold dome rose 62 feet above the rotunda. At the top of the stairs an oval window overlooked the city park. Pretty much everything in the courtroom was from the original construction: the dark walnut furniture was massive, the light fixtures ornate, the railings imposing, and the wall covering oppressive. The dark paneling and dark wooden blinds shut out all light from the outside and made the room seem even smaller than it was.

The judge's bench was opposite the main entrance; the jury box was in the center of the courtroom. The round design of the room created some unique acoustics. Sounds bounced around and echoed strangely. Like the whispering gallery in Congress, one could be sitting right next to someone and not hear them, whereas someone across the room could hear every word.

Despite the seriousness of the occasion there was an almost festive atmosphere in the courtroom. The spectator seating area was filled with excited citizens of Tupico Flats. Everyone had a rooting interest in the out come of the trial. Those who supported Mr. Schafer were told to remove their badges and ribbons. There were one hundred and ten people in the jury pool. The bailiff led the first group of prospective jurors into the courtroom and directed them to take a seat in the jury box. The judge reminded each attorney that they were restricted to 15 minutes in which to determine if a prospective juror was someone they could accept. The attorneys alternated examining each prospective juror. Each attorney used their eight preemptive challenges to remove those prospective jurors they believed could the most damage their case.

From the first moments of the jury selection, it was easy to see why Parker won most of his cases. "May it please the Court? Your Honor, may I approach the jury?"

"You may."

Reggie paused and made eye contact with each member of the panel. He had memorized the names of each prospective juror and knew that the sound of their own names was sweet music to their ears.

"Mr. Johnson, ladies and gentlemen, good morning. As Judge Williams told you, my name is Reggie Parker. As you know I am not a resident of Tupico Flats. However it is an honor and privilege to be here speaking on behalf of Jim Schafer." Parker walked over to the defense table and casually gestured toward Schafer. "Mr. Schafer would you please stand?" Parker had previously instructed Schafer to stand and make eye contact with the panel. By the time Parker got through with them he wanted each juror to feel that Parker was their personal friend.

Throughout the afternoon Parker tried to exclude anyone who had ever been assaulted or who had a personal relationship with a rape victim. Johnson tried to exclude anyone who had a personal relationship with Schafer. It was quickly proven that Johnson was correct in assuming almost everyone in town either knew Schafer personally or knew about him.

Parker glanced at the bio of juror number forty as he got out of his chair and approached the jury box. Shelly Horton was fifty, divorced, lived alone, and played competitive bridge. He asked a few meaningless questions before getting to his main point. "Ms. Horton have you ever been raped or sexually assaulted? She was startled and paused before answering. Parker knew from her survey that she was attacked last year in the parking lot of the local mall. When she answered yes, he asked that she be excluded from the jury.

It took three more prospective jurors before Reggie found one he would accept. Johnson had classified juror number twenty as a definite no. Ronald Griffin, was forty-three years old, had pale blue eyes, washed out brown hair and looked like he needed a good bath. Johnson approached Griffin and asked, "Do you personally know Mr. Jim Schafer?" Mr. Griffin, smiled and said, "Mr. Schafer goes to my church. I've known him since he came to town." When Johnson asked that Griffin be excluded from the jury, Griffin was indignant. He stood and shouted, "Don't you want me to tell you what I think of him? I think he is being falsely accused, that's what I think."

Judge Williams pounded his gavel and announced that juror number twenty was excused and warned the others jurors to refrain from any further outbursts. During the afternoon recess Johnson again met with Sarah and Adam. He told them he was going to have to accept a jury made up of local people who knew Schafer. He admitted to himself that their only hope was if he could get the jury to know and like him. "I've lived in this county my whole life. Most of these folks know my dad even if they don't know me. I need them to believe I am just like them and that Reggie is an outsider," Johnson said. "Then I have a chance of getting them to accept our theory of the case." Although Johnson didn't have a great deal of trial experience, both Adam and Sarah could see that he was a student of human nature. He seemed to understand what makes people tick. They hoped he would be able to seat a fair jury.

Because Johnson thought there was a general negative attitude about Lizzie and a positive attitude toward Schafer, he asked all prospective jurors if they understood that, by law, a juror couldn't consider anything other than the evidence produced through testimony. "You can't consider what you might have read or heard about the case. When you are sworn as a juror, you are taking an oath that you will consider only the law and evidence in arriving at your verdict. I need to know if you can accept and abide by such an oath."

Johnson knew that everyone would answer in the affirmative. He also knew that once selected each juror would do whatever they damn well pleased. However, he wanted to keep repeating this mantra in the hope that it would have an impact on their later deliberations. Johnson asked open-ended questions in order to get each prospective juror talking. He needed to hear them talk in order to figure out how they thought. At the same time he knew that as he was picking a jury, the jurors were picking a lawyer. As each juror answered Johnson's questions he found himself beginning to relax. The jurors picked up on his demeanor and began talking about themselves. He knew that if he tipped his hand as to which jurors were most likely to see things his way, Parker would try to strike them.

Adam's twenty years of trial experience led him to believe that all things being equal, a tree will generally fall the way it leans. He told Sarah that the key issue for Johnson was to eliminate as many people who were already leaning away from Lizzie. Johnson also wanted to identify the leaders in the group. Johnson and Adam agreed that the natural leaders would hold a disproportionate sway over how the other jurors would vote.

After three days, eleven jurors and three alternates were selected and seated. The trial was scheduled to begin on Monday.

Adam was not happy with the jury. Only three jurors had more than a high school education, and all but one were lifetime residents of Tupico Flats. Although the judge had excluded potential jurors who paid taxes in Schafer's school district, the county only had one newspaper and it carried dozens of articles and letters to the editor in support of Schafer. As far as Adam knew, none of the jurors had signed any petitions in support of Schafer.

At the conclusion of the jury selection process Reggie Parker, knowing that he risked judge Williams' wrath, held an informal press conference on the courthouse steps. As he positioned himself in front of the reporters he turned to Jade, his assistant, and whispered, "in Tupico Flats this trial is a bona fide media event. Shoot, it's bigger than their state championship high school football team and almost as big as Jessie Walters' sighting of a UFO." Jade had been with Parker for five years. Most people assumed their relationship extended beyond the workday. She tried to keep a straight face as she leaned near him to prompt him with the names of the two national reporters who were at the front of the pack.

As the reporters crowded around, Reggie nodded and smiled making them believe that he recognized each one of them. The first question sailed at him like a huge softball. "Mr. Parker, what is it about this case that made you come all the way to Tupico Flats?"

Reggie hit it out of the park. He slowly shook his head, smiled sadly, and replied, "Teachers work hard. They're underpaid.

Each of us owes a huge debt of gratitude to all our teachers. Mr. Schafer deserves the best defense possible. I can't be a bystander and watch an innocent teacher be convicted of a crime he didn't commit. I've made it my life's mission to keep the wrongly accused out of jail."

A reporter from the local television station asked, "Why would this girl accuse Mr. Schafer of rape if he's innocent?"

"My client doesn't understand why Mrs. Sutton and her daughter are attempting to destroy him. However, we are both very confident in the wise deliberation of the jury. Jim is obviously looking forward to being able to resume his life as a beloved husband, father, and music teacher."

Adam and Sarah watched Parker's performance from the other side of the stairway. It was clear to Adam that Parker understood exactly how to feed the news beast. When Reggie concluded his media blitz, Sarah and Adam headed for their car. As they walked Adam looked back at Parker. "He's learned to speak in short quotable messages. He's a master at giving the reporters the sound bite that fits his message. I'll bet he knows which of his quotes news editors will select to be broadcast before the reporter sends them in."

"You sound like you know him," Sarah said.

"Yeah. I know him, all right. He defended a serial rapist in a case I worked in Rhode Island five or six years ago."

"What happened?"

"You don't want to know." Adam grimaced and continued, "Sarah, I've watched guys like him for years. They've learned how to script their words to sound like they're spontaneous quips. I doubt if he cares if Shepherd is guilty or innocent. First and last, Reggie is interested in polishing and refining his image as the most famous trial lawyer in the country. Although he's taking this case pro bono, don't be fooled. The publicity from this case will get him a few million dollar retainers."

"Isn't what he's doing unethical? Isn't he tampering with the jury? There's no way the jurors aren't reading the papers."

"Sarah, this trial has become a media circus. The Bar Association's policy of prohibiting lawyers from making statements that may be disseminated to the jury has gone out the window. I'll ask Johnson to complain to the judge, who said he wouldn't permit the case to become a spectacle, but Reggie will argue that he didn't seek out the media. He'll say he was just responding to legitimate media questions."

When they were half way down the steps another commotion erupted at the courthouse door. Johnson's badly timed exit put him in the middle of the reporters who hadn't had time to leave the courthouse steps. For Reggie Parker facing a pack of reporters shouting out questions, jockeying for position, and racing to meet deadlines was the high point of his day. For Gordon Johnson it was a frightening gauntlet he was forced to run, courting disaster with every step. It was immediately apparent to Adam that Johnson wasn't even close to being in Reggie's league. Johnson's body language made it clear that he dreaded every encounter with reporters. When Johnson saw the reporters he tried to dodge them and head for his car. They were on him like a pack of wild dogs before he got ten yards. The next ten minutes were like watching jackals ganging up on a defenseless baby springbuck. As painful as it was to watch, they couldn't turn away. Johnson's answers were long and convoluted and filled with legal jargon. He walked backwards toward his car as he answered their questions looking more like a Mafia don trying to escape than a county attorney.

"He's oblivious to the fact that his terrified demeanor made Lizzie's case look even weaker than it is, " Adam said shaking his head as they once again headed for their car.

On the morning of the trial the courthouse steps were crowded with people who weren't able to get a seat in the courtroom. They were escorted into a small auditorium where folding chairs had been placed before a big screen television. News vans and television trucks surrounded the building.

Charles James, the middle school janitor, sat in a witness room in the far corner of the building. He had come to believe that Mr. Schafer had fooled him, that Schafer did have someone in the band room. He wondered what was going on in the courtroom and looked forward to his turn to testify against Schafer.

When Gretchen Cocan heard about the trial she knew she had to be there. She drove to Tupico Flats the night before the trial. Halfway up the courthouse steps she remembered she would have to pass through a metal detector in order to get into the courtroom. She turned and walked back to the parking lot and put her single action Smith & Wesson under the front seat. Lately, Gretchen's dreams of revenge had resumed.

At nine o'clock sharp the bailiff entered the courtroom and commanded, "Please rise. The court in and for Tupico Flats County is now in session, the Honorable Lawrence Williams presiding."

Williams entered with a flourish of his black robe, stood behind the bench, and gazed over the courtroom making it clear he was the prince of all he surveyed. Williams loved this moment. He relished the fact that the bench was the focal point of the courtroom, and that he controlled the proceedings. He looked down on the clerk's desk and the witness stand.

The bailiff escorted the jurors to the jury box where they were sworn in. Williams asked the bailiff to call the case and inform the attorneys it's time to begin their opening statements.

Johnson rose from the prosecution table and approached the jury box. He was wearing his lucky sport coat, brown tweed with patches on the elbows that contrasted nicely with his yellow shirt and tie. He reminded himself to speak clearly and slowly. He wet his lips, cleared his throat, and began his opening remarks.

"Today, each of you is a temporary officer of the court. Many of you are serving on this jury at great personal sacrifice." He scanned the faces of the jurors. By now he knew the life stories of each of the six women and five men. As he spoke he tried to make eye contact with Bill Kennedy. Kennedy sat ramrod straight and looked much like he did twenty years ago when he was a captain in the marines. He was short and wiry with close cropped steel grey hair. He had a strong sense of right and wrong and understood his duty. Johnson knew if he could persuade Kennedy to vote against Schafer, there was some hope for a favorable verdict.

Agnes Welch, a tiny grandmother, wore a dark blue suit with a stiff high-necked blouse. Her eyes seemed to lose focus through her thick glasses, but she was listening intently to every word, aware of everything going on around her. Johnson saw her as his next best hope. He knew she had daughters and granddaughters. She might be able to identify with what happened to Lizzie.

Johnson moved closer to the jury. "The defense is going to tell you that Mr. Schafer is a great teacher. Many citizens of Tupico Flats will come forward to tell you what a good person he is. Look at him. He looks like a really nice man, the kind of guy you would like to invite to lunch, and the kind of guy you might want teaching your children. Don't be fooled by his appearance. James Schafer raped a fourteen-year old girl who lives in this town. What's more he did it in a school, the very institution that parents trust will protect their children."

Juror four, Mitzie Palmer, had a round face and long curly blond hair. She would have been pretty except for her crooked smile. She smiled and nodded her head each time Johnson said something positive about Schafer, frowning and shaking her head when he was critical.

Johnson was worried about Julie Summons, juror number ten. In spite of the air conditioning, perspiration was forming on her florid face. She looked like a heart attack about to happen. She was known as the town gossip. Her café was a hotbed of rumors. She had promised to keep an open mind, but Johnson saw her smile and nod at Schafer when he entered the courtroom.

"We will present an expert who will testify that child molesters get away with their heinous crimes because they are the last people you would suspect. Seldom do they fit the stereotype of the guy in a trench coat that hangs around playgrounds and offers candy to children.

"James Schafer selected a young, impressionable child and took advantage of her innocence. He told her that he loved her. He even told her that when she got older he was going to divorce his wife and marry her. Tragically, Lizzie Sutton believed him." As Johnson spoke he realized his first impression of Kaitlin Romin, juror number five, was correct. He could see it coming but hoped he was wrong. Romin had been the center of attention since she entered the courtroom. She was a beautiful red head with very large breasts. She wore a green sweater that was two sizes too small and a half-a-dozen gold bracelets dangled from each wrist and jangled every time she moved her arm. Just as Johnson attempted to make his main point, she tossed her hair out of her eyes and smoothed her short skirt. The jingle of her bracelets caused everyone to look in her direction. Johnson's opening statement was all about telling a story and getting the jury to come to care about Lizzie. Kaitlin, whether innocently or not, had broken his fragile narrative.

Trying not to show his displeasure, Johnson continued, "The defense will tell you that Lizzie consented to having sex with Mr. Schafer. You need to understand clearly that in Nevada the age of consent is sixteen. Lizzie is only fourteen. She was legally incapable of giving her consent. The defense may use phrases like 'inappropriate relationship,' or 'an affair,' or 'a bad decision.' Don't be fooled by these word games. You'll come to see by law, and through common sense, that James Schafer raped a child who trusted him." Johnson looked at juror number twelve. Debbie Royce's round face and short blond hair reminded him of a bobble head doll. Her constant smiling and head nodding was distracting. Johnson hoped she was really listening.

"During this trial we are going to be forced to talk and think about subjects that will make all of us uncomfortable. I promise you I will speak only of those things that are necessary for you to understand all aspects of the case. For example, in Nevada statutory sexual seduction means ordinary sexual intercourse, anal intercourse, cunnilingus, or fellatio committed by a person 18 years of age or older with a person under the age of 16 years. I remind you that Lizzie Sutton is only 14 years old and James Schafer is over 50." The look of distaste on Kathy Hutten's face caused Johnson to end his litany of sexual perversion. By then Hutten's arms were crossed over her chest, her lips were pursed, and she was sighing deeply, clearly indicting she was offended by the subject of sex. Johnson was not sure if this was good or bad for his case.

Johnson couldn't help wondering what was going on with juror number eleven, Jeff Powell. Johnson had never seen Powell smile. He didn't look well. Tall, thin, and angular, he looked like he might fall asleep at any time. Johnson tried not to be discouraged by Powell's constant frowns and sighs.

"In conclusion, it is important for us to remember why the age of consent law was passed. It protects young and easily impressed youth by prohibiting adults from having sex with children, regardless of whether or not the child agrees. Schafer's sexual abuse of Lizzie Sutton has traumatized her and will undoubtedly negatively influence her for the rest of her life. The damage done has been physical and psychological as well as sexual. It is your duty to make it clear that society will not tolerate such abuse, and most especially from teachers. James Schafer seduced Lizzie Sutton, just like he has seduced this community. When you hear from our witnesses and from Lizzie herself, you will have no choice but to find James Schafer guilty of all charges." Johnson almost managed a confident smiled as he walked to his chair knowing he was facing an uphill battle.

The judge called on Reggie Parker to make his opening remarks. Parker casually stood up and ambled toward the jury. He paused and smiled confidently as he surveyed the jury. Most of the jury members leaned forward in their chairs clearly expecting something memorable. "Mr. Johnson has just told you it is important for you to understand Nevada's age of consent law. Mr. Johnson is wrong. The case isn't about how old Lizzie Sutton is or how old Jim Schafer is. You don't need to understand that law because Jim Schafer didn't have sex with Lizzie Sutton. He did not seduce her. He did not molest her. I'm not here to attack Lizzie Sutton or her mother, however, it is my job to point out the misunderstandings, misstatements, and outright lies that have been spread by Lizzie Sutton, her mother, Assistant County Attorney Johnson, and others. We will prove that Jim is innocent of all charges brought against him.

"I want to tell you a true story, a very frightening story. In 1983 the mother of a child attending a preschool in California charged a teacher with sexually abusing her child. After the teacher was arrested, the police sent a letter to the parents of all three hundred students in the school. The parents were asked to question their children to see if they had been a victim or had witnessed a crime. The parents were told that their children could possibly have been the targets of criminal acts including: oral sex, fondling of genitals, buttock or chest area, and sodomy. Several hundred children were then interviewed. The children were repeatedly asked suggestive and leading questions. Eventually over fifty children accused the teachers at the day care center of sexual abuse.

"In 1990, after months of testimony and weeks of deliberation by the jury, the teacher was acquitted on all counts. After the trial some of the children who had previously said they had been molested recanted. Several children admitted they told of many things that didn't happen. One child said he lied to please his parents."

"We are facing a similar situation here. We will show that this case is really about a woman who doesn't even live in Tupico Flats. Sarah Abbott is an outsider who has her own agenda and is not above using Lizzie to get what she wants. We will prove that Lizzie Sutton lied to please her mother and Sarah Abbott."

Reggie shifted his gaze to Sarah who was sitting directly behind Lizzie and her mother. "Sarah Abbott has an unjustified hatred of Jim Schafer. Sarah Abbott has been on a witch-hunt for over a year. She has slandered Jim Schafer's name and hurt his reputation. She has damaged Jim Schafer's marriage and confused his young daughter. Don't let Sarah Abbott mislead you, the citizens of Tupico Flats, into doing her dirty work for her."

Sarah inwardly flinched at Parker's accusations. Her mind was racing; she couldn't believe what she was hearing. She could feel everyone's eyes on her back as Parker attacked her. Parker was trying to make this a trial about her character, just like Johnson said he would.

"This case is also about another outsider, Adam Faulkner. He is a private investigator brought in by Sarah Abbott. He has not only laid the groundwork for the charges we are looking at today but has made a career of traveling around the country bringing charges against innocent teachers. He has worked behind the scenes getting parents to bring cases against teachers in Pennsylvania, Ohio, Colorado, and a half dozen other states. Now he is here trying to lynch your friend, Jim Schafer.

"These two outsiders want you to convict an innocent man of an unspeakable crime. Jim Schafer is innocent of all charges, but because of Lizzie Sutton, her mother, Ms. Abbott, and Mr. Faulkner, Jim Schafer's reputation is permanently damaged, his life turned upside down, and his freedom is at risk."

Jurors stared at Sarah and Adam while Parker was talking about them. From across the room Sarah heard a spectator whisper, "That bitch should get out of town, if she knows what's good for her." Several people nodded in assent.

Johnson knew it was highly irregular to interrupt an opening statement, but he couldn't help himself. He jumped to his feet and objected. "Your honor Mr. Parker is taking us on a bird walk that has nothing whatsoever to do with the facts of this trial. I move that all of these statements be stricken from the record and the jury be directed to disregard them."

Judge Williams' face turned red. "Mr. Johnson, sit down! You know better than to interrupt an opening statement. The jury will ignore Mr. Johnson's remarks. Please continue, Mr. Parker."

Reggie paused and looked at the jury with an injured expression. In a quieter, more soothing tone he continued, "Young girls often have crushes on teachers." He smiled at each of the female jurors as he said, "I'll bet some of the women in this courtroom today can remember an innocent crush they had on one of their teachers. However, Lizzie Sutton didn't have an innocent crush on Jim Schafer. She came to believe he is in love with her. We are here today because Lizzie Sutton developed an intricate fantasy world around Jim Schafer. She wrote about her fantasies in her journal. Then a bitter, unstable woman from Boston and a hired gun from Colorado came to town and convinced Lizzie and her mother that her fantasies were real.

"For a moment, let's look at what Mr. Johnson is asking you to believe. You are being asked to believe that Lizzie's journal is an accurate description of sexual abuse at the hands of a teacher. You are being asked to believe that Barbara Sutton believes this abuse occurred, even though she never called the school or the police to report it. In fact she never called anyone about the abuse. What would you have done if you believed a teacher had sexually abused your daughter? Would you have remained silent? Of course not. You would have immediately acted to protect your child. Mrs. Sutton did nothing until Sarah Abbott and Adam Faulkner talked her into defaming Jim Schafer.

"Jim Schafer and I are totally confident that you will see this case for what it is, a witch-hunt initiated by a disturbed woman from Boston. This is a case that should never have gone to trial. When you have listened to all of the facts you will find Jim Schafer not guilty of all charges."

After the morning session as Sarah and Adam were walking to lunch, Sarah expressed her outrage and fears, "He's made the case about us, Adam. Are we jeopardizing the outcome by attending the trial?"

"Johnson told us he thought Parker would drag us into the case," Adam reminded her. If we stop going to the courtroom now, everyone will think Reggie was telling the truth and has scared us off."

"Yes, but..." Sarah was interrupted by the buzz of her cell phone. She noticed the ID was blocked as she accepted the call. A male voice said, "You better watch your back, bitch." Sarah held the phone to her ear for a few seconds after the caller disconnected. Adam noticed her distress. "Sarah. What's wrong?"

"This call. It was from a very angry man. He hung up. I don't know who it was. It might have be the same guy who yelled at me in the courtroom."

After she told Adam what the man said, she admitted that this wasn't the first threatening call she had received over the past week.

"How many others?" Adam asked.

"I've had hang up calls and heavy breathing calls a couple of times a day since my name was in the papers. I have no idea how they got my cell number."

"Sarah, why didn't you tell me?"

"Adam you know how much I care for you and how much I appreciate all that you've done for me. But sometimes you treat me as if I were your daughter. You act like a knight who wants to ride up on a white horse and save me. I have to know I'm capable of saving myself. I knew if I told you about the calls you'd spring into action and try to fix things."

Outwardly, Adam was silent. Inwardly he was disheartened. *A couple of weeks ago we almost became lovers. Now she thinks of me as her father,* he thought. *I guess she's right. That's what I do. I try to save people.* "You're right, Sarah. Sorry."

"Adam. I didn't mean to hurt your feelings, but I can't find my own voice if I'm your prodigy."

"You're right. I understand what you're saying. Do you want to talk about the calls?"

Sarah nodded. "The caller never stays on the phone more than a minute. I know it would take longer than that to trace the call."

"That's what the television would lead you to believe, but the problems of keeping wacos on the phone are relics of the old manual switchboards. Since the start of electric switching systems, a caller's phone number can be identified almost instantaneously."

"But, Adam, what's the point of finding out who is calling?"

"What do you mean? We could catch him and have him punished."

"Adam, the only person I care about punishing is Tony Shepherd, and right now it doesn't look like that's going to happen.

Chapter 34

When the court reconvened after lunch Johnson called the first witness for the prosecution, Dr. Dennis Ross. Ross was a college professor right out of Hollywood casting. He was tall with hair as white as a snowdrift. He wore a conservative blue suit; gold wire-rimmed glasses, and spoke in a clear, scholarly voice. He was self-deprecating as Johnson asked him about his degrees, publications, and awards. Johnson led Ross flawlessly through his testimony. Ross answered all questions directly and with precision. He made it clear that teachers who molested children were able to do so because they were beyond suspicion. Johnson glanced from time to time at the jury. It was clear that they liked Ross. They were paying attention to his every word.

"The vast majority of teachers are competent, capable, caring people doing a very difficult job," Ross testified. "However, some aren't. If administrators, other teachers and parents are looking the wrong way or aren't vigilant enough they won't see what's going on right in front of their eyes."

Johnson was very pleased by the way Dr. Ross' testimony was going. He was rejoicing inwardly as he posed his final question. "Dr. Ross, relying on your research of the relevant literature, your personal experience, and your professional judgment, is it your opinion that James Schafer molested Lizzie Sutton?"

"It is my expert opinion that......."

Reggie leaped up, interrupting Dr. Ross, and shouted, "It is the jury's duty to determine if Mr. Schafer is guilty."

Judge Williams responded, "Objection sustained. Do not answer that question, Dr. Ross."

Ross looked confused. Johnson looked defeated. Johnson had momentarily forgotten that an expert was not permitted to offer his opinion as to guilt. Most of Johnson's previous work was in civil court and he did not know there were different rules in criminal cases. Johnson turned to Ross and quietly said, "Thank you Dr. Ross. I have no further questions."

Adam was nonplused. What a rookie mistake, he thought.

Reggie Parker could hardly contain his glee as he approached the witness. He loved expert witnesses. Eviscerating pompous experts was his forte. In fact, other attorneys often retained him solely for the purpose of taking down opposing experts. As he approached Dr. Ross, Parker had one goal, to destroy Ross' credibility. He sauntered up to Ross and smiled warmly.

Ross tried to regain his composure and smiled back confidently.

The smile remained on Parker's face, but his approach was immediately sarcastic and mean spirited. When Johnson was doing the questioning, Ross was calm and seemed very comfortable on the stand. That all changed when Reggie began his cross-examination. Reggie opened by sneering at Ross, "Well, Mr. Ross, the court is led to believe you are a 'so called expert.'" Is this correct?"

Ross immediately bristled, "It's Dr. Ross. And yes, I'm a nationally recognized expert in the area of sexual abuse of children."

Parker immediately began badgering Ross by asking him to respond with a simple "yes" or "no" to very complex questions, cutting him off in mid sentence, and then turning his back on Ross in the middle of his answer. The rude treatment was having the desired effect. Ross became frustrated and argumentative.

Sarah and Adam looked at each other and simultaneously mouthed, "Oh, shit."

Just when it looked like Ross's testimony couldn't get any worse, Parker moved in very close to him. He paused and then asked, "Is it appropriate for a teacher to meet in isolated areas with students, travel out of town with students, or communicate with them by e-mail or Instant Messaging, Mr. Ross?"

Ross smiled and seemed to relax; he was back on solid ground. "Absolutely not. Those are all red flags. No teacher should do any of those things you mentioned."

Parker suppressed a smile, walked over to the defense table, and withdrew a book from his briefcase. He opened the book and with a puzzled expression began slowly shaking his head as he walked back to Dr. Ross and handed him the book.

"Mr. Ross would you identify the book that your holding?"

Again smiling confidently, Ross answered, "Why yes, it's my book on sexual abuse. It's used as a text book in over seventy colleges and universities across the country."

"Please open the book to the page that is marked and read the material that is highlighted."

Ross found the passage. His face blanched. He looked around like a trapped animal.

"Mr. Ross, have you found the passage?"

"Yes, but you're taking this out of context," Ross said meekly.

"Please read the marked passage for the court," Parker persisted.

Ross started to read. "Many of...."

Parker interrupted him. "Louder. Mr. Ross, so that the court can hear your expert testimony."

Ross cleared his throat and started reading again. "Many of the behaviors that are sometimes associated with grooming can be legitimate activities. For example, music teachers often tutor students after school, and today most teachers are connected electronically with their students."

"Please read the last sentence again, Mr. Ross." Parker requested smugly.

Johnson jumped to his feet, "Asked and answered, your honor."

Williams sustained the objection, but the damage had already been done.

Parker looked at the jury and then turned to Ross. "Mr. Ross, I'm confused. Which is it Mr. Ross? You can't have it both ways. Is it reasonable for music teachers to spend time after school with students, or not?"

"Well, it is not that simple...." Ross began.

With a dismissive gesture Parker turned his back to Ross. "That is all that I have for this 'expert.'"

Johnson didn't want the jury to remember Dr. Ross' last words, so he tried to rehabilitate Ross' testimony in his redirect. After several minutes of moderate success, he decided to move on and excused Ross.

Dr. Ross' complexion was gray and his suit looked rumpled as he vainly tried to smile as he walked from the stand and out of the courtroom.

When the court adjourned for the day, Lizzie and her mother left for home. Adam, Sarah, Johnson and Dr. Ross walked down the steps of the courthouse in silence. Dr. Ross had five hours before his flight home. Typically, Johnson would have invited Ross to join them for dinner. Instead, he asked his paralegal to drive Ross to the airport. Adam, Sarah and Johnson headed for the bar across the street. By now they had become a team that worked together on analysis and strategy planning.

"I might have seen a worse expert testimony, but I don't think so," Adam said.

"Boy, I didn't see that coming," Johnson lamented. "Ross seemed so competent when I was preparing him for his testimony. Boy, Parker really took Ross apart today."

"Yeah he did," Sarah agreed mournfully. "But what's more important, I was watching Lizzie and Mrs. Sutton during Reggie's attack. They're both scared to death. Reggie smells blood in the water. He'll attack them with a vengeance, and I'm afraid they'll crumble."

Adam listened quietly. He refrained from pointing out that it was Johnson's incompetence that allowed Parker to do so much damage.

"We definitely need to spend some time with Barbara and Lizzie tomorrow morning before they get on the stand. It's all going to come down to Lizzie's testimony," Johnson innocently predicted.

Chapter 35

That night Lizzie lay awake worrying about what tomorrow would bring. She was afraid that Mr. Parker was going to get her all confused. At three a.m. her cell phone vibrated. When she saw the caller ID she jumped out of bed and went into her closet so her mom wouldn't hear. She was trembling.

"Hi Lizzie, I miss you so much. Are you doing okay?" Schafer's voice dripped with concern.

Lizzie didn't answer his question. Her questions tumbled out. "Why haven't you returned my calls? I've left hundreds of messages."

"People have been watching me, Lizzie. This is the first time I've had a chance to call you. How are you holding up?"

Once again Lizzie ignored his concern. She was focused on what was going to happen in the morning.

"I don't want to go to court tomorrow. I don't want to say bad things about you, but, my mom says that I have to." Lizzie was sobbing softly by this time.

"You know that everyone in this town loves me," Schafer comforted. "They won't be able to get a jury to convict me if you tell everyone that what you wrote in the diary isn't true. You have to make the jury believe we didn't do anything wrong. Remember, if they believe I am guilty they will also believe you did something wrong. If it looks like I am losing the case, my lawyer will show everyone the photos you sent me. Don't make him do that, Lizzie. I don't want him to do that. You know how much I love you. We'll be together forever after this is all over. I promise."

Lizzie panicked. "You still have the photos. You told me you deleted them. Please don't let anyone see them," she begged.

Schafer immediately knew he'd made a mistake. "I won't let Reggie show them, Lizzie I promise. I love you and would never let anyone hurt you."

Lizzie so much wanted to believe him. Instead she said, "Everyone is telling me you're lying to me. They say you have done things to other girls. That's not true. Is it?"

"Of course not, Lizzie. When you get on the stand, just look at me, and you'll know that I love you and no one else. But, Lizzie, you have to go on the stand. If you just don't show up they might continue to investigate me. Go on the stand but you can't admit anything. Do you understand what I am saying?"

"I'm really afraid of Mr. Parker. Can't I just say nothing happened?"

"Yes, that's exactly what you need to say. But, you have to say it on the stand." Schafer was emphatic. After one more "I love you," he hung up, pleased with his performance yet fearful for what the morning might bring despite his best effort to sway Lizzie.

The prosecution team met the Suttons for breakfast. They took a corner booth out of earshot of the other customers. Lizzie scrunched down in the booth shredding her napkin into confetti. She wouldn't make eye contact with anyone.

Sarah put her hand on Lizzie's. "You're going to be fine. You're so brave. Thank you for what you're going to do today. You're going to keep Mr. Schafer from hurting any more girls."

Lizzie shrugged Sarah's hand away. "I'm afraid of Mr. Parker. He's mean. He's going to try to trick me and get me confused."

"I'm nervous, too." Mrs. Sutton admitted. "Is there any way you can keep Lizzie off the stand? If I do a good job, will that be good enough?"

"Your both going to be fine," Johnson assured them. "Just tell the truth. Keep your answers short, and answer only the question Parker or I ask. I'll protect you. I'll object if he tries to intimidate you."

Adam had been watching Lizzie. Red-rimmed eyes peered from a chalk white face. Her appearance combined with her repeated plea not to testify, told Adam that they were in big trouble. He knew Lizzie wasn't ready to testify. She was a time bomb waiting to go off. No one really had any idea what she was going to say.

As they walked across the street to the courthouse, Sarah pulled Adam aside. "Lizzie is even more upset than she was yesterday. I can't put my finger on it, but something's happened. I have a bad feeling about Lizzie's testimony."

"I know. I saw something in her eyes, too," Adam said grimly.

Johnson had planned on calling several teachers and Mr. James before he called Mrs. Sutton, but he decided he needed to get the jury on his side fast. Mrs. Sutton's testimony would establish the discovery and authenticity of the journal, give a history of Lizzie's behavior, and hopefully, gain the sympathy of the jury.

After some general questions to calm her down, Johnson asked, "Mrs. Sutton, before last year, what kind of student was Lizzie?"

"She's always been a good student. Made mostly A's. She loved going to school."

Reggie quickly stood up and said, "Judge, please have the witness speak up. I can't hear a word she says."

"Please move closer to the microphone, Mrs. Sutton," Judge Williams admonished gently.

Mrs. Sutton slid her chair closer to the microphone and repeated her answer.

"Is Lizzie an honest child?" Johnson asked.

"Yes, I have never known her to lie to me. She has always been very responsible."

Adam turned to Sarah and said, "She's giving more information than the question elicits. This could be trouble when Parker gets a hold of her."

"How was her school attendance?" Johnson asked.

"Last year she had perfect attendance. She got an attendance award signed by the principal. We are so proud of the award we hung it in the dining room." Mrs. Sutton smiled at the memory of a happier time.

"When you confronted Lizzie with her journal, did she admit that it was a truthful account of what happened to her?"

"Not at first. At first, she said she made the stuff up. She didn't want to get Mr. Schafer in trouble."

Parker objected that the answer was not responsive to the question asked. The judge sustained the objection.

Johnson continued, "Did Lizzie subsequently admit that the material was true?"

"Yes, she did. After she learned that Mr. Schafer had mol...."

Mr. Parker jumped to his feet, "Objection, Your honor," he shouted. "The witness is about to discuss alleged former bad acts that you have ruled could not be presented."

"Objection, sustained. Mrs. Sutton, you must confine your the testimony to what you know first hand."

"Your honor, may I remind the court that Mr. Parker is the one who brought Ms. Abbott and Mr. Faulkner into the discussion during his opening statement, thus opening the door for my questions."

Williams gave Johnson a withering look and said, "Yes, that's right. I'll allow the witness to answer the question."

Johnson asked the court reporter to read his question. After the question was read, Mrs. Sutton continued, "Ms. Abbott told Lizzie that Mr. Schafer had molested her. That's when Lizzie admitted that Mr. Schafer molested her, and agreed to testify."

Johnson paused hoping the jury would feel the impact of Mrs. Sutton's statement. "Mrs. Sutton would you please describe how you came to know about Lizzie's journal?"

"I found it when I went in to clean her bedroom. It was a disaster area. I tried to ignore the mess, but eventually I gave in, and decided I had to clean it."

Several of the female jurors smiled and nodded indicating they knew exactly what Mrs. Sutton was saying.

Mrs. Sutton continued, "There was a spilled a carton of pop that had leaked into one of her dresser drawers. While I was emptying the drawer the journal fell onto the floor."

Johnson then asked her, "Are you in the habit of reading Lizzie's journal?"

"No. I didn't even know she had a journal."

"Why did you read it this time?"

"When I saw Mr. Schafer's name on the cover I got concerned."

"Why did Mr. Schafer's name cause you concern?"

"It wasn't just his name. Lizzie had written 'Mrs. Lizzie Schafer' and put a ring of hearts around the name."

"Thank you Mrs. Sutton. I only have a few more questions. Do you think what is written in the journal is true?"

"At first I hoped it wasn't, but now I believe it is. I believe that Mr. Schafer raped my little girl." Mrs. Sutton Sutton's voice cracked and she began to cry.

Before Parker could object Johnson said, "Thank you for your testimony, Mrs. Sutton, I know it's been difficult for you." Johnson turned to address the judge, "Your honor. I request a brief recess so that Mrs. Sutton can compose herself before cross examination."

"The court will recess for 15 minutes and resume at 10:00." Judge Williams banged his gavel and the previously silent gallery began to buzz.

At 10 o'clock Parker stood up, walked to the witness stand, and gently began his cross-examination. Parker's actions were choreographed. He was aware of his every movement. It had taken him years to perfect a style that some described as a 'magnetic.' He knew it was critical that he not alienate the jurors by seeming to attack Mrs. Sutton or her daughter.

The jury and most of the spectators hung on Parker's every word. He was the biggest celebrity that ever had come to Tupico Flats. Gordon Johnson was just like them, a small town good old boy, but Parker was exotic. They probably couldn't explain their feelings but most of the jury instantly liked him.

In a very soft voice he introduced himself to Mrs. Sutton and reminded her that she had sworn to tell the truth. With an understanding smile aimed at putting Mrs. Sutton at ease, he said, "I'd like to revisit the subject of Lizzie's journal. Mrs. Sutton, tell us again, please what your daughter told you when you first showed her the journal?"

"She said that she made it all up."

"Did she tell you that some of it was true?"

"No, at first she said none of it was true."

"You told Mr. Johnson that at first you didn't believe the journal was true, but you later came to believe that it was. Is that correct?"

"Yes."

Parker picked up the diary from the prosecution table and said, "Mrs. Sutton. Is this your daughter's journal?"

"Yes."

He handed the diary to Mrs. Sutton. "Please turn to the marked page and read the highlighted section."

"Mrs. Sutton took the journal and looked at the page that had been marked. Her face reddened and her voice quivered. "I'm embarrassed to read this out loud."

"Your honor. Please instruct the witness to read the passage."

Judge Williams said, "Mrs. Sutton, he said gently but firmly, you are required to read the passage Mr. Parker has indicated."

Mrs. Sutton began to read. Her voice was barely audible. "'Dear Journal, something really freaky happened today. Mr. Schafer and I were in the band storage room, and he put his hand down the back of my skirt and panties. When he touched me before, he just rubbed my bottom. Today he put his finger inside me. It hurt. I pulled away." Mrs. Sutton closed the journal and sobbed.

Parker waited for her to regain her composure. "Mrs. Sutton. Let me be sure that I understand what you previously stated.

When you read this passage the first time, did you believe it was true?"

Tears ran down her cheeks as she softly said, "I hoped it wasn't."

"That is not what I asked you." Parker was relentless. "Did you believe this passage described something that actually happened?"

"I didn't know if it was true."

"Your honor, please direct the witness to answer my question."

"Mrs. Williams, please answer Mr. Parker's question."

"Yes, I thought it was true."

"If it was true, would this be a behavior you would tolerate?"

"Of course not, this is why we are here today," Mrs. Sutton answered sharply. "Mr. Schafer sexually molested my daughter."

"After you read the journal and talked with Lizzie, did you call the police and tell them Mr. Schafer was molesting your daughter?"

"No."

"Did you call Social Services and tell them that Mr. Schafer was molesting your daughter?"

"No."

"Did you call the school and tell them that Mr. Schafer was molesting your daughter?"

"No"

"Mrs. Sutton. Isn't it true that if Ms. Abbott had not come to your house, you would never have told anybody about the journal?"

"I don't know. I think I would have contacted someone."

"Is it true that your daughter told Mr. Faulkner and Ms. Abbott that Mr. Schafer never behaved inappropriately?"

"She told them it happened."

"Mrs. Sutton. My question was did your daughter ever tell Mr. Faulkner and Ms. Abbott that Mr. Schafer never behaved inappropriately?"

"Yes, but...."

"Did your daughter tell Mr. Johnson that the material in the journal was 'made up?"

"Yes."

"Please tell us why you did not report Mr. Schafer's alleged behaviors to anyone."

"I did report it to the police and Mr. Johnson."

"Mrs. Sutton. How long after you found the journal and talked with your daughter did you make these allegations against Mr. Schafer?"

"I reported him as soon as I was sure."

"Mrs. Sutton. Isn't it true that Mr. Faulkner and Ms. Abbott came to your house and told you that they believed Mr. Schafer was abusing your daughter?

"Yes."

"So, tell us again why you didn't report your suspicions earlier." Parker's voice had lost much of its patient tone.

"Bringing up all these horrible acts is very painful and embarrassing for us. Both Lizzie and I strongly resisted all efforts to go public. I didn't want to make Lizzie the poster child for molested children. I didn't want her to be embarrassed in front of her friends. I didn't want to have to face my neighbors. Lizzie is very traumatized by what Mr. Schafer did to her. He must be stopped...."

"Your honor. Parker interrupted. "Mrs. Sutton's answer is not responsive. I request that the answer be stricken from the record, and that the jury be instructed to disregard it. And please, your honor, direct Mrs. Sutton to confine herself to answering the question I ask her."

"The jury is directed to disregard the last response from the witness. Mrs. Sutton, you must respond only to the question you are asked."

Parker continued, "Mrs. Sutton, did Ms. Abbott tell you that she believed Mr. Shafer had molested her twenty years ago?"

Johnson objected, "Your honor this question is irrelevant. I ask that you direct the witness not to answer.

"Overruled!" Williams said with authority. "The can's turned over and there are worms everywhere. He said sardonically. Mrs. Sutton, answer the question."

Mrs. Sutton asked to have the question repeated and then answered, "Yes."

"Did it strike you as odd that Mrs. Abbott waited so long to report this alleged molestation?"

"Mrs. Abbott said she tried to put the whole experience behind her. She said that all the recent publicity about teachers and priests molesting children brought it all back for her."

Parker raised his hands in a helpless gesture and looked at Judge Williams. Judge, please?"

Williams voice had lost all of its patience, "Mrs. Sutton answer yes or no! You are not permitted to editorialize."

"Yes. It struck me as odd," she said meekly.

"Mrs. Sutton. You waited to come forward after you read Lizzie's journal. Why did you wait?"

"When I first found out that Lizzie had been abused, I had a jumble of emotions. At first, I wanted to wring Schafer's neck.

I wanted to torch his house with him in it. I wanted someone to tell me what I was supposed to do to get my happy healthy child. I don't think she'll ever trust an adult again. It was so emotional, I just wanted the floor to open up and suck me in. I didn't want to face what had happened. When Lizzie started school I told her to 'mind her teachers.' This is all my fault."

Parker looked at the jury and rolled his eyes. He turned to Judge Williams and said with painstaking agitation, "Judge, could you please remind the witness once again that she must answer the question she is asked, that she is not permitted to give a speech."

Judge Williams was obviously annoyed. "Mrs. Sutton, do you understand the question?"

"Yes."

"Then please answer the question."

Mrs. Sutton looked Parker squarely in the eyes. From some remote source of inner strength she drew the courage to say, "You tell me, Mr. Parker. What parent wants her child on the front page of the local newspaper and on everyone's television screen saying, 'I had oral sex with a 50-year-old man in the band room?'" She continued to fix her gaze on Parker, daring him to answer.

Parker knew he had gone too far and was treading on very thin ice. He couldn't risk getting the jury upset with his be-havior. He pretended to look at his notes so that he could allow a few seconds to pass. "Are there any other reasons why you didn't come forward?" His voice was calm and his smile was back.

"Yes. Child molesters are smart. They don't molest their victims in front of witnesses. And, I've seen how lawyers, like you, act. I knew that a trial would be just like this one...

horrible." Her voice remained strong and her demeanor had been transformed to confident and justified.

Parker walked close to the witness stand and said, "Other than the journal which your daughter has said is a fabrication, do you have any direct evidence that Mr. Schafer did anything to your daughter?"

Mrs. Sutton looked confused. She stared at Parker and then said, "No."

Parker started to walk back to the defense table when he turned to Mrs. Sutton and asked. "Mrs. Sutton did you take your daughter to a doctor for a gynecological exam after you read her diary?"

"Yes, I did."

"And did the doctor have any opinions about whether your daughter was still a virgin?"

"Yes, he did."

"And what did the doctor say?

"He said Lizzie is still a virgin."

Parker wheeled around and strode to the defense table. "I have no further questions for this witness."

Sarah and Adam weren't sure how to regard Sutton's testimony. On the one hand Reggie got Mrs. Sutton to show that she didn't take any immediate action and that she really didn't have much evidence. On the other hand, Mrs. Sutton came across as a sincere mother who was devastated by what had happened to her daughter. The question about Lizzie's virginity caught them both by surprise. Since Lizzie never said that she and Schafer had had intercourse, the issue of her virginity never came up.

"I think we lost more than we gained." Adam whispered to Sarah. "Now it's all up to Lizzie."

Johnson stood, "I have one more question for this witness on redirect, your honor."

Judge Williams nodded his assent.

"Mrs. Sutton, is there anywhere in Lizzie's diary where she said she had vaginal intercourse with Mr. Schafer?"

"No."

"Thank you. I have no further questions for this witness."

Judge Williams excused Mrs. Sutton and adjourned court for the day.

The next day Johnson called three teachers to the stand. One told of often seeing Mr. Schafer and Lizzie alone in the music room. Another testified she frequently saw Lizzie riding in Mr. Schafer's car. The third said he remembered Lizzie having a hall pass from Mr. Schafer almost everyday excusing her from study hall to go to the band room.

When Parker cross-examined these witnesses he asked each one if they knew they were mandatory reporters of suspected child abuse. All acknowledged that they understood the law. Parker then asked each of them why they had not reported their suspicions to the police or to their principal. All said that it was only now, after they thought about what they had seen that they had suspicions. Each said at that at the time it just never crossed their mind that Mr. Schafer would harm a child.

Johnson's final witness before Lizzie was Mr. Charles James, the school janitor. After the arrest of Schafer began to get publicity Mr. James called Johnson and told him that Mr. Schafer's actions were suspicious when he came out of the music closet. James also told Johnson that he thought he saw a pair of girl's panties on the floor of the music closet. When Johnson had interviewed James he had to admit he thought the guy was scary. He didn't know how a jury would respond to him. James was huge. He looked like he belonged in the boxing ring or in the World Federation of Wrestling. Six foot six over three hundred pounds, shaved head, full beard, diamond stud earrings, and a gold tooth. After talking with Mr. James, Johnson became convinced that he could help Lizzie's case.

A murmur ran through the courtroom as James walked into the courtroom and up to the witness stand. For some he seemed vaguely familiar. They thought he might be a famous professional football player. He was dressed in a pressed brown work shirt and a pair of brown pants. He sat looking at his hands while he was being sworn in.

Johnson smiled as he approached the witness. He led James through questions about his education, his military service, and his combat injuries. James answered all questions with a soft, polite voice, never looking up from his hands.

"Mr. James, please tell the court where you are currently employed and what your job responsibilities are."

"I work at Tupico Flats Middle School. I'm the head custodian."

"How long have you worked at this school?"

"I've been there since I got home from my last tour of duty in Iraq, three years ago."

"Do you know who Mr. Schafer is?"

"Yes."

"If you see him in this court room, would you please point him out."

James pointed at Schafer and said, "That's him."

"Have you had occasion to observe Mr. Schafer in the music room?" James finally looked up from his hands and stared at Schafer. "Yes, I have."

"Could you please tell the court what you observed?"

"A while back I was making my rounds after school emptying wastepaper baskets and checking to be sure all the doors were locked. I went into the music room, emptied the wastepaper basket and then went over and rattled the handle of the music closet."

"Why did you do that?"

"The closet holds uniforms and band instruments. One of my assigned tasks is to check to be sure that all doors are locked at the end of the day."

"And was the music room closet locked?"

"Well, yes and no."

"Could you please tell the court what you mean by 'yes and no?'"

"Well, when I jiggled the doorknob I could see that the door was locked, but while I was still holding the door knob Mr. Schafer pushed the door open and jumped out at me. Gave me quite a start, actually."

"What do you mean, Mr. Schafer jumped out at you?"

"Well, I still had my hand on the doorknob and he whipped the door open and stepped out of the storage room right in front of me. It was as if he was trying to keep me from entering the closet."

Parker stood and said, "Objection witness is speculating beyond his personal knowledge."

Williams sustained the objection.

Johnson continued, "What happened next?"

"Mr. Schafer said he had put something in the music closet and that he would lock it up."

"Did you see anything that struck you as being strange or out of place?"

Parker objected, "Mr. Johnson's leading the witness your honor."

Williams sustained the objection.

Johnson rephrased his question, "What did you see in the music closet?"

"I caught a glimpse of a pair of girl's underpants in the middle of the room on the floor."

There was a buzz in the courtroom. Johnson waited a moment and said, "How did Mr. Schafer seem to you?"

"I don't know what you mean?"

"How did he look? How did he behave?"

"He was sweating. His shirt was un-tucked. His hair was mussed up. He seemed very nervous."

"Mr. James, what did you think was going on in the music closet?"

"I wondered if he had a girl..."

Parker jumped up. "Objection, your honor! This last question calls for speculation on the part of the witness."

"Objection sustained," Judge Williams said wearily. "Don't answer that question, Mr. James."

"Were you suspicious that there might be something sexual going on in the locked music room?"

"Yes."

Reggie started to object and then thought better of it and sat back down.

"No more questions at this time, your honor."

Adam and Sarah watched Parker for some sign that he was knocked off stride by James' testimony. Parker was smiling while he drew little stars all over his notebook pages. His staff had done a very through background investigation on all of Johnson's witnesses.

Parker walked rapidly to the witness stand and began his cross-examination. "Hello, Mr. James. Thank you for agreeing to testify today. And thank you for your service to our country. I have only a few questions. Is it true that you have been under the care of a psychiatrist for the past several years?"

James seemed surprised by the question. He looked Parker in the eyes. "Yes."

It was obvious that Johnson, Sarah, and Adam were caught off guard by this information.

"Is it true that sometimes you get confused?"

"Sometimes. Over one-half of all soldiers who have seen combat suffer some symptoms of post traumatic stress syndrome."

"What are some of these symptoms, Mr. James?"

Johnson objected. "Your honor this line of questioning is irrelevant and calls for a medical opinion."

"Overruled. You may answer the question Mr. James." Williams instructed.

James paused and resumed looking at his hands, which were folded in his lap. "I used to have flashbacks, wouldn't eat much, and I used to get angry over every little thing."

"Do you ever think you are back in Iraq, Mr. Parker?

"Sometimes. I used to."

Parker said, "Has your doctor prescribed any medications to help you?"

"Yes, I take Zoloft and Prozac."

"Mr. Parker. Do you know of any side affects of either Zoloft or Prozac?'

"My doctor told me that some people have headaches and get dizzy."

"Have you ever had any of these symptoms, Mr. James?"

"I got nauseated and had some dizziness."

"I am happy to know you're your doctor has found some drugs that have helped you. Were you on drugs the day you say you saw Mr. Schafer in the band closet?"

"I don't abuse drugs." James said angrily. "I have a prescription."

"Yes, we know you have a prescription." Parker reiterated condescendingly. Then his voice hardened. "My question was were you using Zoloft or Prozac the day you say you saw Mr. Schafer in the band room?"

"Maybe. I can't remember. I don't take the medicine every day."

Parker looked at the jury and sighed. "Mr. James have you ever gotten confused between what happened in Iraq and what is happening now?

"Not any more. I told you. I have a prescription."

"Mr. James do you believe that Mr. Schafer molested Lizzie?"

James was silent.

"Your honor will you direct the witness to answer the question."

"Answer the question, Mr. James, " Williams said.

James stared at Parker with a look of pure hate. "Yes, I believe he molested Lizzie. I think he should be in prison."

"Do you hate Mr. Schafer enough to lie about him?"

Johnson shot out of his chair, "Objection, "Your honor. Mr. Parker is baiting Mr. James."

Parker turned away from James, shook his head and said, "Your honor I have nothing further for this witness."

James left the witness stand, not quite sure what had just happened. But he knew that Parker had disrespected him. His anger toward Parker served to intensify his hatred of Schafer. That S.O.B had better not got off scot-free, he thought. He glared at Schafer as he walked past the defense table.

Chapter 36

Johnson called Lizzie as his final witness. He had saved her for last, knowing her testimony would be the most dramatic moment of the trial. Up until now Lizzie sat quietly at the prosecution table, an ordinary adolescent. She kept her hands crossed and her head down. As Sarah watched Lizzie walk to the witness stand she thought, now everyone is going to get a chance to judge for themselves, if they believed her.

Lizzie was terrified. Everyone was looking at her. She felt like she had one foot on dry land and the other on an iceberg. She was being pulled apart. No matter what she said it was going to be wrong. She knew her mother and Ms. Abbott said that Mr. Schafer was taking advantage of her, but they just didn't understand. He loved her and they were going to be married. Once in the witness box Lizzie stole a glance at the defense table. Schafer was smiling at her. She smiled and blushed when he winked at her.

"Lizzie," Johnson began, "do you understand you are under oath and are required by law to tell the truth?"

"Yes."

"May I call you Lizzie?"

"Yes."

"Do you know the difference between telling the truth and telling a lie?"

"Of course I do."

"How old are you, Lizzie?"

"14"

"What grade are you in?"

"Eighth."

"Lizzie, are you a student in Mr. Schafer's music class?"

"I used to be when I went to school. Now I go to school at home and I don't have any friends."

"You don't go to school any more?"

"No, I do my school work at home."

"Lizzie do you like school?"

"I used to."

"Why didn't you like it when you were going to school?"

"Everyone was mean to me."

"Lizzie, when you were going to school did you like being in Mr. Schafer's music class?"

"Yes."

"Did Mr. Schafer ever give you private instruction?"

"Yes?"

"How many days a week would he tutor you?"

"Sometimes one day a week, sometimes more."

Were there weeks when you had private lesions every day?"

"Yes"

"Lizzie, is it true that Mr. Schafer took you into the closet at the back of the music room for your lessons?" Johnson asked.

"It wasn't a closet. It was a storage room," Lizzie said defiantly.

The hair on the back of Adam's arms stood up. Something was wrong. Lizzie had an attitude. It was clear that Johnson was also surprised by her answer.

"Excuse me, Lizzie. Is it true that Mr. Schafer took you to the 'storage room' in the back of the music room?"

"Yes," Lizzie said.

"Why did you go into the storage room? Why weren't the lessons in the band room?"

"We went into the storage room so we didn't disturb any-one else in the school." Lizzie stole a peek at Schafer as she spoke. He was smiling and subtly nodded at her.

"When you were in the storage room with Mr. Schafer, did he ever rub your back?"

"Sometimes."

"Did you like him to touch you?"

Adam couldn't believe what Johnson had asked. If he wasn't careful he was going to single handily get Shepherd off, Adam thought. The last thing he should be doing is getting Lizzie to say she liked what Shepherd did to her.

Sarah looked at Adam questioningly, "What is Johnson doing?"

Johnson seemed to realize he had taken a miss-step and got back on track. He had prepared Lizzie on exactly how to answer the next question. Without waiting for Lizzie to answer his previous question he moved on.

"Lizzie, did Mr. Schafer ever touch you in an inappropriate manner?"

Parker got to his feet, "Your Honor, I object. He's leading the witness."

"Objection sustained," Judge Williams said.

Johnson came at his objective from another angle. "Lizzie, other than rubbing your back, what did Mr. Schafer do when you were in the band storage room?"

"I don't understand what you mean."

Johnson's heart began beating faster. What was she doing? They had gone over her testimony a half a dozen times. She knew the correct answers.

Sarah and Adam looked anxiously at one another.

"Well, Lizzie, when you were in the storage room with Mr. Schafer, did he ever put his hands on your shoulders?"

"Yes."

"How often would he put his hands on your shoulders?"

"Almost all the time."

Now we're back on track, Johnson thought. Before he could ask his next question Lizzie added, "My shoulders got stiff so Mr. Schafer gave me a shoulder massage."

Johnson ignored her comment, "Did Mr. Schafer put his hands under your clothing?"

Lizzie didn't answer.

Johnson repeated the question.

Lizzie looked at Mr. Schafer and answered meekly, "No."

Johnson saw that Lizzie was looking at Schafer and moved into her line of sight. "Did Mr. Schafer ever touch your breasts or bottom?"

"No, he never did any of those things."

Johnson' felt weak in the knees. He leaned on the witness railing. "Now, Lizzie, this is very important. Before the trial you told us that Mr. Schafer touched your breasts and your other private areas. Your journal details dozens of times when Mr. Schafer touched you inappropriately at school and in a hotel room on a band trip. You told us he put his finger inside of you and had oral sex with you. You wrote about it in your Journal. Let me ask you again."

Parker stood up, "Your honor, who is testifying here? It sounds like its Mr. Johnson. He's not a witness, is he?"

"I don't appreciate your sarcasm, Mr. Parker." Williams said sharply. "However, you had your opening statement, Mr. Johnson. If you have anything else to say save it for your summation."

Johnson turned back to Lizzie. She wouldn't look at him. He tried to convey to her with his the tone of his voice the importance of her answer. He slowly and precisely repeated the question moving slowly toward the witness stand as he spoke. "Lizzie, did Mr. Schafer ever put his hands under your clothing while you were with him in the storage room?"

Lizzie tried to see Schafer's face, but Johnson kept blocking her view. She shook her head slowly, and repeated her previous answer, "Mr. Schafer never did any of those things."

Johnson was having trouble breathing. He considered asking for a recess but that would make it even more obvious that his star witness was killing her own case. He was confused, but remembered Adam telling him he thought this might happen. Johnson held the railing tightly to keep the jury from seeing his hands shaking. Johnson turned to Lizzie and asked, "Lizzie, have you spoken with Mr. Schafer since the trial began?"

Lizzie looked around the room for somewhere to escape.

"Lizzie did you hear my question?"

Silence.

Adam squeezed Sarah's hand, "Here we go."

Adam and Johnson had discussed the possibility of asking the judge to declare Lizzie a hostile witness. It was a dramatic and seldom used strategy but he had run out of options. "Your honor, I'd like permission to treat Lizzie as a hostile witness."

Sarah was livid. She turned to Adam and through clinched teeth asked, "What in the hell is he doing. He's attacking our only hope for a conviction."

Adam replied, "A lawyer can't impeach his own witness unless the witness is declared hostile. This is the only way Johnson can challenge Lizzie's denials."

There was a rustling in the courtroom. Although most spectators didn't know exactly what this meant, most sensed something unusual had just happened.

Parker tilted his head and smiled wryly, it won't work, but nice try, he thought.

Judge Williams looked annoyed. But declared a fifteen-minute recess, and directed both attorneys to meet him in his chambers.

When the three were settled in the judge's office, Williams began, "Mr. Johnson, your request is highly irregular. Explain yourself."

Johnson knew he was skating on thin ice. "Your honor, Lizzie is clearly upset and confused. I need to be able to ask leading questions in order to help focus her testimony. I had no idea that she was going to change her testimony. It is critical to the county's case that I am able to show that Lizzie was telling the truth earlier and is lying now."

Parker continued, "Judge Williams, Mr. Johnson is trying to confuse you. It seems clear that Lizzie lied before and is telling the truth now."

"Mr. Parker, Williams said sarcastically, I really appreciate your concern that I may be too stupid to understand what Mr. Johnson is doing. However, I agree with his assessment. I am going to allow him to treat Ms. Sutton as a hostile witness."

Johnson had to control his joy. He had finally won a battle.

Parker tried to look disappointed. However, he believed the war was already won.

When the court reconvened and Judge Williams announced his ruling, the room buzzed. The sound of reporters' texting could be heard. Johnson knew his case probably came down to the next few minutes.

Judge Williams banged his gavel for order. He turned his gaze on Lizzie who had been reseated on the witness stand. "Ms. Sutton, please remember you are under oath."

Johnson resumed his questioning. "Lizzie. Did Mr. Schafer contact you last night?"

Judge Williams leaned forward in his chair and looked back and forth between Johnson and Parker. Any attempt to intimidate a witness into changing her testimony is a federal offense and grounds for a mistrial. He wondered if Johnson was going to be able to show that Schafer had intimidated Lizzie.

Lizzie hesitated. Finally, in a voice so faint it could hardly be heard she said, "Yes."

Judge Williams and Parker both sat straighter in their chairs. Williams reached for his gavel and Parker grabbed Schafer's forearm.

"How did Mr. Schafer contact you?" Johnson continued.

"He called my cell last night."

"What did he say to you?"

Lizzie squirmed in her chair. "That's private. I don't have to tell you about personal calls," she said.

Johnson looked at Judge Williams.

"I want to hear her answer before I decide if we have a mistrial here," Williams said angrily. "Lizzie you must answer the question."

"Tell us what Mr. Schafer said to you, Lizzie?" Johnson repeated.

"He asked me how I was holding up."

"What else did he tell you?"

"That's all he said."

"Lizzie you are still under oath. You must tell the court the truth. He told you not to tell us what he did to you. Didn't he?"

"No. He just said that he was worried about how I was doing."

The buzz in the courtroom grew louder. Mindy Hailer, juror number fourteen, looked from Lizzie to Williams to Johnson and back to Lizzie. In another place and time her befuddled look would have been humorous. The other jurors were as nonplused as Hailer. They all wondered if Lizzie was telling the truth now or was she lying?

Johnson felt he had done some damage to Schafer. He wanted to get away from the topic of the phone conversation before Lizzie said more. She had now become a loose cannon. The first rule of examination was never to ask a question where the answer was unknown. Johnson had no idea what she might say next.

Johnson picked up Lizzie's journal and walked to the witness box. He was well aware that he needed to have the jury sympathetic to Lizzie. He also was aware that anything he did from this point on could make him the villain. His next move, though necessary would be tricky.

"Lizzie, is this your journal?"

"Yes."

"How long have you been keeping a journal?"

"Since the second grade."

"How often do you write in your journal?"

"Almost every night."

"What kind of things do you write in your journal?"

Lizzie didn't answer right away. She saw the trap. If she said she wrote important stuff in it, she would be admitting what she wrote was true.

"I just write about things I'm thinking about."

Johnson handed Lizzie the journal. "Please turn to the page that is marked with the red tab and read what you wrote."

Lizzie's hands were trembling as she took the journal and opened it. She read in a soft voice. "Today was the first day of school. I like all of my teachers. I'm excited to be taking band. Middle school is not as scary as I thought it would be."

"What is the date of that entry?

"September 15."

"Is that a true statement?"

"Yes."

"Please read what is marked with the blue tab."

Lizzie read, "Mrs. Walker is really funny. She makes us all want to learn math."

"Is that a true statement?"

"Yes."

"Please read what is marked with the yellow tab."

"Music is really fun. I like Mr. Schafer. All the kids think he is the best teacher in the school."

"Is that a true statement?"

"Yes."

"Please read what is marked with the orange tab."

"Mr. Schafer is really popular. I'm so lucky to be in his class."

"Is that a true statement?"

"Yes."

"Now, please go to the section that is marked with the purple tab."

Lizzie's voice became even softer. "I never want to go to school again. Mr. Schafer was so mean to me today. He made fun of me and said I was the worst student he ever had."

"Is that a true statement?"

"Yes."

"Turn to the black tab and read what you wrote on that page."

Lizzie looked at the page and frowned. Her voice was almost inaudible. "I don't want to read this."

"Your honor, please direct the witness to read the passage," Johnson requested.

Judge Williams patiently instructed Lizzie again. "Ms. Sutton please read what Mr. Johnson has asked you to read."

Lizzie's face got red. She read softly, her voice thin and panicky. "I love Mr. Schafer. Today he told me he was going to marry me when I got to be sixteen. He must really love my butt. Today he touched my butt all during our practice."

"Lizzie, is that a true statement?"

Adam and Sarah squeezed each other's hand. They knew how much was ridding on this answer.

Lizzie paused and tried to look at Mr. Schafer. Once again, Johnson had placed himself to block her line of vision. She looked at her mother who was nodding her head up and down.

"No! That's not true. That never happened, " Lizzie shouted.

Johnson felt sick to his stomach. His throat was so dry he was afraid to try and speak. He had to get Lizzie to change her story. He would have to continue to attack her.

"Lizzie, why did you write what you did in your journal?" Johnson croaked.

"Mr. Schafer is the most popular teacher in school. All the girls have crushes on him. I was just making up stories."

"Lizzie, we have talked about what Mr. Schafer did to you many times over the past months. Didn't you tell me that Mr. Schafer molested you?"

"Yes."

Adam was watching the jurors as Lizzie spoke. She had their complete attention. Their faces reflected the same shock that everyone else in the courtroom felt. They were all asking themselves, "What had just happened?"

"Lizzie, earlier you told us that you knew the difference between telling the truth and telling a lie, didn't you?

"Yes," She murmured.

"Do you remember when we talked yesterday and you told me what Mr. Schafer did to you?"

"Yes."

"Do you remember when you told me that what you said was true?"

"Yes."

"Then please tell us why you told me that Mr. Schafer molested you, if it wasn't true?"

No! No! That's not how to ask that question, Adam thought.

Lizzie wiped the tears from her eyes, looked directly at Johnson, and said, "Because you, Mr. Faulkner, Ms. Abbott, and my mom kept telling me that Mr. Schafer had hurt other girls and it was up to me to put him in jail." Lizzie was choking back tears. "I can't lie and say what you told me to say. You knew I didn't want to say anything bad about Mr. Schafer. Why did you make me come here?"

Lizzie was becoming more and more agitated. At the defense table Schafer began to relax. Lizzie is actually going to pull this off, he thought. She is going to save me. He knew the cameras were watching him, so he was carful not to show any emotion, but inside he was cheering Lizzie's performance.

Johnson was desperate. "Lizzie do you still love Mr. Schafer?"

Lizzie looked at him quizzically, wondering if this was another trick. Softly she said, "Yes."

"Do you want to marry him?"

"Yes."

"Are you afraid that he might go to jail if he's convicted today?"

"Yes."

Johnson paused and then said, "Do you think people who are in love should be faithful and loyal to one another?"

"Yes."

"Should people who are in love protect one another?"

"Yes."

"Lizzie, do you love Mr. Schafer so much that you are lying to keep him out of jail?"

Lizzie saw the trap too late. She looked around the courtroom in panic. Then she started to cry. She sobbed so hard her shoulders shook.

"Thank you, Lizzie. No further questions for this witness," Johnson said. He grimly walked back to his seat, not able to even pretend he wasn't devastated.

The courtroom was electric with tension as everyone waited for Parker to cross-examine Lizzie. Sarah sat silently, tears streaming down her cheeks. Adam put his arm around her. She shrugged it off. "By God, I swear he won't get away with what he has done," she said through clinched teeth.

During Johnson's questioning Parker was debating his options when his turn came. He knew that there was a danger that he would look like he was badgering or attacking this Lizzie. He considered not cross-examining her. After all, Johnson had done a pretty good job of casting reasonable doubt on Lizzie's testimony.

Parker rose, smiled at the jury, turned to judge Williams, and said, "The defense has no questions of this witness, your honor." Parker remained standing and continued, "Your honor, the defense moves that the charges against Mr. Schafer be dismissed. The prosecution has not presented sufficient evidence that a crime has been committed."

"Motion denied," Judge Williams said.

Johnson rose and stood by his desk for a moment. He then said, "The prosecution rests, your honor."

"The court is adjourned until 9:00 a.m. tomorrow morning,"

There was a murmur in the courtroom as reporters began to post their blogs. Jake Fowler, a well know local blogger, wrote. "The defense has not even begun presenting its case. But to this reporter the outcome is clear. This trial is over. James Schafer is not going to jail."

Chapter 37

Reggie Parker spent the hours before heading to the courthouse on the phone talking with his Las Vegas staff about his next case. There was nothing left for him to do to prepare Schafer's case. He was ready to begin his defense. He had twenty witnesses who were prepared to testify that they had never observed Schafer doing anything inappropriate. But, Lizzie's testimony caused him to change his mind about his strategy.

Judge Williams called the court to order at precisely 9:00 am. He peered up over his half-glasses at Parker. "Is the defense ready?"

"Yes, Your Honor." He turned and whispered to Schafer. "Remember. Keep your answers short when Johnson cross examines you."

Then Parker turned to the bench, "Your honor the defense is only going to call one witness. I call Mr. Jim Schafer to the stand."

There was a gasp from the spectators. The bloggers began writing furiously.

Johnson was stunned. He had spent months preparing to question each of the twenty people on Parker's witness list.

Schafer was incredibly nervous. Yet, he smiled confidently at the jury and tried to act casual as he walked to the stand. He was used to lying. He knew he was a consummate actor. He also knew that this was his most important performance.

The bailiff approached Schafer. "Please put your left hand on the Bible and raise your right hand. Do you swear or affirm to tell the truth the whole truth and nothing but the truth so help you God?"

"I do."

"State your full name for the court."

"James Richard Schafer."

"Be seated."

Parker wasted no time, "Mr. Schafer, I have only a few questions for you. How many years have you been a teacher?"

"Thirty years."

"During these thirty years, how many teaching awards have you won?"

"I've won ten teaching awards."

"Tell us about some of them."

"Well, in the five years I've been at Tupico Flats I've been named the outstanding teacher in the district twice, and I was named the outstanding middle school teacher in Nevada two years ago. Last year I was a finalist for national music teacher of the year."

"During the time you have been a teacher at Tupico Flats Middle School, how many times have your band students received the highest award at the state music competition?"

"My band students won every competition we entered."

"Mr. Schafer, how would you characterize your relationship with your students?

Schafer smiled. Parker and he had gone over this series of questions and his answers dozens of times. "I care deeply about the welfare of my students. With all of the violence, drugs, and teen-aged suicide; I'm convinced that every child can benefit from having a teacher who really cares for them. As far as I know, none of my former students has gotten in trouble with the law."

"Mr. Schafer, have you ever put your hands on a student?"

"Yes. I don't think you can teach music, or any other subject for that matter, without touching the child in a professional manner."

"Please describe a circumstance when you have put your hands on a student."

"I might have to show a student how to hold the instrument properly. I might put my hand on their stomach to be sure they're breathing correctly. I might pat their shoulders to show approval. Research has shown that a brief touch on the arm or shoulder is a strong form of reinforcement and encouragement."

"Thank you." Parker paused and looked down at the floor. He walked near the witness stand, turned and looked Schafer in the eyes. "Mr. Schafer, are you a child molester?"

"No, Mr. Parker, I'm not," Jim responded emphatically.

"Mr. Schafer, are you a pedophile?"

"No, Mr. Parker, I'm not."

"Did you molest Lizzie Sutton?"

"No, Mr. Parker, I've never molested Lizzie Sutton or anyone else. he added," shifting his gaze briefly to Sarah.

Damn! Parker thought. How many times did I tell this jerk not to ad lib?

Adam and Johnson both tried to conceal their surprise. By alluding to other students, Parker may have just given them the chance to bring in testimony about Schafer's other victims. Maybe we have a chance, after all, Adam thought.

Parker paused. "Mr. Schafer, what impact has this trial had on your life?"

Johnson jumped to his feet. "Your honor, I object on the grounds that this question is not relevant to the issue before the court."

"Objection overruled." Williams said, "You may answer the question, Mr. Schafer."

Schafer turned from Parker and addressed the jury, "It is very difficult for me to sit here and describe the impact that this false charge has done to me and my family. I've wondered every day why Lizzie and her mother have made up these horrible, vicious lies about me. Only they and God know the answer to that question."

Shit! Parker thought. Another adlib. Throwing God in made Schafer look far too self-righteous. It's time to get him off the stand.

"I have no further questions for Mr. Schafer. The defense rests."

Sarah turned to Adam, "This is bad. This is really bad," she whispered.

"It's not over yet, Sarah. Reggie may have just given us an opening," Adam whispered back."

Adam nodded to Johnson as he approached Schafer.

As Johnson walked toward Schafer he said, "Mr. Schafer, how many years have you been a teacher?"

"About thirty."

"How many school districts have you worked for?"

"Five"

"How many states have you taught in?"

"Four."

You've worked in five school districts in four states in thirty years?"

"Yes."

"That seems like a lot of moving around. Were you successful at Deer Lake School District?"

"Yes."

"Yet, you left town without even saying good by to your fellow teachers or students."

Parker stood and asked, "Is there a question there somewhere, your honor?"

"When a popular teacher leaves a school isn't there usually some type of going away party?"

"Sometimes."

"Were you happy when you were teaching at New Haven, Pennsylvania?"

"Yes."

"Was there a going away party for you when you left New Haven?"

"I don't like parties very much."

Parker stood and said, "Your honor Mr. Johnson is going on some type of fishing expedition. I object to this total line of questioning on the grounds that it is irrelevant."

Judge Williams paused for a few moments. "I will allow the questions. Mr. Johnson, please get to your point."

Johnson thanked the judge and turned his attention back to Schafer. "Were you happy when you left all of your teaching jobs?

"Yes."

"Why did you leave five school districts where you were successful and happy?"

"I am always looking for a new challenge. In each district the music program was very weak when I was hired. I like to build programs. When they are going well, I get bored and want a new challenge."

"Is it true that in two of your past schools, you left town shortly after one of your students died?"

"That had nothing to do with why I moved."

"Please answer the question I asked. Is it true that in two of your past schools, you left town shortly after one of your music students died?"

"Yes."

"Johnson moved close to Schafer and rested his hands on the witness stand rail. "Mr. Schafer. How long has your last name been Schafer?"

The jurors and several spectators looked confused.

Schafer took a few deep breaths to slow his breathing. He didn't seem as surprised as Jonson expected. "Well, that's my name."

"I know it is your name today." Let me ask the question in a different way. "What name is on your birth certificate?"

Again, Schafer hesitated.

Johnson waited patiently for his answer.

After another moment Judge Williams leaned forward and told Schafer to answer the question.

Looking unsure of himself for the first time in the trial began Schafer answered, "Anthony Robert Shepherd,"

"Is it true that you changed your name shortly after you left New Haven School District?"

"Yes."

"What were you trying to hide when you changed your name?"

Parker got to his feet and objected, "He's badgering the witness."

Williams upheld the objection.

Johnson approached Schafer and continued his cross-examination. "Mr. Schafer, was Lizzie Sutton a student in your music class?"

"Yes."

"What kind of student was she?"

"She was about average."

"Did you give her special treatment?"

"No."

"Isn't it true that you met with her outside of class several times a week?"

"Yes, that's true."

"And you don't consider that unusual, especially for an "average" student?"

"No."

"Is it true that you took Lizzie Sutton into the music room closet and locked the door when you gave her music lessons?"

"Objection! Compound question, your honor," Parker barked.

"Objection sustained."

"Okay, I'll break it down. Is it true you took Lizzie into the music room closet for her lessons?"

"It was a storage room."

Johnson threw up his hands and repeated the question for the third time. Despite his best efforts to hide it, his voice was tinged with irritation. "Did you take Lizzie into the storage room for her lessons?"

"Yes."

"When you took her into the storage room, did you lock the door?"

"Never!"

"Do you recall Mr. James' testimony when he said he found you locked in that same music storage room?"

"Yes, but I have no idea why he would say that. It's not true."

Did you ever give Lizzie a back rub while you were in the storage room with her?"

"I may have massaged her neck once or twice. Sometimes students get tense when they are under stress."

"Did you ever touch Lizzie Sutton underneath her clothing?"

"Certainly not."

Johnson continued asking Schafer questions for the next thirty minutes. Schafer denied any inappropriate contact with Lizzie. For the first time in this trial, the jury was beginning to get bored. They were tuning out Johnson's questions and Schafer's answers. Johnson could feel the case slipping through his fingers.

Johnson looked directly at Schafer and asked one more time emphatically, "Did you molest Lizzie Sutton?"

Schafer replied just as emphatically. "No!"

Johnson turned and walked slowly to his table. He picked up a sheaf of papers and flipped through them slowly. He returned them to the table and gazed off to the back of the courtroom. "So, Mr. Schafer, how many other students *have* you abused over the years?"

Parker shot to his feet. "Objection, your Honor! The question crosses into an area that you have ruled may not be admitted."

Before Williams could speak, Johnson responded, "Your Honor, Mr. Parker and Mr. Schafer opened this area of questioning when Mr. Schafer volunteered that he had quote, 'never molested anyone else.' We have the right to challenge that assertion."

Judge Williams was clearly annoyed. "In my chambers," he ordered. He banged the gavel with a vengeance. "The court is recessed for fifteen minutes."

Judge Williams led both attorneys into his office. His rapid pace and stony silence signaled his anger at the recent development, but before he could speak, Parker began his argument. "You can't get into the issue of alleged past bad acts. It's all speculation and has already been ruled inadmissible."

Johnson shot back, "Schafer opened the door. We're allowed to walk in."

Judge Williams turned and faced both of them. "Quiet! Both of you! Mr. Johnson you were warned not to try and bring in alleged past bad acts. There's no foundation for your question, and I'm not going to allow it."

"But, Judge Williams, Schafer said he didn't molest anyone else. We have a right to challenge that statement."

"Mr. Johnson, you know better than that."

Johnson was not about to give up on his last best chance. "Judge Williams please reconsider your ruling?"

Judge Williams' face was red and his voice acidic as he leaned across his desk and spat, "You are very close to being ruled in contempt of this court, Mr. Johnson. You will confine your questions to those that are relevant to the case before this court. Do you understand, Mr. Johnson?"

"Yes, your Honor." Johnson answered in a resigned tone.

Judge Williams reconvened the court and said, "The objection is sustained. Mr. Schafer, don't answer that last question."

Johnson's disappointment had turned to anger. He was barely able to control his voice as he turned to the judge and said, "I have no further questions for this witness. The prosecution rests."

Adam was angry, too. He'd know all along the case was weak. In addition, everything that could go wrong had gone wrong. Closing arguments represented their last hope of nailing Schafer. Johnson faced a monumental challenge. Adam looked over at the defense table. Both Parker and Shepherd were doing a poor job of concealing their confidence about the verdict.

Parker rose and said, Your honor. If I may, I have a few questions on re-direct.

Williams nodded and Parker approached the witness. "Now, Mr. Schafer, let's get this name change straightened out," Parker said to Schafer. Mr. Johnson has implied there is some nefarious reason behind changing name from Tony Shepherd to James Schafer. He further implied that you changed your name in order to hide your true identity. Is that true?"

"No." Schafer said as he shifted his gaze to the jury. "My father physically abused my mother and me until he deserted us when I was five years old. His name was Tony Shepherd, Senior. I always hated him and hated the name he gave me."

"How did you come up with the name Schafer?"

"I did some genealogy research and learned that in 1916, when my great-great-grand father, Jakob Schafer, came to America, he translated his German surname and given name to English because he wanted to become an American as fast as possible. Schafer is German for shepherd. I am proud that he wasn't the passive victim of an Ellis Island bureaucratic whim, but a striving man who sought to better his life. I decided to disown my father and honor my great-great-grandfather by legally changing my name to James Schafer."

"Thank you, Mr. Schafer." Parker turned to the jury and smiled. He then turned to the judge and said, "your honor, the defense rests."

Chapter 38

Johnson worked late that evening putting the finishing touches on his closing. His head was throbbing and he needed a shower. Today was grueling and he knew the next day would be worse. Just as he was about to turn out the light and head for home District Attorney Sail entered the room. "Hi Gordon, how's it going?" He asked far too cheerfully to suit Johnson.

"Not great. And why are you asking now?" He asked icily. "I mean, I appreciate your interest, but why haven't you given me any help with this trial. You've seldom returned my calls and don't seem to have time to meet with me. We've hardly spoken during this whole trial." Two months ago Johnson would not have dreamed of talking to his boss in such a fashion. Tonight, he didn't care. In fact, being fired almost seemed like a blessing.

Sail was quiet for a few moments. He sat on the corner of Johnson's desk. Ignoring Johnson's outburst he asked, "What do you think about offering Schafer a plea bargain?"

Johnson could only stare open mouthed. If they were going to offer a plea, they should have done it months ago. Before he could censor himself he replied, "You can't be serious!"

Sail said, "We need to be realistic," Sail counseled. "I was in court today. The jury isn't buying what you are selling. You don't have the votes."

"I know I've made some mistakes, but on the whole I think I've done as well as anyone could with what I've had to work with. I don't want to settle this case if there's even a sliver of a chance for a conviction.

Sail said, "I was thinking that the best thing to do might be to have Schafer surrender his teaching license, admit and apologize for a lapse of judgment, and give him a very strict probation. Could you sell this to Parker?"

Johnson's mind was reeling. It seemed that Sail was trying to sabotage the case. However, Sail was his boss so he had no choice but to talk with Parker. As soon as Sail left his office, Johnson called Adam. After all, Adam had been his source of support and advice when Sail abandoned the case.

Adam and Sarah were in the hotel bar commiserating when Adam's cell phone vibrated. A glance at the caller ID told him he needed to answer the call.

"This is Adam."

"You're not going to believe what just happened." Johnson said without bothering to give a greeting. "Sail just stopped by and practically ordered me to offer Schafer a plea bargain."

Adam was speechless.

"What's the matter?" Sarah asked.

Adam rolled his eyes and signaled for her to wait. "He can't be serious. What is he thinking? You offer a deal when you have something he wants. He said into the phone "Parker and Schafer think they are going to win."

"I know. I can't believe it, either."

"What's the point, we both know this case is going south."

"I know, but I don't see that I have much choice. I have to present the idea to Parker. If Parker's interested I'll need to talk with Mrs. Sutton to see how she feels about it. By the way she's acted over the past week and by the way Lizzie's testimony went today, I think she'll agree if we can get an admission from Schafer."

Johnson called Parker and got right to the point. "Reggie, the D.A. has suggested we drop the charges and end the trial if Schafer agrees to surrender his teaching license, admits and apologizes for his laps of judgment, and agrees to be on probation for five years."

"Too little too late." Parker said. "We both know Schafer is going to walk. See you in court tomorrow, my friend. Parker smiled as he hung up the phone.

There was no need for Johnson to call Mrs. Sutton.

The courtroom was packed two hours prior to the start of today's proceedings. The overflow again filled the auditorium where folding chairs and a big screen television had again been set up. Parker was renowned for his eloquent summations. Everyone in Tupico Flats wanted to be able to say they had heard and seen him in person.

Johnson looked around the courtroom as he walked to the prosecution table. Sail was sitting in the back row near the door. Early that morning, Johnson had informed Sail that Parker and Schafer had rejected their offer. Johnson thought Sail overreacted to this news. Sail had told him angrily that his job was to follow directions and get Schafer to agree to a plea. He made it clear that he was not pleased with Johnson's work. He suggested that Johnson might want to consider going back to private practice.

Johnson tried to ignore Sail's comments. However, he could feel his heart rate increasing as he thought about his unfair treatment.

At 9:00 o'clock sharp Judge Williams declared the court in session in an authoritative tone tinged with obvious relief. Ladies and gentlemen, good morning. We are ready to proceed with the closing arguments of counsel in this case. Because the County has the burden of proof in the case, you will hear first from Assistant County Attorney Johnson. Mr. Parker, counsel for the defendant, will have an opportunity to argue, then Mr. Johnson will have an opportunity for a rebuttal argument. Following the arguments, I will instruct you on the law. We will take our usual recess except we will limit the noon recess to an hour today. We want to give a full and fair opportunity to both sides to present their arguments in the case, and we'll also ask counsel to help us with timing the recesses so that we don't interrupt at a time that may be inconvenient for the lawyer making the argument.

"Mr. Johnson, you're going to present the Government's case."

"I am, your Honor."

Johnson was focused on the job at hand as he approached the jury box. He was smiling, but the smile was obviously forced. "Ladies and gentlemen of the jury, clearly Mr. Schafer is a very charming and popular man. It seems that the general opinion is that Mr. Schafer is also an excellent teacher.

Well, Mr. Schafer is not an excellent teacher. Excellent teachers don't sexually abuse their students. Mr. Schafer has used his charm and popularity to fly under the radar of parents, teachers, and this community. Don't let him fly under your radar. Lizzie Sutton has endured more than any young child should ever have to endure. She has been harmed, both physically and psychologically.

Mr. Schafer met with Lizzie Sutton over fifty times in the music room at Tupico Flats Middle School. Over the course of these meetings he touched her breasts, touched her bottom, touched her vagina, inserted his finger in her vagina, and performed oral sex on her. He stole her childhood. The trauma of being molested by her teacher will have a negative influence her entire life and her relationship with others."

Johnson watched the faces of the jury as he spoke. It was clear to him, that despite his best efforts, he was not engaging them. Their faces didn't show the emotion that his words should have provoked. Johnson knew that in order for the jurors to become emotionally connected to Lizzie's experience he would have to help them visualize how they would feel Lizzie's position. "May I ask you to close your eyes for a few seconds and travel back in time to when you were a child. What would you do if the most popular teacher in the school told you how special you were? How would you feel if this teacher told you he was in love with you? What would you do if this teacher told you he would ruin your reputation if you did not do what he told you to do?"

It wasn't working. Johnson could see that most of the Jury continued to stare at him when he asked them to close their eyes.

At the defense table Schafer desperately tried to look confident. He knew that the jury could see his face and he did not want to look worried or afraid. Parker calmly watched Johnson.

"Obviously, Mr. Schafer's abuse of Lizzie Sutton has caused her to be confused and emotional. She still believes Schafer loves her. She's still convinced that Schafer is going to marry her. He has brainwashed her to the point that she can't separate reality from fiction. Please think of your own children. What do you think your young, impressionable child would do if the most popular teacher in the school told her she was beautiful, she was smart, she was very mature for her age, and that he was in love with her. Are you confidant that your daughter couldn't be seduced?"

Johnson's argument was building up steam. His formerly factual tone shifted to one of urgency. "James Schafer spent an inordinate amount of time with Lizzie. He has admitted to taking her into a storage room three or four days a week. We have proven he got her out of her free period and had her meet privately with him in the music room. He molested Lizzie in the school building and in a motel room while on a band trip. Parents who send their children to school have the right to expect that the teachers will be ethical and moral people. Schafer is not ethical. He is not moral. He is narcissistic, selfish, and committed to fulfilling his own sexual fantasies. He is a child molester. You must look past Schafer's image and look at the damage he did to Lizzie Sutton. If you do that, you have no choice. You must convict Schafer of all charges." Johnson paused. He was surprised by the emotions he was feeling. He believed what he was saying and he desperately wanted the jury to believe him. He stepped close to the jury, paused, and then said softly, "It's about justice, really. Thank you, ladies and gentlemen, for your attention and your service on this jury."

He tried to smile as he looked at each juror as he walked past the jury box. Only three or four of the jurors looked back at him. The rest avoided his gaze as he walked to his seat. Johnson could feel the eyes of the spectators. He was certain that Schafer molested Lizzie, but he couldn't suppress his anger at her. She sabotaged him in front of the whole town. When he reached his seat he sat down, leaned back, and whispered regretfully to Adam, "I'm sorry. I don't think the jury bought a word of my closing statement."

Adam silently agreed with him.

Parker stood and confidently walked to the jury box. His smile was genuine and hypnotic. Most of the jurors smiled back at him expectantly. "Ladies and gentlemen, I know you take your responsibility as a juror very seriously. Very fateful charges have been lodged against James Schafer. However, Mr. Johnson and the county have presented a case that has fallen far short of its burden of proof. "You've had the opportunity to hear the evidence presented by Mr. Johnson, such as it was. He presented an expert that contradicted himself. He presented a journal that is a work of fiction. And most damning to his case, his star witness, the alleged victim, recanted her previous testimony and denied that Jim Schafer molested her."

Parker walked over to Mr. Schafer and stood behind him. As he spoke, he placed his hand on Schafer's shoulder. "You also had the chance to hear from Jim Schafer. But you already know him. He's an award-winning teacher with stellar reputation. He's beloved by his students and their parents. There are literally thousands of children who have benefited from Jim Schafer's compassion and teaching skill. Let's be honest. Jim Schafer is the best teacher that ever worked in Tupico Flats. He's probably the best teacher that will ever work here. Reggie paused, patted Schafer on the shoulder and then walked to the jury box. "You have a duty to examine the evidence and decide whether, beyond a reasonable doubt, Jim Schafer committed the crimes he is accused of." Parker slowly looked at each member of the jury. "Your decision is easy. I'm confident that you will do your duty and find him not guilty of all charges. It has been a pleasure speaking with you. Jim Schafer's fate is now in your hands. Thank you for your time and attention."

Judge Williams adjourned the court for the day.

Chapter 39

The next morning Judge Williams called the court to order and gave his instructions to the jury. "A jury plays an important role in the search for justice. It is your duty to follow the law as contained in these instructions and to apply it to the facts that you believe have been proven from all of the evidence in the case. In performing your duty you must not permit yourself to be influenced by sympathy, bias, prejudice, or favor to any party.

"Your first responsibility, when you go to the jury room, is to select one of your fellow jurors to serve as your foreperson, to preside over your deliberations, and to speak for you here in court. You will take the verdict form the bailiff will give you to in the jury room. When you have reached your decision, your foreperson will fill out the form, date and sign it, and return it to the courtroom."

Bill Kennedy marched into the jury room first and took a seat at the head of the long conference table. He smiled and nodded at each of his fellow jurors as they filed into the room and took their seats. He knew he was the smartest person in the room. Jurors looked expectantly at Kennedy, acknowledging the fact that he was their leader. They didn't know that Kennedy had business out of town in ten days and needed to wrap up this trial by next Friday. Kennedy watched Katilin as she pranced into the room and thought about how easy it was going to be to hook up with her after the trial was over.

From the first day of the trial Katilin had made it clear that she was interested in him. Kennedy caught her eye, smiled, and winked at her. He then waited for the inevitable.

After a minute or two of silence, Katilin cleared her throat and said, "The judge said our first job is to select a foreperson. I think Bill would do a great job." Katilin waited for a reaction. There were murmurs of assent around the table. "Is there anyone else who would like to be considered as foreperson?" No one spoke. Katilin smiled triumphantly. "Well Bill, looks like you're in charge." Bill nodded modestly. "If you want me to serve, I will. How do you want to proceed?"

Agnes Welch smiled to herself as she looked at Kennedy. She thought he was an egotistical fascist. She hated the way he walked around like he thought he is was still in the marines and like he was god's gift to women. She had been watching the way he had acted around Katilin doing everything short of groping her. Do guys think they can stare at our breasts without us knowing it? I don't freaking care how he wants us to vote, I'm going to go against him, she vowed to her self.

Julie Summon waddled into the room sweating like a pig. Large circles had formed under her arms and she smelled of old lady perfume. The other jurors tried to find seats as far away from her as they could. Mr. Schafer was one of Summon's favorite customers, but she had kept that to her self. She wasn't going to allow him to go to jail.

Kennedy cleared his throat while glancing down the front of Kaitlin Romin's sweater as she bent down to pick up her notebook, and then said, "Let's start by getting a feel for where we are. We'll go around the table and take a straw vote as to Schafer's guilt or innocence."

The vote was seven not guilty and four guilty. The vote surprised and disturbed Kennedy, he worried he would not get a quick verdict. Agnes Welch voted, guilty. In a cigarette-hoarse voice she said with some authority, "I suggest we review the testimony before we vote again."

Kennedy shot her a withering look. He resented the implication that he had done something wrong or that he needed her help.

For the next two days each juror read all the witness testimony. They asked for copies of Lizzie's school records, her doctor's medical records, floor plans of the middle school, and Dr. Ross' report. Welch was pleased to see that a few of the jurors who initially voted not guilty seemed to be wavering. She had become Kennedy's nemesis. Each time he made a point in favor of Schafer she had a counter point.

At the beginning of the third day of deliberation Kennedy was becoming impatient. He was used to giving orders and having his orders followed. "Okay, we've reviewed the all of the transcripts and exhibits, I suggest we make two lists." As he talked he went to the grease board and drew a line down the middle. "Let's start by listing all the points supporting a not guilty verdict. To save time we'll discuss each item as I write it on the board. We'll limit comments on each item to fifteen minutes."

Kaitlin Romin began, "He has a spotless reputation in this town."

"Yes, but the judge told us we weren't permitted to be influenced by sympathy, bias, prejudice, or favor to any party. Most of us know of Mr. Schafer. Don't we?" Debbie Royce's voice faded off at the end of her sentence.

"I'm not talking about prejudice. I'm talking about his reputation. Of course we can consider his reputation." Romin countered with an edge to her voice.

Kennedy wasn't sure who was correct. "Let's move on to the next point in favor of an acquittal," he said.

"Lizzie recanted her earlier testimony and said Schafer didn't molest her. I think this is the key to our decision. Without a complaint how can we convict him?" As Julie Summons spoke her face became even more flushed. She was angry. She didn't like the way the conversation was headed. She thought a not guilty verdict was going to be easy, but some of these people seemed to want Mr. Schafer to go to prison. She absolutely knew he could not have done what he was accused of.

It was clear from the passion in their voices that sides were beginning to form. The discussion was taking on the tenor of a debate.

Mitzie Palmer had not spoken during the trial. In fact, at times she seemed to be asleep. She surprised everyone by saying, "It's not just that Lizzie changed her story. No teachers or students testified that they had seen anything inappropriate. I am sure someone would know if one of his or her colleagues was molesting a student. Frankly, I just don't believe her."

"What about what the janitor said? He said he saw a pair of girl panties on the floor, " Agnes Welch said.

"He's not competent of give an opinion. He admitted he hallucinates," Summons responded.

Kennedy was disturbed by the direction of the conversation. On the one hand, he wanted a quick decision. On the other hand, he wanted to protect the reputation of a fellow soldier. He tried to redirect the discussion. "Okay. Good input. Now let's list some reasons why he should be convicted."

In a less politically correct time Alan Richmond would have been referred to as an old codger, coot or geezer. He must have been eighty years old, had tufts of black hair growing out of his ears and nose, wore hearing aids that apparently didn't work, and had bits of food stuck in his unkempt beard. He stood up and shouted his question, "If she was molested she would have told someone. Sounds to me like she seduced him, not the other way around. She wanted it and he gave it to her. The end, amen, end of story."

"Mr. Richmond, we are asking for reasons why Mr. Schafer should be convicted. You should have made your comments when we were asking for reasons why he should be acquitted," Kennedy said harshly.

"Well then write what I said where it was supposed to be. How hard would that be?"

Kennedy followed Richmond's directions and then repeated his request for reasons to convict.

"Well, like Debbie said, someone would have known. Not only were there no teachers who witnessed anything inappropriate, there were no students, either. I have a teenage niece and now a day there is not a sense of privacy. Where people my age kept secrets, now a day these kids tell everything. Between social networks, blogging, and texting their every thought is shared. I just believe Lizzie would have told someone if it really happened." Richard Martinez said with conviction. Martinez was the only union member on the jury and felt a need express his frustration with what he saw as efforts to railroad a fellow union member.

The top two buttons of Kent Butler's yellow silk shirt opened to reveal a large gold eagle suspended from a thick gold chain. His sleeves were rolled up to reveal a colorful dragon tattoo on his left forearm. His shaved head glistened in the glare of the overhead lights and a small tuft of hair adorned his chin, just under his bottom lip. During the trial no one had seen him smile. It was clear that those who were sitting near him were intimidated by his menacing manner. "Well, wait a minute, peer pressure and loyalty are pretty strong. Just because no one said anything doesn't mean that no one knew what was going on. All we really know is that no one admitted knowing." Butler said.

Kathy Hutton turned toward Butler and spoke for the first time. "I disagree. I think that if what Lizzie says happened really happened another student would have seen or heard something. It's hard to believe that Lizzie wouldn't have told a friend if what she first said was true."

"That's crazy. She knew her relationship had to be kept a secret. Hell if she hadn't written in her journal we wouldn't be here now," Butler responded.

"I'm hung up on the fact that Lizzie is still a virgin. Come on! If some guy were molesting a girl for a year, there would be some evidence. Don't you think?" Powell was twenty-two, good-looking, levelheaded, and never married, seemed somewhat naïve about sex.

"No one ever said he had regular sex with Lizzie. If he just had oral sex, she would still be a virgin," Martinez corrected.

Richmond responded, "Wait a minute. In her journal she said he put his fingers in her. Wouldn't that likely have broken her hymen?"

Kathy Hutton couldn't take it any longer. "Stop it. Just stop it. We don't have to keep harping on sex. Do we? Let's move on."

Richmond glared at Kathy and said, "Most of us have had kids in his class. I think Jim was totally believable when he was on the witness stand."

Over the next two hours Kennedy wrote their comments in the right and left hand columns.

As the list was completed Debbie Royce asked, "Honestly, I've changed my mind. I don't think Mr. Schafer is capable of what he is accused of?"

"Let's not rush to judgment. I've already listed some of the points for and against conviction," Kennedy responded. "Who wants to add to the list?"

Kathy Hutton was first to speak, "He's moved from school to school and state to state. To me that looks like someone who is trying to cover his trail."

"That doesn't mean anything." Agnes Welch said.

"What about his name change? His explanation seemed fishy to me," Hutton responded.

"I don't know. If his father really abused him, getting rid of his father's name makes sense to me. And honoring his great-great-grandfather is sort of cool," Ken Butler said.

"I think we all need to re-read Mr. James testimony. I think it was pretty convincing. What was Mr. Schafer doing in a locked band storage room, and what were a pair of girl's panties doing on the floor?" Jeff Powell said.

"Clearly, this guy is suffering from some sort of post traumatic stress. I don't think we can put much weight on what he said. He admits he forgets things and might have been on some type of medication," Welch said.

"I don't think we can dismiss Lizzie's Journal. Yes, she recanted, but she is obviously distraught," Alan Richmond replied.

"The journal is really the only hard evidence we have. And all it proves is that she wrote it. It doesn't prove it happened. Young girls do have crushes on their teachers. I know I had a crush on my math teacher in junior high school. I had his name written all over my notebooks. Thank God, my parents never saw my doodling. Honestly, I even dreamed about the guy. Did you watch Lizzie? She seems confused, afraid, embarrassed, and really sorry this trial is happening. I don't think Mr. Schafer ever touched her," Julie Simmons said.

"I'm really concerned about Schafer calling Lizzie during the trial. He was told not to have any contact with her," Hutton responded.

"Yes, and why would a grown man tell a young girl he loves her? This is something Lizzie admitted happened and Parker didn't challenge her on this point," Kennedy said.

"I think Ms. Sutton was telling the truth. Why would she come all the way out here from Boston if she hadn't been raped? Parker tried to make her out as some type of fatal attraction stalker. I just don't buy it. She seems like an honest person to me," Agnes said.

Richard Martinez had been furiously taking notes on everything that was being said. "Reggie didn't challenge Lizzie's statement that Schafer called her. That seems pretty weird to me."

The jury engaged in another day of heated discussion. By the morning of the fifth day every point had been examined, debated, and debated again. Kennedy called for another vote. This time the vote was unanimous.

At 11:00 a.m. on the fifth morning, Kennedy filled out the verdict form and sent word to Judge Williams that the jury was ready to pass judgment on Schafer. When it was announced that the verdict was in the spectators filed back into the courtroom where they were briefly united in anxious silence awaiting the verdict. Johnson grimly smiled at Lizzie.

He couldn't bring himself to speak with her. Reggie smiled confidently at the jury. Schafer looked at his hands as the jury filed back into the jury box for the last time.

Judge Williams wasted no time upon his entry into the courtroom. "Has the jury reached a decision?" he asked.

Bill Kennedy stood and said, "Yes, we have, your Honor." He then handed the written verdict to the clerk. The clerk passed the verdict to Williams who read it and handed it back to the clerk who passed it back to Kennedy.

Williams then asked Kennedy to read the verdict. The courtroom was silent. Although most thought they knew what Kennedy was going to say, they couldn't be sure. At the defense table Parker was the picture of confidence, but Schafer's façade of composure was eroding. His face was white, perspiration glistened on his forehead and upper lip, and he was holding his hands together to keep them from shaking.

At the prosecution table Johnson quietly prayed for justice. He was also wondering why Sail hadn't helped him with this trial. He put his hand on Lizzie's shoulder. She pulled away. She was silently crying. She knew there was not a decision that would make things the way they were before. She didn't want Mr. Schafer to go to jail, but she knew she would never see him again regardless of the verdict.

Adam sat with his hands clinched with no illusions about the outcome. Sarah and he both knew that Schafer was going to go free. Adam pledged to himself that if Schafer were found not guilty he would make sure he never taught again. He thought back over the past year and saw the faces of the young women who had been molested by Schafer and who were helpless to stop him. His thoughts turned to Julie. I've let her down again, he thought.

Sarah felt cold inside. She stared at Schafer. For most of her life she had pretended that what happened to her was no big thing. She couldn't pretend any longer. Schafer had damaged her just like he had damaged so many others. And these people were going to let him get away with it. She wanted him to look over at her, but he kept his eyes down.

The reporters, so confident of the outcome, had already written their stories and were waiting for the verdict before pushing the send buttons on their PCD's.

Kennedy stood and said, "On the charge of rape, we find the defendant not guilty."

Cheers and applause filled the courthouse. Williams banged his gavel to restore order.

Kennedy continued, "On the charge of lewdness with a child under the age of fourteen, we find the defendant not guilty."

This time, despite the excitement in the courtroom, the spectators remained quiet and orderly.

"Your honor, may I have a the jury polled in open court?" He hoped that at the last instant one of the jurors would become conscience stricken, or that someone would admit to having been forced by the other jurors to "go along" with the verdict.

Judge Williams stared at Johnson in disbelief and then asked the court clerk to poll the jury.

The clerk began with Kennedy, "Was this then and is this now your verdict?" "Yes." Kennedy answered without hesitation. The other ten jurors each responded to the question with a confident "yes."

Judge Williams acted quickly. "The finding of not guilty stands. The jury is dismissed with the court's thank you for your service on this case. Mr. Schafer you are free to leave. As he slammed his gavel he said, "Court is adjourned."

Chapter 40

Reporters pushed digital recorders in Bill Kenney's face as he left the courtroom. "Why did the jury vote the way it did, Mr. Kennedy?"

Kennedy answered decisively, "Because of Lizzie Sutton's inconsistent statements and her demeanor on the stand. We believed her when she said that Mr. Schafer didn't do it."

Johnson, too, faced reporters' questions as he left the courthouse. "Several of the jurors are saying they didn't believe some of your witnesses, Mr. Johnson. Did you prepare your witnesses adequately for their testimony?"

Johnson was annoyed at the stupid unproductive question. What did they expect him to say? "Absolutely. My team met with each witness five or six times. You can never totally predict what a cross-examination is going to bring. And you're never sure how a witness will respond to the stress of cross-examination."

"Mr. Johnson, were you surprised by the verdict?"

Johnson deflected the question. "We believe that James Schafer molested Lizzie Sutton. The jury did not agree with us." He could not resist adding, "Schafer was not convicted, but that doesn't mean he is innocent. It's like the O.J. Simpson case. He was never proven innocent. He was just found not guilty."

The reporters continued their questioning, "Why did you put Lizzie on the stand if you knew she was going to deny that Schafer raped her?"

Johnson tensed. "We didn't know that she was going to change her story." Other reporters shouted questions. "I have no further comments, " Johnson said as he turned and walked away.

Mrs. Sutton and Lizzie tried to get past the media gauntlet outside the courtroom. They had almost reached their car when several reporters cut them off. "Are you going to file a civil case against Mr. Schafer and the Tupico Flats School district?" One reporter called out as another thrust a microphone in front of Mrs. Sutton.

Mrs. Sutton squeezed Lizzie's hand and tried to get between Lizzie and the reporters. "My daughter and I are going home to try and heal from this terrible ordeal. Of course, we're very disappointment. Please just leave us alone?" She steered Lizzie to the passenger side door.

As Lizzie got in, a reporter shoved a tape recorder in her face and yelled, "Lizzie! Lizzie! Do you still love Mr. Schafer?"

Lizzie pulled the car door closed. She had lost the ability to feel anything.

On the other side of the courthouse steps Parker and Schafer held an impromptu news conference. The crowd noise made it difficult for them to be heard. It seemed more like a pep rally than a press conference. Several band members and former band members had brought their instruments to the courthouse and began playing the Tupico Flats fight song. Dozens of well-wishers crowded around Schafer. Someone began a chant, "We love you Mr. S. We love you Mr. S."

Parker waved and headed for his limousine. In fifteen minutes he would be in his jet high over the Nevada desert.

Schafer accepted the accolades and stayed until his last fan left.

Adam and Sarah sat in the empty courtroom long after everyone else had left. Adam's back was throbbing; pain was radiating down both legs. The pain pills had stopped working. He needed a scotch. "This 'Passing the Trash' bull shit has got to stop," Adam said. "They could have stopped him in Ohio, Pennsylvania, or Missouri. They could have nailed him here in Nevada several times."

Sarah nodded. "It seems like we've been tracking Shepherd forever. I know what he did to me. We've met his other victims. We know he's guilty. We have to find a way to stop him."

"I don't know who makes me more angry," Adam mused, "Shepherd, or the jury who failed to convict him. From the start the prosecution of this case was strange. I still can't figure out why Sail didn't take the lead. He has a reputation as a strong prosecutor. Johnson is a nice guy, but he was in way over his head."

As they drove away from the courthouse Sarah tuned the radio to the local news station.

"I am Ronald Brett, station manager of WXYZ, with today's editorial. We agree with today's jury decision to find Mr. Jim Schafer not guilty the rape charges. The jury made it clear that they were not swayed by the prosecution's attempts to frame the case as the molestation of an innocent child. One thing is certain – the jury knew its mind. Members deliberated for less than five days.

"Although the prosecution expressed shock and astonishment at the verdict, I, for one, think the justice system worked properly. The prosecution's case was lost when the key witness, Lizzie Sutton, recanted her previous testimony and contradicted the testimony of her mother. There were a sufficient number of holes in the case to doom it from the start. This case was bogus and would never have gone to trial without the interference from outside agitators, Sarah Abbott and Adam Faulkner."

Adam reached over and turned off the radio. They rode to their hotel in silence.

The front page of the *Tupico Mercury's* morning edition the next day carried two strikingly different photographs. One was of Schafer jubilantly raising a fist in the air. The other was of Lizzie Sutton's tear stained, forlorn face.

Chapter 41

"Thank you God, thank you God, thank you, thank you, thank you! I'll never do it again, I promise," Schafer repeated as he turned onto his street. He smiled as he saw the large banner that was strung between the two Lombardy Poplars in his front yard. "Welcome Home, Mr. S. We love you!" He'd done three radio interviews and a national television remote spot since being found not guilty. Everywhere he went supporters greeted him. He had heard "I knew you didn't do it Mr. S." so many times it was almost a chant. People shook his hand in the grocery store and as he filled up his gas tank at the Quick Shop.

Grace had taken Ashley to stay with her mother during the trial. She was pretty upset when she left. Schafer knew the marriage was over. He was grateful that Grace didn't choose to testify against him and for the spousal testimonial privilege that prevented Johnson from forcing her to testify. I'll miss Ashley, but it's best that she go with her mother, Schafer thought. At first he thought he should try to get Grace to come back for appearances sake but realized it was time to get out of town and it would be easier if he were alone.

As he turned into his driveway, he flipped open his cell and called her. When she answered he said cheerfully, "Hi Hon. It's over. Not guilty! I told you everything would be okay." Grace was silent. "Are you there?" Schafer asked.

"Yes, Jim. I'm here. Congratulations."

"You don't sound very happy."

"Jim, I want a divorce. I think the jury made a mistake. I'll drive down tomorrow morning to pack up the rest of our things."

"Okay, fine," he said as he pulled into his garage. Schafer was not surprised or particularly saddened by this news. He'd miss Ashley, but Grace was no great loss. Lizzie really came through. Thank God.

Schafer was exhilarated and exhausted by the trial and the phone call. The ordeal had taken a toll. He'd lost fifteen pounds. Although he'd worried about the verdict, he'd never really believed he would be convicted in this town. He thanked God again. He knew he held a wild card. He knew his fellow traveler wouldn't let him go to jail. Still, Schafer realized that he needed to slip away from Tupico Flats before anything else happened.

Schafer didn't notice the shadow of someone slinking into the garage as he lowered the door. He got out of the car and then reached into the back seat for the teaching job announcement he printed off at the library on his way home. He had almost memorized the first two paragraphs. "Wanted, energetic person who loves children to start a music and band program at St. Gonzalez Academy. St. Gonzalez Academy has existed as a private elementary school for twenty years. The board of directors has voted to start a middle school next year. The starting salary is competitive with other local schools, and there is a housing allowance provided.

"Teach in Puerto Rico! Live overseas and get paid to be a world traveler! Experience a land, its people, and culture firsthand; see the sights and sample the local cuisine; and make friends you'll have for a lifetime. This is a 100% English immersion environment. You don't need to know the local language first."

Schafer smiled, bent over and touched his toes, then stood and stretched. He could feel the stored up tension began to slowly leave his body. As he walked toward the door that connected the garage to his house he caught himself trying to picture his Puerto Rican band students. As put his key in the lock he heard a muffled scuffing sound behind him. He froze. His mind raced to identify what made the sound. When he heard the sound again he knew someone else was with him in the garage. Schafer saw fleeting images of Mr. James, Adam Faulkner and Sarah Abbott.

Suddenly the intruder was right behind him. He could feel the hot breath on his neck. "Hello Jim. Feeling pretty good, I bet."

Schafer didn't immediately recognize the voice. He held his breath, too frightened to move.

"Go ahead, asshole. Turn around."

Schafer slowly turned and instinctively smiled. With a sigh of relief he held out his hand. "Christ! You scared the shit out of me." Then he saw the gun and the cold eyes. I'm not going to get out of the garage, he thought.

The intruder said, "I only went to one freaking meeting and you were there. I knew it was stupid and dangerous for me to meet with others like us. But you know how it is. We really can't control our actions. Can we?"

"Thank you. You did it. You got me off."

"I did what I could, Jim. But, you really didn't give me much choice. Did you? The case against you was so weak you probably would've gotten off without my help. But, I couldn't take any chances. Could I?"

"What are you doing here? What's the gun for?" Schafer asked.

"Do you remember what you said to me? No? Well let me refresh your memory. Let's see now. How did it go? Oh, yes. I remember, 'If I have to name names, I will.'"

Schafer's mind was racing. "That was just talk, Mr. Sail. I was out of my mind with fear. You know I'd never tell anyone about you."

"Jim, Jim, Jim. You are a very stupid man. I get the fact that you can't stay away from young girls. I have the same problem. But, to screw students that you teach, how stupid is that? I'm amazed they hadn't nailed your ass years ago."

"I swear I'll never tell anyone about you. I am taking a job in Puerto Rico. I'll never come back to Nevada. I swear. You'll never see me again. Please, Mr. Sail, don't hurt me," Schafer whimpered.

"You know, Jim, I was in the courtroom today. There are quite a few others who want to kill you. You're lucky I got here first. I'm just going to shoot you. It will be over quick. You won't feel a thing. Who knows what some of your victims might want to do to you?"

"I won't tell anyone, I promise. I've got a wife and a daughter. Please don't hurt me."

"Get down on your knees, you fucking idiot."

Schafer was crying as his knees hit the cool concrete floor. Sail reached into his back pocket, pulled out a small notebook and pen, and tossed them on the floor in front of Schafer. The only sounds were the clicking of the car engine cooling down and Schafer's rasping breath. Sail stared at him. Finally, he said. "Jim, there may be a way I can help you. Pick up that pen and write the names of every one of your little girls."

"You know I didn't do anything wrong. We're the best things that ever happened to them, Mr. Sail. You know they're not as innocent as people think. They all wanted it. They all wanted me."

"Yes, I do know that. Most people don't understand what we do."

"That's right. We understand each other," Schafer said hopefully.

Sail grimaced. "Certainly you can understand why I can't let you leave this garage. I have to send the police off looking for one of your former victims. You can understand that, can't you?"

Jim sobbed quietly.

"It's very simple, Jim. If you write the name of every child with the date beside it I'll shoot you in the back of the head. It'll be quick and painless. If you refuse, I'll make sure that you suffer for a long time. Either way, no one is going to suspect me. You'll be dead."

Jim started to protest, thought better of it, slowly picked up the notebook, and started writing. When he finished there were ten names on the page.

Sail smiled with his mouth. His eyes remained deadly serious. "Don't fuck with me, Jim," Sail said. "I want all the names."

Five minutes later, thirty-three names were scrawled in the notebook.

"That's much better. Don't you think?" Sail asked. "Now write today's date at the top of the page and sign at the bottom."

Schafer did as he was told and then started to stand up. "The discharge knocked Schafer on his ass. It took a few seconds for him to realize he'd been shot. He looked down at his crotch and saw a pool of blood spreading out on the garage floor. It took another few seconds before the excruciating pain hit. Schafer grabbed his crotch and started screaming.

Larry Sail stayed in the garage long enough to watch Schafer bleed out. "Sorry Jim. I had to make it look like a crime of passion," Sail said as he left garage by the side door. Sail took off his gloves as he walked the five blocks to his rented car. At the car he stuffed the hospital booties, stocking cap, sweat pants and shirt, and rubber gloves into a black plastic garbage sac. To be safe, he drove out to the local reservoir and tossed the gun and silencer as far out as he could throw them. Next he stopped at a truck plaza, paid nine dollars for a freshly laundered towel, washcloth, bathmat and soap, and got in the shower. He knew he probably had hundreds of lead, barium and antimony particles on his face. Gun shot residue is easier to wash off than cop shows would lead you to believe, he thought as he got in his car and headed home. He pulled into a trailer park and placed the bag of clothes in a trashcan that was at the curb waiting for tomorrow's pick up.

As Sail arrived in his own neighborhood his thoughts turned to Johnson. Thank God he is so naïve, he thought. I'll find him a job in Las Vegas and he'll move on with his life. As he drove up his driveway and prepared to greet his wife and two daughters Sail thought about how sweet and vulnerable Lizzie Sutton looked as she sat in the courtroom.

The next afternoon Sarah and Adam were having drinks at the airport bar waiting for their flights to be called when they heard the news about Schafer. The lead story on the local news television station began, "The body of James Schafer was found in the garage of his Tupico Flats home at nine o'clock this morning, the day after a jury found him not guilty of molesting a female student in his music class. Schafer was one of the most accomplished and popular teachers Tupico Flats has ever known.

"According to Detective Rich Santano, Schafer's wife found his body in their garage when she returned home from a visit with her relatives. Santano said a single shot to the groin, fired at close range, caused the death. Dr. Richtain, the medical examiner, said that it probably took ten to twenty minutes for Schafer to bleed to death. She speculated that if Schafer had received immediate medical attention he probably would have survived. It is reported that the police found a notebook at the scene of the crime. They have not said what was written in the notebook. Schafer's neighbors report that they did not see or hear anything out of the ordinary. At this point, the police have no suspects."

For a few minutes Adam and Sarah sat quietly staring at their drinks. Sarah spoke first. "Adam, I have something I've got to tell you. It is pretty embarrassing,"

"I would think by now we could tell each other just about anything," Adam replied.

"I haven't been completely honest with you."

"Go on. What is it?" he said.

"During all the time we have been together I've kept a secret from you. When I was going through counseling I realized how badly Shepherd had hurt me. I blamed him for so many things that had gone wrong in my life. From the minute I contacted you until now, I had planned on killing Schafer if we ever caught him. I am so sorry I lied to you. Can you forgive me, Adam?"

Adam wasn't as shocked as Sarah had expected. "I totally understand what you're saying. I've kept the same secret from you. Shepherd changed the direction of my life. He took Julie from me and took away my childhood. When I was fifteen I vowed I'd find him and kill him. For the last fifteen years I substituted every scumbag I tracked down for Shepherd. I really didn't think I had anything to lose by killing him. I planned on turning myself in and taking my punishment. So, I forgive you if you'll forgive me."

"If someone else didn't do it, do you think one of us would really have gone through with it?"

"I'm not really sure about you, but during our search I've turned loose of most of my hatred of him. I'm pretty sure I wouldn't have killed him. I've really enjoyed life these last months. Being with you has been great and made me realize that there were good people out there and that I could get interested in a woman again. I'm in a much better place now than I was a year ago."

"I think I would have tried to kill him. I am grateful that I'll never have to find out. I want to put Shepherd behind me and get on with my life. Who do you think did it? Do you think it was Gretchen?"

"Could be. It's not like there aren't dozens of likely candidates. Did you see the way Mr. James looked at Shepherd during the trial? It wouldn't shock me if he did it.

TABERNASH, COLORADO
ONE YEAR LATER

Relaxing on his deck, sorting through his mail, Adam watched the clouds change shapes as they drifted over Indian Peaks. Before he lost so many trees to the pine beetle infestation, he couldn't see the clouds or much of the mountain. His cabin was always in the shade. Now, the morning sunshine warmed his great room and the deck. In the evening he can watch the sun set over Byers Peak.

Callie brought a tray of sandwiches to the teak picnic table. Lately, she'd been spending almost as much time at Adam's cabin as she did at Doc Susie's. Their relationship had changed from friends with benefits to something much more important to both of them. Adam learned a lot about himself over the past year. He felt he could finally close the door on Julie Romano. They both could rest in peace now that Shepherd was dead.

Adam opened a letter postmarked Tempe, Arizona and pulled out a single sheet of lined pink paper. The note was from Lizzie Sutton.

Dear Mr. Faulkner,

I am sorry I didn't tell the truth at the trial. The kids at school were so mean to me. Everybody hated me. Mom couldn't stop crying. I believed Mr. Schafer loved me. I was so confused and scared. They say his funeral was the biggest Tupico Flats has ever seen.

They had to hold it in the school auditorium. I heard almost everyone in town was there.

Mom and I have moved to Arizona to live with my uncle Gary and aunt Kathy. I have a new puppy. Her name is Ruby. I love my new school. I'm thinking of going out for track next year.

I'm really sorry it has taken me so long to write. You and Ms. Abbott were right about Mr. Schafer. I'm sorry that he died, but I hate the fact that he was my first kiss. He tricked me. I'm seeing a counselor every week and she has been great.

Thanks for making me not afraid to go to school.

Your friend,
Lizzie

Adam handed the letter to Callie. She read it, came over and gave Adam a hug, and said, "You can't save every child, but you're making a real difference in the world. I love you for it."

Adam smiled to himself. A girl friend and a dog, this is more like it he thought as reached down to scratch Willie behind his ears. Willie is a six-month-old Border Collie Adam rescued from the pound. He felt that adopting Willie and spending more time with Callie was a sign that he had begun living with an eye to the future rather than the past.

Lizzie's letter caused Adam to think about Sarah. She lives in Maine and calls Adam every few months. In her last call she promised to come out to the cabin for a visit as soon as she can get away from her new job at the Woman's Crisis Center. She's started dating Mike, a professor of sociology at one of the local universities. In her last call Sarah confided to Adam that her relationship with Mike felt pretty good. She said she's happier than she's been since she was a little girl.

They never talk about Tony Shepherd.